Full TILT

BECCA SEYMOUR

HE'S READY TO
PROVE THAT HE'S
NOT JUST A
DISTRACTION—
HE'S THE REASON
TO STAY

Full Tilt

BECCA SEYMOUR

RAINBOW TREE PUBLISHING

For information, contact the author:
hello@beccaseymour.com

Editing: Hot Tree Editing

Cover Designer: Story Style Cover Designs

Alternative Edition Cover Designer: BookSmith Design

Publisher: Rainbow Tree Publishing

E-book ISBN: 978-1-923252-47-9

Original Paperback ISBN: 978-1-923252-53-0

Alternative Paperback ISBN: 978-1-923252-55-4

1

Camden

MY LEGS SHAKE, MY CORE SCREAMS AT ME, WHILE my neck's so taut I feel the strain in places I didn't know could cramp. One more set and I can cool off, collapse, and—if the rugby gods are kind—crawl into bed tonight with my dignity mostly intact.

"Come on, Crawford. Five more." Joyce bobs his head, watching me like a hawk.

I grunt something that might be agreement—or a death rattle—and hold the neck bridge. It feels like my skull's about to launch off my spine and roll into the squat rack, but I grit my teeth, knowing I can't get away with not completing today's training.

"Four more," Joyce says, cheerfully ignoring my slow descent into rigor mortis. The strength trainer stays by my side, counting down like it's the easiest thing in the world. The man's basically a walking slab of optimism in trackies.

By the time we're on the last hold, every muscle in my neck and core is singing the national anthem of pain.

"That's it. Hold."

The vein in my temple pulses. Maybe it'll burst and take me out of training early.

"And done."

"Fuck." My back hits the floor with the grace of a sack of potatoes, arms splayed out. I should stretch, but I might need a priest first. Or a forklift.

Joyce chuckles. "You're dramatic today."

"Today?" I mutter, still trying to locate my soul somewhere near my spine. "You say that like I'm not always two reps from a full existential collapse."

He snorts. "You love it. You just hate admitting it."

I give him a slow blink. "That's not true. I hate it, and I will never admit to anything."

There's a familiar shuffle behind me before someone nudges my side with the toe of their trainer. I don't have to look.

"You dead, Cap?" Lachie, our hooker, my best mate, and resident pain in my arse peers down at me. "You look like roadkill someone politely dragged off the A38."

I lift one arm and flip him the finger. "Just visualising what peace might feel like."

Lachie drops down beside me and offers a bottle of water, which I accept like a man who's not had a drink for days rather than the fifteen minutes it has been. He's still annoyingly fresh, sweat barely breaking on his forehead, while I look like I've fought a bear. Naked. In a sauna.

Wednesday's our long grind day, and we've earned tomorrow off. Not that my legs care—they're threatening to secede from the rest of me.

"Joyce has a vendetta," I mutter as the demon master takes off with a far-too-upbeat bounce in his step. "Took something personally in a past life."

"You do look especially tragic today," Lachie says with a grin, resting on his elbows. "I should take a photo for that 'dicks out' chat you're in."

If I had the energy to flip him off again, I'd do so. I shouldn't react, but... "We don't use the chat to jack off together, arsehole, *which* I will say *again,* you're far too invested in the idea of. And that's *not* its name." The group chat my butthead friend is referring to has an impressive collection of international queer athletes—most I met in the flesh last year at a photoshoot. Hell, if I suggested a group jackoff session, it's likely one of the horny arseholes would think it's a good idea. Cosmo, probably. I manage to arch my brow at Lachie. Though since

I'm still flat on my back, I'm not sure how effective it is.

"Whatever." He sighs. "Perhaps I'll send it to the team chat instead. Rather than finding this"—he waves his hand in my general direction—"a thirst trap, they'll see the tragedy as God intended."

I snort as he smirks. "They already think I sleep hanging upside down in a cold cellar. Not sure they need any more proof of just how tragic I am."

"True." Lachie rolls his eyes. "But they respect the hell out of you, so it's probably a very majestic cold cellar. Big, echoey. Fancy torch lighting."

I roll my eyes, but it's true. The Seagulls are my team in almost every sense. Nine years with Lachie by my side, more seasons than I care to count with most of this squad, and I'd still throw down for any one of them without hesitation. They're family. Not just in the cliché way—actual family. Not something I say lightly.

My blood family's up in the West Midlands, and I love them, I do. But this lot? This scrappy, foul-mouthed, endlessly loyal crew? They're my people, my chosen family. The older guys had my back when I came out at twenty-two, when the noise got loud and the headlines tried to twist it. I'd be lying if I said I didn't carry a bit of that bitterness still. It's quieter now, duller around the edges, but it's made me wary. Guarded.

As a result, I trust who I trust. That circle is small, and I like it that way. It's also why tonight's going to be such a ball ache.

I'm meeting someone new—something I try to avoid... like open bars and emotional vulnerability. Tank, my tattoo artist of the last five years, has decided to bugger off to Canada. Says it's for a "fresh start," which I think is code for "I'm sick of your grumpy arse, Cam."

Before he goes, he's insisted I meet his replacement. Some guy named Brent. Which sounds more like a bloke who sells discount patio furniture than someone I'd trust to put a needle to my skin. But Tank knows me, knows how picky I am about ink—and people.

So yeah. Tonight, I get to grimace awkwardly at a stranger while pretending I'm not already imagining bailing out the back door while wondering if they're going to sell a story to the press about how I whimpered or got a hard-on while getting ink.

I sigh, then wince as my hip pops when I try to sit up.

Lachie offers a hand. "Want help, old man?"

"Touch me and die."

He grins. "There's the ray of sunshine we all know and tolerate."

The gym's a humid mess by the time we limp out, sweat-slick and cursing softly, every one of us in some stage of broken.

The locker room's already buzzing. Lads are stripping off kit, chucking socks into corners with surgical accuracy, snapping towels like feral schoolboys. The familiar stink of sweat, liniment, and that one mystery protein bar someone dropped behind a bench three weeks ago wraps around me like a weighted blanket. Disgusting. Comforting.

"Oi, Cap," someone calls. "You survive the Joyce Special?"

It's Rafi Khan—our rookie winger with lungs for days and legs like he's got rockets strapped to his boots. He's fresh out of the Under-18s England squad, and damn if he doesn't have the makings of something massive. He's already tearing up the pitch in his first pro season like he owns it. And the best part? He's not a knob about it.

"Barely," I grunt, tossing my kit bag into my locker.

"He cried," Lachie adds, peeling off his shirt. "Tears of pain. And maybe a little shame."

"I will end you," I say mildly.

Rafi laughs and drops onto the bench beside me, towelling off his hair. "Well, you still looked cool doing it. Like a dying gladiator."

"Appreciate that. Put it on my gravestone."

He grins, wide and easy. It's the kind of smile you can't help rooting for. We all are, really. Kid's got the game in his blood, and if things go right, we'll be seeing him on that England squad for the World Cup in three years. He's already got the attention of scouts and press. I just hope he keeps his head down and his ego in check—which so far, he's managed.

Me? I gave up that dream years back. I never made the England cut, and at thirty-one, I'm not holding my breath. But seventy-two caps with Exeter and a captaincy that's lasted longer than some of our sponsorship deals? I'll take that. Honestly, I'm proud as hell of what we've built here and the part I've played. And this year, we're third in the Premiership table, with six games left. It's tight, and staying in the top four could go either way. But we're playing our arses off to make the play-offs, and I've never seen the boys hungrier.

Lachie thumps down beside me, cracking open a sports drink. "Anyone seen Tommy?"

"Nope," Rafi says. "He left early. Said his dog ate something dodgy and puked on his game boots."

"Again?" Lachie blinks. "That dog needs therapy."

"That dog needs to stop eating socks," I mutter, peeling off my damp shirt and resisting the urge to just lie down right here on the floor and melt.

Lachie passes me a bottle. "You going out tonight?"

"Nah." I shake my head, already picturing the blessed solitude of my flat. "Gonna veg at home. Might cook. Might stare at the wall. Big plans."

"What about that thing with the new ink guy?" he says casually, but I clock the glint in his eye.

"Brent," I reply, voice flat. "Yes. Later. A thrilling social engagement I'm deeply excited for."

Rafi perks up. "New tattoo?"

"Not tonight," I say, knowing better than having a new piece when I'll be pummelled in a game a day or two after. "Just meeting the guy before I get new ink when the season ends. Tank's leaving and wants me to bond with his hand-picked successor before he runs off to the land of syrup and apologies."

Lachie snorts. "Bet Brent's a sweetheart. You'll love him."

I arch my brow in his direction at his weird optimism. "I won't."

"You might."

"I absolutely won't."

"Cap," Rafi cuts in, still half damp and very entertained, "do you ever like new people?"

I pause, then raise a brow. "No."

"Not even a little?"

"Not unless they come with a rugby ball and an injury report."

Rafi laughs again, and Lachie leans back against the locker, still grinning. I've got a reputation around here— dour, dry, loyal to a fault. But the lads, especially those who've been here for a few seasons, know the truth. They've seen the worst of me and stuck around. That makes them mine. And in return, I'd take on the world for them.

The showers hiss in the background. Someone's singing off-key. Probably Jules. The mood's light, but under it all, there's a current—quiet intensity and shared purpose. Six matches left. Every point matters. Every tackle counts.

After hosing down, I towel off, drag on some fresh clothes, and start to head out.

"Hey, Cap," Rafi calls as I pass.

"Yeah?"

"Don't scare this Brent dude too bad, yeah?"

"No promises."

Rafi grins as he waves me off.

The sun's dipping low by the time I get home from the supermarket. The sky's streaked in that soft kind of gold that makes even the car parks look poetic. Not that I'm in the mood to get all sentimental—my lower back's barking, and my stomach's doing its best impression of a hollow drum.

My flat's not far from the club, a short enough drive that I've got muscle memory for every traffic light and pothole. It's nothing flashy—two-bed, second floor, tucked in a quiet corner of Exeter in a block where mainly other blokes, and a couple of older women, live solo and seem to enjoy silence as much as I do. We nod in the stairwell, maybe exchange a line or two about the weather, but no one pushes for more. It's ideal.

I let myself in, toe off my trainers, and take a breath, which feels heavier than it should. It's quiet, which is how I've set things up. How I like it.

Or how I've told myself I like it.

Solitude's a funny thing. I've always needed space to reset, to breathe, to not be "Camden Crawford: Captain, Bloke Who Came Out in the Spotlight, Still Has a Solid Tackling Percentage." I've carved out this little corner of the world where I can just *be*, and for the most part, it's a relief.

But sometimes—nights like this—there's an edge to it. It's a bit like silence with teeth.

Coming out at twenty-two damn near gutted me. The press had a field day. Fans, strangers, pundits with opinions no one asked for. I couldn't so much as step outside for a takeaway without someone trying to snap a photo or shout something clever about my "bravery." That or they hollered something gross that made it hard not to knock them flat on their arses. It took me years to stop flinching every time a flash went off. Years longer to stop trying to shrink myself in public.

And dating? Hooking up? Forget it. I don't do clubs.

I don't trust people easily. And I sure as hell don't need another twink with an Instagram account selling a "Hot Night with England Hopeful Camden Crawford" to *The Sun*. Once was enough, thanks. Six years ago, and it still makes my skin crawl.

So yeah. Maybe I've built this quiet life for myself. And maybe I've forced myself to like it a little more than I actually do.

I head into the kitchen and put my groceries away. Once the space is tidy, I pull out a pan and toss in some chicken and veggies, the sizzle a small comfort. Cooking helps. Simple, focused, physical. It's a little like training, but with less screaming from Joyce or Coach.

I'm halfway through chopping basil when my phone buzzes on the counter. I smile, seeing my brother's name.

I wipe my hands and answer. "Yeah, Joel, I'm alive."

"I did start to wonder." His voice is bright, his Walsall accent thicker than mine these days. "Been trying to call you all week, you miserable git."

"I've been busy being professionally pummelled."

"Well, I'm getting professionally pummelled by wedding planning. So we're both suffering."

That gets a small smile out of me. "July's coming fast."

"Don't remind me." He groans. "Tasha's got me

choosing napkin colours. *Napkins*, Cam. Like it matters what shade of beige they are."

"They definitely matter. Pick the wrong one and society collapses."

"Exactly." He snorts. "How's the body holding up?"

I shift, stretching out my shoulder. "Neck's tight. Legs are pissed. Otherwise fine."

"You still third?" he asks, and I roll my eyes. Joel is a Villa supporter, which yeah, in our family, it's criminal not to be, but he's very much a football fan and not a hardcore rugby fanatic.

"Yep. Just six games left. Could all go tits up, but we're holding on."

"Reckon you'll make the play-offs?"

My grin stretches that he's using terms I've spent years drilling into him. "If we keep playing like we did last weekend. Rafi's on fire."

"That's the kid with the ridiculous speed?"

"That's the one. Whole team's rooting for him to make England. He's got it in him."

Joel's quiet a beat, then says, "You seeing anyone?"

I bark a laugh. "What, in my spare time between being a hermit and dodging tabloid scum?"

His grunt of agreement travels through the speaker. Joel had been ropable during all the bullshit coverage when I came out. Like my team, he's always had my back. "You've got a decent beard now. Someone out there must be into grumpy cavemen. Or bears—is that what some guys call you?"

I bark out a laugh and stir the pan. "Fuck off. I am not a bear. And perhaps never talk to me about bears again." My brother means well. He also loves stirring me up. And as for being a bear.... I hold back my sigh. Sure, I may look the part, and at work, I can be grizzly and protective as fuck, but in the bedroom, what I wouldn't give to be railed by someone who knew what they were doing and was strong enough to handle me.

I clear my throat and shake thoughts away that I absolutely don't want to have while on the phone to my brother.

Joel's laugh is loud. "Okay, okay, no grizzly talk. I got it. Are you good for tonight? You're meeting the new tattoo guy, right? Which I haven't told Mum about, by the way, and you're welcome."

He laughs again, warm and easy. It softens something in me. Reminds me I'm not just the player or the captain or the wall people bounce off. I'm also a brother. A son. A man with people who love me even if I vanish into myself sometimes.

"Yeah, I'll be okay," I say, a little quieter. Joel knows

all about my aversion to strangers. Sure, there are times he'll take the piss while singing "stranger danger" at me, but he knows all too well how people try to get close for all the wrong reasons. He's also one of the few people who really know how meeting people like this Brent guy, someone who's going to be in my space and I'll inevitably spend hours alone with, makes me truly stressed.

Put me on a pitch with fifteen rugby players who I've never played before, my face squashed against theirs in a scrum, and I'm just peachy. Outside of rugby is a whole different story.

"I know. Just give the guy a chance. You trust your old tattooist, right?"

"Right," I agree, albeit a little reluctantly.

"So I'm sure he wouldn't hand over his client list to a wankstain."

I huff out a laugh. "Here's hoping he hasn't."

"I'm sure it'll be bostin. Listen, I best get gone. I just wanted to check on ya."

"Thanks, Joel. 'Preciate it, bro."

"Take care of yourself, Cam."

"You, too, man."

We hang up, and the silence creeps back in, but it's softer now, a little less isolated. I finish cooking, plate up, and sit down at my little table, phone facedown beside me.

Outside, the light fades, while inside, I eat alone. And in a couple of hours, I'll be meeting Brent.

Here's hoping the guy doesn't turn out to be a prick.

2

Brent

I WIPE DOWN THE LAST CHAIR, SET THE SPRAY bottle back on the shelf, and let out a slow breath through my nose. It's been a day. Back-to-back bookings, one walk-in who wanted an entire phoenix up his ribcage today, and a guy who nearly passed out mid-wrist tattoo because he forgot to eat lunch. Classic.

I stretch my arms overhead, tattoos pulling across my skin, and look around the studio—Black Salt Ink. It still doesn't feel like mine, not entirely. Not yet. The floors are scuffed in places that don't match the rest of the wear, the back room light flickers when it rains, and Tank's artwork is everywhere. But I like it here. There's something steady in the bones of the place. Solid. Like it's used to people coming in with all their noise and walking out a little quieter.

Tank's behind the desk, balancing his laptop on one knee and drinking the last of his lukewarm coffee. He looks like the ghost of a rock band roadie—long hair, sleepy eyes, covered in even more ink than I am. He's got one foot out the door already. Canada calls.

"So," I say, leaning against the counter, "tell me again why we're still open after hours?"

Tank glances at me over his mug. "You're meeting your problem."

"Excuse me?" I'm pretty sure this is the first time he's mentioned a "problem" client to me. Sneaky asshole.

"Camden Crawford," he says, with all the dramatic weight of a soap opera character about to reveal the secret twin. "Prop. Captain. Big deal at Exeter Seagulls."

"Rugby." I nod. "The one that's like American football but with fewer pads and more visible violence."

Tank chuckles. "That's the one."

I've lived in the UK long enough to recognise the sound of rugby fans yelling at a pub TV. It's like a primal chant. A lot of vowels. Some war cries. Camden's name's come up once or twice when I've been out—usually followed by someone saying, "Oof, he's a unit," or, "Wouldn't want to meet him in a dark alley."

I smirk. "So, what I'm hearing is: I'm meeting a massive, brooding man with a neck like a bridge support and the personality of a slightly pissed-off cat."

Tank chuckles again. "More or less. You'll be fine."

I twirl the ring through my lip piercing. "What's he getting?"

"Not sure. That's between you two. But it won't be tonight."

Thank fuck, since it's late and I'm not sure I have anything left to give this evening.

"He's just meeting you. I told him you don't suck."

I huff out an amused laugh. "That was generous."

"Don't make me regret it."

I grin. "Nah, I got this. Oldest of five, remember? Two twin brothers who treated everything like a wrestling match, a younger brother who's half golden retriever, half human spotlight, and a sister who can murder with a glare. I know how to deal with complicated personalities."

Tank raises a brow. "This isn't summer camp, Brent. Camden doesn't do small talk."

I wave that off. "Everyone does small talk. You just have to find the right language."

"Yours being relentless optimism?"

"Exactly. It's unsettling. Breaks down defences."

He snorts and closes his laptop. "If he punches you, I'm not covering dental." He shakes his head. "You know how hard it is getting an NHS dentist these days?"

I roll my eyes, knowing full well that for all its faults,

the NHS is a damn lot better than what we have back home in the US. "If he punches me, I'm getting it tattooed."

Tank just shakes his head. "God help you."

I walk the floor again, checking needles are boxed, stations clean, lights low but not spooky. The shop's good at night. It feels calm. Still. Like it knows it's about to be part of someone's story, even if just the beginning.

And yeah, I've been tattooing long enough to know this matters. For some people, it's a design. For others, it's a declaration. A line drawn in ink that says, *This is mine. My story. My skin. My control.*

Tank's headed out next week, and this? Tonight? This feels like the big test. I'm leasing the space, taking over the books, and hopefully will keep the clients happy —but Camden's the one Tank's most protective of. If I pass this test, I'm golden, and he's already said in six months, he'll look at selling the place to me if I'm still interested.

I slide behind the desk, flick on the playlist—something mellow but not sleepy—and check the time.

Camden Crawford should be walking in any minute now. And hey, if he turns out to be the intimidating, scowly, tighthead of doom everyone says? Well, I've got charm, tattoos, and a well-honed ability to wear people down with friendship.

Let's see how long he lasts.

The bell above the door gives a soft jingle. It's nothing dramatic, but it still hits me like a cymbal crash in a yoga class. I glance up, and my gut does this weird little flip.

Holy shit. The man who steps in is big. Not just tall, though he's definitely got a couple of inches on me. No, he's built—broad across the shoulders, chest like a battering ram, thighs that look like they've won arguments with steel beams. There's a quiet power to how he moves. Controlled. Deliberate. Like he could level the whole block if he wanted to, but he's choosing not to, for now.

And then I catch it—the peek of black and red ink curling just beneath the sleeve of his right arm. Sharp lines, heavy shading. Something floral maybe? I can't quite see, but it's enough to tell me he doesn't do his tattoos on a whim. They mean something. They're his.

I'm still cataloguing all that when my gaze skims up past the beard—which, by the way, is excellent—and I hit his eyes.

Jesus. Tank wasn't exaggerating. They're dark and sharp, narrowed just enough to make me feel like I'm on trial. Not cold exactly, but watchful, like he's measuring me, assessing, maybe even deciding whether I'm worth his time, his trust, possibly even his breath.

It hits me right in the chest. Not fear. Not even nerves, really. Just this overwhelming urge to wrap him in a hug. Which is ridiculous, because he looks like the kind of guy who'd throw a punch at anyone who tried. And also because there's every chance he outweighs me by a good thirty pounds, and I'm not a small guy.

But still, there's something in him. Something hurt and guarded, stitched into the line of his jaw, the tension in his shoulders, the way his mouth doesn't quite settle. He looks like someone who's been cracked open before and decided *never* again.

Yeah. He calls to something in me. That soft spot I try to hide behind the piercings and ink and my "whatever, man" vibe.

Tank stands and gives me a quick nod. "Cam, this is Brent Parks. Brent, this is Camden Crawford."

Camden looks at me like I'm a puzzle he didn't ask for.

"Hey," I say, stepping forwards, smile easy. "Nice to meet you, man."

He eyes the hand I offer like it might bite him, but after a second, he takes it. His grip's solid, warm, a little slow to let go.

"Thanks for staying open," he says, voice low and gravelly. "I know it's late."

I shrug. "You kidding? I live for late-night introductions with quietly intimidating blokes."

Tank snorts quietly behind me. Camden just grunts. It's not exactly a laugh, but I'll take it.

He steps further in, eyes scanning the shop. There's a tension to the way he holds himself, like he's keeping everything tucked tight under the surface. I can't tell if he's uncomfortable or just built like a human fortress. Maybe both.

"I heard you've got opinions about ink," I say lightly. "I respect that. You've got great work from what I can see."

His brow lifts, just slightly. Not quite a thank-you. More like *noted*.

"I didn't pick you," he says. "Tank did."

I nod. "Right. No pressure." I hold back from raking my gaze over him again, confident he wouldn't like that. Instead, I aim for a relaxed smile despite his short words.

"I'm particular."

My lips lift a little, and I try to figure out the best way to handle this guy, because fuck me, I really think he could do with some kind of handling. I wrestle those thoughts away, settling on "So am I."

That earns me another long look, and I swear I see the corners of his mouth twitch. Barely, to the point it's almost nothing. But it's there.

Tank gives Camden a nudge. "I'll leave you two to chat. Just talk tonight, yeah? If you want to book, Brent's got the schedule."

Camden grunts again. I think that means yes.

Tank claps me on the shoulder as he heads for the exit. "Good luck."

"Thanks," I murmur. "I think I'm gonna need it."

Camden crosses his arms, big forearms flexing under the sleeves of his hoodie, eyes still on me like he hasn't quite figured out whether I'm the real deal or a liability. I take a breath and step back just enough to give him space without making it obvious.

"Want a drink?" I ask. "Water? Coffee? Something stronger? I make a killer herbal tea that would totally ruin your street cred."

That earns a definite eye twitch. "Water's fine."

I grin and grab him a bottle, then gesture towards the chair nearest my station. He doesn't sit. Of course he doesn't. Standing means control, distance. I've met enough guarded types to know the drill.

Still, I'm not worried. I've got time. And I've got charm. I can wait him out.

I pass Camden the bottle of water and tilt my head towards the portfolio on the counter. "Want to see some of my stuff? Or are we just here to glare at each other until someone blinks first?"

He gives me a flat look, but after a second, he nods towards the binder. "Might as well."

I slide it over and flip it open to a few pages I've marked—stuff that's clean, bold, and not too flashy. Strong lines, careful shading. One is a full back piece I did a year ago, a Norse mythology spread that took weeks to finish. Another's a minimalist series I inked on a couple who'd been together twenty years. Not everything's dramatic. Some of it's quiet, but meaningful.

Camden leans over slightly, water bottle still unopened in his hand, and starts flipping.

He doesn't say much. He doesn't need to. The little pause he gives on a shoulder mandala, the way his eyes linger on a crow piece I did last spring, that's enough. It's not enthusiastic praise, but for a guy like him? I'm reading it as: *Yeah, all right. Not bad.*

"So," he says finally, still looking at the binder, "how long you been in the UK?"

"About eight years," I say, leaning back against the edge of the counter. "Moved over when I was twenty-two. Originally lived in London, then Brighton, now here."

He glances up. "Why?"

I shrug. "Felt like the right time. Got itchy feet after college. My mom said I always needed to touch every hot stove once before I believed it was hot. Figured if I was gonna make mistakes, might as well make them some-where cool with better beer."

Camden hums like that answer's passable.

"I actually went to community college. I've got four not-so-little-anymore siblings, so I thought I'd give my parents a break from crazy college fees," I add, seeing the flicker of surprise on his face. "Staying local also meant I could start apprenticing right away. Got a part-time job sweeping floors and scrubbing equipment in this old-school shop when I was seventeen. Worked under a guy named Dutch who smelled like motor oil and menthols. Taught me everything."

He raises a brow. "Oldest of five, you said?"

"Oh yeah." I grin. "Twin brothers—chaotic energy, the both of them—then a younger brother who's basically TikTok incarnate and plays ice hockey at a college like he's on a personal mission to become a legend. And my baby sister? She's the scariest of us all. One look from her could end empires."

Something shifts in his face at that. Maybe recognition. Maybe curiosity. "You always knew you wanted to tattoo?"

"Pretty much," I say. "Started sketching in middle school, tattooed a banana once in science class. Went downhill from there. But yeah, art was always the plan.

Skin just made sense. It's permanent in a way most things aren't."

Camden gives a slow nod and finally—*finally*—lowers himself into the chair. It's careful, deliberate, but it's a start. It also feels like a win.

I don't react, not outwardly. Internally, I'm doing a little touchdown dance. Quietly, respectfully, but with spirit. "So," I say, keeping my tone light, "talk to me about what you're thinking of next. Design? Placement?"

He leans back a little, arms folded, eyes scanning the wall behind me. He's probably still on the defensive, but less tightly now. A crack, maybe. A sliver of light. "I've got a few ideas," he says. "Haven't decided yet."

"Got a general vibe? Meaning behind it? Space you're thinking?"

Another pause.

My brain helpfully suggests, *Ask him to take his shirt off so you can see the canvas.*

My brain is also stupid and clearly trying to get me murdered.

Instead, I keep it professional. "You've already got some nice work started," I say, gesturing to his right arm. "If you want to keep building around that, I can work with what's there. Or start fresh, if it's something different entirely."

He nods again. Quiet. Thoughtful. It's like trying to talk to a boulder that occasionally grunts back.

But he hasn't left. He hasn't shut down. And that? That's something.

I give him another smile, one that's calm and open. "Take your time. No rush. Just talking tonight, remember. No needles. No pressure. If you've got ideas you want to bounce around, we can do that. Or I can just walk you through how I usually work with repeat clients. It's up to you."

His sharp, thoughtful eyes flick up to meet mine again. There's definitely something ticking behind them, even when he's giving nothing away. And I'm convinced he's sizing me up. Not just about whether I'm good enough for the work, but whether I'm someone he can stand to sit with for hours at a time. Which, to be honest, is fair.

He doesn't answer right away. He simply watches, still guarded, but doesn't appear to be quite as closed off. Not anymore.

I hold his gaze without pushing, then nod once and glance down at my tablet. "You mentioned you had a few ideas. Want to tell me about them? Even broad strokes are a good start."

His mouth twitches. Not a smile—God forbid—but

something loosening. Barely. Maybe just a twitch of tolerance. But I'll take it.

Thank fuck we're getting somewhere, slowly and steadily.

Camden sits in silence for a beat, then finally leans forwards, resting his forearms on his thighs. His fingers tap lightly against the water bottle, like he's weighing something up. "I want a full sleeve," he says, voice level but low, like he's not entirely sure if he's allowed to want that. "Left arm."

I nod, reaching for my sketchpad and pencil without a word. "Any particular concept?"

He shrugs one thick shoulder, then glances towards his right arm, where the existing ink peeks out. "Balance, maybe. Something that complements this side without copying it. Clean lines, nothing too busy. No colour."

I jot notes, head tilted, keeping my expression neutral. I don't want him shutting down again. "Theme?"

"Still figuring that out," he admits, though the way he says it sounds more like *I have an idea, but I'm not ready to share it with a stranger*. Fair enough. I've seen enough guarded clients to know when to push and when to let the idea breathe.

"Got it," I say. "I'll put together a few design directions, and you can let me know what hits and what doesn't."

He nods once. I can feel the weight of that tiny motion. It's the closest I've gotten to trust all evening.

I glance up from my notes. "If you're happy with what I come up with—my style, the direction—when would you want to get started?"

He doesn't answer immediately. His jaw shifts. That hesitation returns. "End of the season," he says eventually.

I just nod like that makes total sense. "June?"

"Mid-June, most likely."

"I can pencil it in loosely. We'll firm up details later."

He gives a grunt of agreement, then looks away. Tense again. I try not to frown, but I feel the shift. Like a breeze just moved through the room.

"Tank mentioned you play rugby," I say carefully, aiming for conversational more than interview.

The effect is instant. Camden fully tenses—shoulders, jaw, even the set of his mouth. His whole body locks up like someone flipped a switch. My eyes narrow slightly, not in challenge, just curiosity.

Who the hell hurt this guy? Or maybe it wasn't just one person. Maybe it was a crowd.

I try again, lighter this time. "Are you thinking short

sessions or just two or three long ones? I can work around your schedule either way."

"Long ones," he says after a second. "I have a wedding in July, so I want it done by then. Then I'm in the States for about eighteen days."

"Nice," I say, keeping my tone easy. Does he mean his wedding? Is he getting hitched? My gut tightens in a weird clench of disappointment. He doesn't offer more about his travel plans—honeymoon, maybe?—and I don't push. If he wanted to tell me why, he would've.

"Timing works," I add. "I'm heading back to the States too. Just for a week—family thing. I try to head home for the Fourth of July celebrations whenever I can. Just not every year."

Camden doesn't respond with more than a basic up nod before he starts to stand, brushing his palms over his jeans. The chair creaks under his weight. He doesn't meet my eyes as he reaches for the bottle, his fingers flexing like he's preparing to leave the conversation behind with everything else.

I slide one of my cards across the counter. "Here's my number," I say, tone staying low and casual. "If you think of anything you want added, or you've got questions—or hell, even if you want to just send reference images—text me. We can chat about ideas anytime."

He takes the card without looking at it and pockets it. He turns to leave, pauses near the door, then glances back over his shoulder. "How about...," he says slowly, like it physically pains him, "I'll let you know if I'm interested?" Then he's out the door before I can respond.

The bell jingles behind him, far too cheerfully, and I blink after him, still holding my pen, still half leaning on the counter.

Well, damn.

He's fascinating. All carved-out tension and hidden edges, like he's got a second skin under the one everyone sees. He's the kind of man who makes you want to figure him out, even if it takes a freakin' decade.

But also... please, let him be talking about being interested in tattoos and not me. Because if it *was* me, I'm already a little screwed. And yeah, of course he was talking about my ink work and booking me.

I exhale through my nose and push away from the counter, stretching my arms overhead. I've spent the day inking strangers and talking to one emotionally fortified rugby captain. The silence of my flat doesn't sound appealing.

Tank's gone, the shop's clean, the playlist's looping something vaguely lo-fi in the background. I pull off my gloves, grab my hoodie, and lock up behind me.

I need a pint and maybe a few friendly voices that don't feel like decoding ancient runes. Off to the pub I go.

3

Camden

Mud clings to everything—boots, kit, skin. I'm also pretty sure it's wedged between my arse cheeks. The pitch has turned into a swamp disguised as a rugby field, all thanks to the steady drizzle that started before sunrise and hasn't let up since. We're soaked through, our jerseys hanging heavy, while the scent of wet turf and sweat is thick in the air. This is the part of the game where it gets feral. Ugly. Honest.

I crouch down, fingers splayed against the slick grass, my body taut with effort and tension. My head's supposed to be clear, locked in, dialled into this exact moment. I'm the tighthead. This is my battle zone. The scrum is one of the most brutal elements in rugby, and I'm at the heart of it. My job is to anchor, to hold the line, to keep our pack driving forwards when the only thing between us and collapse is raw power and grit.

Instead, my brain's tripping over something stupid.

A text.

Images.

Fucking artwork.

It's been three days since I met Brent.

Three days since I walked into Black Salt Ink and tried not to flinch under the weight of someone actually looking at me—not the player, not the captain, not the tighthead, but *me*. And now I'm standing in the middle of a close match against Bristol, and instead of focusing on keeping the scrum upright, I'm mentally flashing back to a pair of sketches he texted me late last night.

He thought I might like them. Said he was just "noodling around," wanted to see if anything sparked.

They're good, and I've been staring at them ever since. I haven't even responded, because my heart did this stupid, traitorous stutter when I realised he'd texted.

I'm thirty-one years old, have held my own against world-class locks, and here I am, rattled by a bloody tattoo artist with a lip ring and a lopsided grin.

"Crawford!" Jules barks from the back row, yanking me back to the moment.

Right. Game. Rain. Mud. Bristol.

I shake my head, suck in a breath, and dig in.

"Bind!" the ref calls.

I reach out, lock on. Fingers grip wet fabric like it's the only solid thing in the world.

"Set!"

We crash.

Bodies slam together with the force of a head-on collision. My shoulder screams, but I hold. My boots slide half an inch in the mud, but I reset, dig deeper. The opposition's loosehead is burly and scrappy, driving in at a brutal angle, trying to catch me high. I shift my weight, adjust my bind, and shove right back.

The pitch squelches beneath us, our footing unstable. Rain slicks down my back, mixing with sweat. The grind of the scrum is pure chaos—grunting, swearing, eight bodies locked in a mechanical hell—and still, I hold. Anchor. Absorb. Control.

This is mine.

We edge forwards. Slow, inch by inch, clawing ground with stubborn weight and willpower. Bristol resists, but we've got the better shape. Jules roars behind me, driving the second row, and I feel Lachie lock in tighter at the hook. My spine burns with the pressure, but we're winning the push.

Yes.

The ref's whistle blasts, sharp and clear. Penalty. Our ball.

I drop out of the bind, staggering upright, mud streaked down my arms, thighs, caked under my nails. My lungs drag in damp air, and I can't tell if my heart's hammering from the adrenaline or the ghost of those sketches still rattling around in my skull.

Lachie claps a heavy hand on my back. "Nice shove, Cap. Nearly drove the poor bastard into next week."

I nod, still catching my breath. "Wet pitch helped."

"Sure it wasn't tattoo dreams spurring you on?"

I glare at him, and he smirks. Bastard knows me too well. Add in that I'm a dick for even showing them to him when my head's been a mess since meeting Brent.

"You gonna text him back?" he adds, quieter now as we jog to reset. "Or just keep brooding like a half-drowned crow?"

I grunt. "I'll think about it."

"Yeah. That'll be new."

I shove him lightly, and he stumbles just enough to make it worth it.

Rain keeps falling, steady as ever. The crowd's a blur beyond the pitch, a wall of noise and waterproofs. We're away at Bristol, which means less home love, more jeers, but it's close enough not to feel hostile. Devon fans still made the drive.

We reset the play, and I shake out my arms and stretch my neck, trying to shove everything else aside.

Brent's sketches. His easy tone. That half-smile. The way he looked at me like I was worth his full attention, not just a job.

It's ridiculous. I've got bigger things to worry about. Like this match. Like holding third place on the table. Like proving to myself, and to the team, that we've still got it with six games left.

And still... I think of the text again.

Let me know if anything in these speaks to you. No pressure. Just ideas.

I haven't replied.

Because I'm not sure which part of that didn't speak to me.

We're five metres out from Bristol's line now. The ball's ours, and the tempo's picking up. The lads are working like a machine—grinding forwards in brutal little surges, the kind of hard graft rugby that wins games, not headlines.

The ball snaps out from the back of the ruck and we recycle fast—clean hands, good momentum. Rafi blazes up the wing like he's jet-propelled, and for a heartbeat, it looks like he might get through.

Then the tackle comes—high, legal, but savage—and the ball pops loose.

Instinct kicks in, and I charge. It's reflex, pure and simple. I get there first, throwing myself into the mess to secure the ball. A boot clips my thigh as I go low, and someone's shoulder lands hard into my ribs on the way down.

I hear the crunch.

Not bone—*thank God*—but something pulls tight in my side, sharp and hot like a wire yanked too far. I land awkwardly, skidding a few feet in the mud, the ball tucked to my chest.

The ref's whistle pierces the air—our penalty—and the guys cheer.

But I'm still down. Only for a second. Just one.

I roll to my knees, jaw clenched as I breathe through the white spike of pain in my side. Bones aren't broken, the injury's not deep, but my ribs burn like hellfire, and every inhale has me gritting my teeth.

Lachie's beside me in a flash. "You all right?"

"Fine."

"You don't look fine."

"I'm fucking fine," I growl, pushing to my feet. I wobble, just a little, then plant my boots and square my shoulders. My left side screams, but I shut it out. There's no time for this. No space for injury. Not now. Not while we're pushing this close, not when the lads are looking at me like I'm still unshakable.

No one needs to know the captain's running on stubbornness and spite.

I suck in a breath through my nose, adjust my stance, and fall back into formation for the next phase.

Lachie gives me a sidelong glance. "You're limping."

"Barely."

He shakes his head, muttering something under his breath about pig-headed bastards, but he knows better than to push it now.

The ref signals. The ball's back in. And I'm back at it—pain or no.

Rain keeps falling. Mud sucks at my boots. Every contact jolts something raw under my ribs, but I grind through it. It's not about pride—it's about responsibility. This team's mine. I don't sit out unless something's hanging off.

Play carries on in a blur of bodies and breath, and I hold fast. Still standing. Still here. And no matter what's throbbing under my ribs, nothing is taking me out of this match.

THE COACH HUMS BENEATH US AS IT RUMBLES DOWN the wet motorway towards Exeter, the windows fogged with the ghosts of forty soaked bodies. The game's behind us now—a close one, too close for comfort, but a win's a win. We needed that.

The lads are wrecked. A couple of them are nodding off already, headphones in, legs sprawled in the aisle like wreckage. Rafi's curled into his hoodie at the back, and Lachie's got his head tipped against the window, eyes half-shut, lips moving around whatever song he's mumbling.

It's mostly quiet. Just the occasional murmur or snore, the soft percussion of rain on glass.

"Cap," Jules says from a few seats up, "couple of us might grab a pint when we're back. You coming?"

I should say no. My ribs are killing me, and all I want is a hot shower and a cold pack. But we're closing in on the end of the season. The table's tight. The mood's tight. And whether I like it or not, I'm not just the tighthead— I'm the glue. I don't have the luxury of silence.

"Yeah," I say. "I'll come."

A few voices echo their approval, and then it's quiet again.

I shift in my seat, trying to stretch without grimacing, and finally dig my phone out of my bag. I shouldn't, but I do.

The screen lights up, and the unanswered text from Brent stares back at me.

He sent it last night, at around ten. Two images—black and grey mock-ups. Crisp, clean, but there's depth there too.

Layers. They're not exactly what I want, but they're close. Impressively so since I gave him shit-all information to go off. His design is close enough to make my fingers twitch with the need to stroke my fingers over them, to talk about them.

I've looked at them a dozen times already, but it's time to pull my head out of my arse and finally reply.

> Me: These are solid. Close to what I had in mind.

I hit Send, thumb hovering just a second longer than necessary, then tuck the phone into my lap like it might bite me.

It buzzes back immediately.

> Brent: Didn't I just see you on the pitch?

> Brent: What, were you snuggling your phone between tackles?

I almost choke. The corners of my mouth twitch, and I press a knuckle to my lips to hide the smile trying to sneak through.

Another buzz.

> Brent: Also—finally. Thought maybe you ghosted me because my seagull looked like it was doing a tax return.

I stare at the screen.

How the hell is he like this already?

Cheeky, relaxed, no edge of expectation—but sharp enough to cut through the post-match fog still hanging over me. He doesn't come on too strong. Just hits the exact level of... him.

> Me: I was busy wrestling a pack of blokes in a rainstorm.

> Brent: And still managed to find time for me. I'm touched.

> Me: Barely.

> Brent: It's alright. I thrive on minimal emotional engagement. Oldest sibling survival instinct.

The mood shifts just enough to make me blink, and then his next message lands.

> Brent: Seriously though—hell of a match. I'm no expert, but it looked like a war zone. You alright?

I pause, fingers hovering again. My first instinct is to dodge. Joke. Minimise. That's usually the rule with people outside the team—especially when it comes to injuries.

But this doesn't feel like someone fishing for gossip.

There's no "hope you're okay 🙂 " undertone. Just genuine concern.

Still, it pays to be careful.

> Me: Ribs are bruised. Nothing major.

> Brent: Glad to hear it. I was ready to design you a commemorative "I survived the scrum" tattoo.

> Brent: Limited edition.

> Me: I'll pass, thanks.

> Brent: You say that now, but wait till I add glitter shading.

I snort quietly.

> Me: I don't do glitter.

> Brent: Blasphemy.

A small beat follows until another text appears.

> Brent: So you're the captain, right? No pressure or anything.

> Me: You googled me?

> Brent: Nope. Tank mentioned it. Also, it's on the team website. Along with your scariest press photo. You look like you're considering murder.

> Me: It was a media day. We're all thinking about murder.

> Brent: Fair.

> Brent: I was raised in a hockey house— ice hockey, not the kind where people run around on fields with sticks and curse a lot. So I don't know all the rules, but the vibe? I get it.

I raise an eyebrow.

> Me: Ice hockey?

> Brent: Yes. On skates. Fast. Angry. People in cages.

> Me: I thought hockey was just that PE lesson where everyone loses a tooth.

I grin as I hit Send, completely full of shit.

In the Love the Game group chat I'm in with a bunch of other queer athletes—guys I met last year during a photoshoot for *Queervolution* magazine—this line would've caused chaos. At least two of them play ice hockey professionally and are aggressively proud of their mouth guards.

I don't usually do media. I keep my head down, let the sport do the talking. But when *Queervolution* approached me for a piece on openly queer male athletes, something in me said yes. Maybe it was the timing. Maybe it was just about wanting to make a stand, however quietly. There still aren't many of us out in rugby. Fewer still who talk about it. And someone's got to.

The photoshoot itself was chaos—with some thinking shirts were optional while the energy was off the charts—but that night, a few of us started a group chat to coordinate dinner. It's still going, all this time later. Memes, questions, venting, check-ins. Half the time, it's nonsense. The other half, it's a lifeline.

I haven't mentioned Brent in the chat, obviously. Plus, they're a pack of bloody gossips, and the second I drop a name, I'll be fielding questions, innuendo, and at least three memes involving rainbows and rugby balls.

Better to keep it to myself. But right now, the idea of telling them I'm texting a tattoo artist who makes me laugh, who looked at me like I was worth seeing... yeah, they'd definitely have something to say.

Brent: Not totally wrong.

Me: How the hell is that a family sport?

Brent: Oh, it's not. It's a cult. My little brother plays, and I'm gonna tell him a professional rugby player thinks his "sport" is PE with extra bruises.

I huff out a breath that's almost a laugh. The pain in my side tugs when I do, but it's worth it.

> Brent: Alright, gotta run—client coming in soon. Let me know if you want me to tweak anything, or if you want more options. No pressure. Just ideas. Talk soon, Captain.

I stare at the last message a second longer than I need to.

It's early evening. Saturday. The bus is still rumbling through drizzle and quiet laughter. I should be thinking about the pint I promised the lads. Instead, I'm wondering what Brent's client looks like.

I'm also wondering what Brent looks like when he's relaxed, at home, sketching. And—stupidly, quietly—I'm wondering if he's even queer.

I think I got a vibe, but I've been wrong before. Not that it matters.

Right?

4

Brent

"KEEP IT CLEAN, KEEP IT DRY. UNSCENTED moisturiser after two days. No picking. No swimming, no hot tubs, and no saunas, even if someone tries to seduce you into one. Trust me."

The guy, who's mid-twenties, maybe, and fresh off a dare with his mates, laughs and nods as I tape down the wrap over his new forearm piece. "Got it. No sexy saunas."

"None. I'm serious," I say, walking him to the front and handing him a care sheet. "You wouldn't believe what people admit to once their tattoo gets infected."

He thanks me again and heads out, still smiling, and I finally let myself exhale. It was an easy session—simple walk-in, clean lines, no complications. The kind of client

I like: cheerful, chill, not trying to convince me to ink their ex's name or a misspelled quote they found online.

It's been interesting, stepping into someone else's shop mid-flow. Tank's client list is long and loyal, but everyone's been welcoming so far. No drama. Just a few raised eyebrows, some light interrogation, the usual.

The trickiest one? Camden. Though "tricky" doesn't really feel like the right word. Careful, maybe. Guarded. And hell, who wouldn't be, living in the UK with those gossip-rag tabloids and photographers who lurk in trash cans?

He's got every reason to keep his walls up.

Doesn't stop me thinking about him.

Again.

I don't usually have the TV on when I'm working—it's distracting, and most of the time, I'd rather vibe out to music—but today I made an exception. I'd asked Flick—another tattooist here—and my client if they minded, and neither did. Flick gave me a long look, though. One of those eyebrow-raised, *I know what you're doing, but I won't say it* looks.

That's on him. He's not wrong. But still.

Camden intrigues me.

There's something beneath that tough exterior—beneath the beard and that slablike chest and the way he only seems to smile like it costs him money—that makes me want to look. Not in a nosey, tabloid way. Just... look.

We're heading to the pub tonight—same one we've been to a few times now. It's an easy walk, with good beer, decent fries, and a cosy sort of vibe that makes it feel like more than a stop between work and home. Flick's coming, and so are Carrie, who came in to do a few piercings, and Christy, the receptionist. The usual suspects.

We walk together, our chitchat light and pleasant as the four of us head down the narrow pavements. The night's got that late-spring nip in the air—sharp enough to bite at your fingertips but not freeze you outright. It's dark and cloudy, drizzle hanging in the air like a threat, but for now, it's just enough to dampen my hair and cool my skin.

By the time we get to the pub, the sound hits first.

It's louder than usual. Laughter spills out onto the street, conversations overlapping, and bodies are packed tighter inside. It must be post-match buzz. Makes sense since the training grounds aren't too far from here.

We step into the warmth, and the heat and noise hit me all at once. It's rowdy in the best way—shoulder to shoulder, elbows at the bar, friends crowded into booths with pints and stories spilling over the tables.

I smile without thinking. Yeah. This? This I like.

At the bar, I lean my forearms against the wood while Christy and Carrie start debating some new piercing trend they saw on Instagram. I half listen while ordering my pint, but my gaze starts drifting almost immediately.

And then I see him, Camden, tucked into a booth towards the back. It's dimly lit, but he's still unmissable. He's surrounded by a handful of guys—his teammates. I don't need a briefing to figure that out. Their energy, their size, the bruises on a few of their faces. Rugby men, through and through.

But I barely see them.

Because he's looking at me. Eyes locked, beard hiding half his expression, but not enough to miss the fact that he's watching me like he wasn't expecting me... but isn't all that mad about it either. And maybe it's stupid. Maybe it's nothing. But he doesn't look away, and neither do I.

My stomach does this strange little flip—tight, warm, not unlike the rush of dropping a stencil perfectly onto someone's shoulder. It's a precise kind of thrill. Fuck, he's gorgeous. And in my defence, he's the one holding my gaze.

I smile, subtle but definite. And when a hesitant, almost reluctant smile fires back, low and quick like a twitch he didn't mean to let happen, I feel it like a punch to the chest. The bartender hands me my pint, and I barely remember to thank him before turning, casting a quick glance towards Flick. I jerk my chin in Camden's direction, and Flick just lifts one brow, like *Are you seriously doing this?*

Yeah. I'm seriously doing this. Ill-advised? Possibly. But I swear, those text exchanges were leaning just a little flirty. And I'm not walking away from here tonight without saying hello.

I weave through the packed pub with my pint cradled carefully, dodging elbows and half-shouted jokes. My pulse thuds in my throat with every step I take towards Camden, still perched in that booth like a storm cloud with arms.

As I approach, he stands, and I swallow hard.

Fuck, I knew he was big—saw it in the flesh just three days ago—but seeing him like this—upright, broad, filling the space around him like it's his by default—does something to my insides that should absolutely not be happening in public. He's all shoulders and solid muscle, thighs like tree trunks, beard sharp enough to file metal on. And his presence? It's magnetic. Intense.

And fuck if he doesn't tick every damn box I didn't realise I still had.

We're barely two feet apart in the crush of bodies. Maybe less. This place wasn't made for tall blokes with commanding stares and nervous artists trying not to blush.

"Hey," I say, managing a smile that doesn't feel completely wrecked by nerves. "Didn't expect to see you here."

"Same," he says, voice low, rough. His gaze flicks down, then up again, like he's checking I'm real.

I hold out my hand, and he takes it—calloused palm, firm grip, but not trying to crush me. We're practically on each other thanks to the wall of humans pressing in around us, and I have to tilt my head just a little to meet his eyes. It's... a lot. In a good way. In a *very* good way.

"Good game," I say quietly. "Slippery as hell, but you held your own."

He nods, but his mouth tightens ever so slightly.

Noted. Right—rugby is off-limits.

I switch gears without missing a beat. "So"—I lean in, dropping my voice just enough—"you ever tattoo a seventy-nine-year-old woman with a pet iguana named Nigel?"

His eyes narrow slightly. "Can't say I have."

"Well," I say, grinning, "then you haven't lived."

He blinks at me, expression flat.

"For real," I say. "This woman—Edna—walks in last year while I was guesting at a shop in Manchester. Wants a tattoo of Nigel. She pulls out a photo of this majestic bastard in a little Santa hat, says, 'He hates it, but he looks adorable.' I swear on my life, she said adorable like she'd kill anyone who disagreed."

Camden releases a low chuckle—genuine, warm, unguarded—and Christ, it hits me like a jolt. I feel it in my spine. That sound should be bottled and sold for therapy.

His shoulders shift, almost like he's shaking off the instinct to pull back. But I clock the curve at the corner of his mouth. The glint in his eyes. There is something soft there—buried deep under years of careful caution—but it's real.

Someone nearby snorts, and I catch the movement of one of his teammates standing. He's shorter than Camden, wiry strong, and sporting a neat little cut just under his eye. He eyes me like he's already halfway through working out my life story.

"I'm Lachie," he says, grinning as he sticks out a hand. "The prettier one."

"Brent," I say, shaking it. "The tattooist."

"Ah." He nods, looking between us. "The artist. Heard about you."

"Should I be worried?"

"Always." He winks, and Camden makes a sound that might be disapproval or amusement—or both.

I glance briefly at the cut on Lachie's face, and it

reminds me that Camden was hurt. There's a bruise just visible now, darker under the collar of his shirt where it curves towards his side. Geez, he's hurt more than he let on. My gaze flicks back to his face—and that's when I catch it.

Both of his eyebrows lift slightly.

Caught out.

Right.

I lift my pint and take a slow sip, playing it casual. "You two look like you went ten rounds with the weather," I say to both of them. "And the other team."

Camden's still watching me, that subtle, unreadable expression firmly in place. But it's not cold. Not shutting me out. More like he's... weighing something.

And Lachie? He just smirks. "Welcome to rugby," he says. "Mud, bruises, and regret. Stick around long enough and you'll get used to it."

I nod, but my attention flicks back to Camden. He hasn't moved, hasn't said much, but his eyes haven't left mine once.

"So," Lachie says, turning to me fully with the gleam of someone who's just found a new toy, "you're definitely not from around here, right?"

"The accent gave it away, huh?" I reply. "Grew up in the States. Been in the UK a while now."

He nods, satisfied for all of a second. "You live alone?"

I blink. "Uh—yes?"

"Any pets?"

"Nope."

"Family nearby?"

"Nope."

"Got a girlfriend?"

I laugh. "Nope."

He doesn't miss a beat. "Boyfriend?"

There's no edge to it—just curiosity, open and shameless.

I smile and shrug. "Not for a while."

He hums like he's filing the answer under *Interesting, Possibly Important,* and I chance a glance at Camden.

He's still watching me. Still unreadable. But something flickers across his face. Just for a second. Like maybe he wasn't expecting me to say that. Like maybe it caught him off-guard.

Lachie hums thoughtfully. "So, you're single, charming, and good with your hands. That's the trifecta."

"You always interrogate strangers in bars?" I ask, raising my pint.

"Only the ones who might be spending time with my

BFF," he says cheerfully. "Gotta make sure you're a good guy. We've got a vetting process."

That actually lands softer. He's still full of humour, but there's something warm under it that's loyal, protective.

I glance at Camden again, more out of instinct than anything, and find him looking not at me but at Lachie— with that sort of long-suffering fondness that says *I'm going to kill you in your sleep, but I'll still cook you break-fast in the morning.*

I snort. "So, this is the interview, huh? Should I have brought references?"

"If you've got a glowing review from your mum, I'll accept it."

"Tragically, she thinks I'm a delight."

Camden shifts beside me—finally—and says drily, "Ignore him. He thinks he's subtle."

Lachie clutches his chest. "That hurts."

"Good."

Before Lachie can go full inquisition again, Camden says, his voice low but clear, "All right." He steps in with a tone that walks the line between exasperated and dry amusement. "That's enough interrogation for one night."

"Oh, come on—"

"I'll buy you a pint," Camden cuts in, turning to me. "To apologise for him."

I raise an eyebrow. "Apologise or escape?"

"Bit of both."

I grin. "Tempting."

He gives me a look that dares me not to follow, and when he turns, his hand brushes the small of my back—barely a touch, just enough pressure to guide me through the crowd, but hell, my brain short-circuits. Camden's hand is big and warm and right there, and I don't care how packed this bar is, I'm pretty sure I could float to the other side of the room.

I keep walking, trying very hard not to think about the fact that my jeans are now about thirty seconds away from being classified as a health hazard.

Christ. I need to focus, but it's not easy. Not when the gruff rugby captain with thunder in his laugh and bruises under his shirt just hauled me out of a conversation and laid a claim with nothing more than a half-smile and a hand at my back.

Camden moves to my side as the crowd thins while we weave towards the bar. "Lachie means well. He just thinks every conversation is a contact sport."

I snort. "So... rugby, but in words?"

"Exactly."

And God help me, I like this man more with every step.

Camden doesn't say another word as he threads

through the crowd. He just keeps that steady hand at the small of my back until we reach the bar. He orders without looking at me, like this is just another part of his job as captain—ensure the newcomer isn't traumatised by Lachie's enthusiasm, provide alcohol, return to strategic silence.

But when he turns and hands me the pint, his fingers brush mine—brief, accidental maybe, but definitely not missed.

I follow him without a word, and he leads me towards a quieter spot near the back—half tucked behind a pillar, one of those tables that's slightly too small and too round to be comfortable. But right now, it feels like the only bubble of calm in the whole damn pub.

He slides into the bench seat and nods for me to take the opposite side.

No fuss. No small talk. Just him, quiet, watching.

I let the silence sit for a few beats as I take a sip, then lean my forearms on the table. "You always let Lachie do your PR?"

He snorts. "Can't stop him."

"I like him," I say. "He's a menace. But the good kind."

Camden grunts. That might be agreement.

I smile, unbothered. I'm not here to crack him open

or dig too deep. But I am here. And he *did* lead me here. That has to mean something.

The quiet stretches between us, but it's not uncomfortable—not for me anyway. He's got that rare kind of presence, the kind that doesn't need to fill every silence with words. Still, I need to steer us towards safer ground.

"So," I say, "the sketches... you said they were close to what you had in mind. Want to talk specifics?"

He nods slowly. "The second one—more of that. Cleaner lines. Bit more structure through the elbow."

My eyebrows lift, impressed. "You know exactly what you're after."

"Had time to think it through."

"That helps." I pause, then tilt my head. "And you've got a good eye. Most people don't catch structural flow through the joints unless they've done a few themselves or stared at too many bad tattoos."

His mouth quirks—barely, but it's there. "I've seen enough to know what I don't want."

"That's half the battle."

He nods again, sips his beer, and I take the opportunity to just watch him.

His beard is neatly trimmed, not a speck out of place, and he's changed out of his kit—clean and put together in a way that still somehow feels effortless. There's something about the way he sits, like he's *always* ready to move—solid, firm, coiled quiet. His knuckles are rough, bruised. There's a tension in his shoulders that never really leaves. And then there's that *voice*—low, gravelly, threaded with that deep West Midlands drawl that I *definitely* shouldn't be this into.

"So, you're from the Midlands?" I ask.

"Yeah," he says. "Just outside Wolverhampton."

"I still haven't made it up that way," I admit, leaning back. "London, Brighton, bits of Devon now—but I've yet to venture further north. One day."

He huffs, not quite a laugh. "Depends what you're after. If you like post-industrial towns with a half-decent curry and endless rain, it's a dream."

I grin. "Sounds like home, honestly. Just swap rain for snow and add one loud hockey rink."

That gets a flicker of something—amusement, maybe. Recognition. It's always subtle with him, but it's there if you're watching.

The conversation winds on in gentle turns, nothing too deep, but enough to give me flickers—glimpses—of the man behind the press photos and the guarded looks. Camden's still clipped with his words, still watching me like he's measuring out trust by the ounce, but there's warmth under the surface. A dry wit that slips out in tiny, unexpected sparks.

We talk about the differences between Devon and

the Midlands, about his mum's obsession with feeding people, and about how his sister once threatened to break his nose for stealing the last custard tart at Christmas. He tells me all of this in the same deadpan tone, like it's barely worth sharing, and yet each piece feels like a little stone passed across the table. Carefully placed. Quietly offered.

I'm just about to tell him about the time I accidentally tattooed a mirrored symbol on a guy's ribs—his fault for holding the reference sheet upside down—when a pair of voices stumble into our quiet space.

"Camden! Mate, hell of a game!"

We both turn as two guys, who are probably in their mid-twenties with pints in hand and clearly a few deep, wobble over to our table. One's got a club scarf half hanging off his neck; the other's already half spilling his beer.

Camden shifts, subtly but instantly. His shoulders stiffen just enough for me to notice. His pint stays on the table, untouched, but his posture changes. Alert. Ready.

He gives them a small nod, smile tight. "Cheers."

"Thought you were gonna break that guy's ribs in the first scrum," the scarf guy says with a laugh, clearly unaware of the tension on Camden's shoulders.

Camden's smile doesn't move. "No need. Ref handled it."

They linger for a moment too long, and I feel something twist low in my stomach. Not fear, not exactly—but something protective, a flicker of frustration on his behalf. This isn't hostile. But it's intrusive. Like watching someone push past a boundary they can't see.

Camden stays calm and still.

"Appreciate you coming by, lads," he says when the drunker of the two starts trying to replicate a huddle, "but I'm catching up with someone."

A beat.

Another.

Then scarf guy claps the table once. "Right'o. Cheers, mate. Good luck next game." They shuffle off without fuss, back into the crowd.

Camden exhales through his nose, and when he looks at me, there's the faintest flash of apology.

I tilt my head. "That happen a lot?"

He shrugs. "Sometimes. Less now."

I glance back at the booth where a few of his teammates are still sat, mostly unnoticed. "I'm honestly amazed there are so many of you just... hanging out here."

"It's our local," he says simply. "Unwritten rule not to hassle the players. Most people stick to it."

"And when they don't?"

He lifts one shoulder again. "They get bored when we're not dramatic."

I sip my pint, watching him over the rim. "You handled it well."

His mouth twitches. "You expecting a headbutt?"

"No," I say, grinning. "Well, maybe from Lachie."

That gets me a proper snort. It's short-lived, but it's real.

I told myself this move to Exeter was about work. About carving out a quieter, more stable kind of life. But the truth? I've been restless. Something in me has been waiting—for what, I'm not sure. Maybe for a reason to stay in this country beyond just liking the people, the pace, the grey skies that made ink colours pop. I miss my family, yeah. But I want to build something that's mine. And maybe, finally, I'm closer than I thought.

The mood settles again, if not a little quieter. I study him for a moment—his steady hands, his careful posture, the way he always seems like he's bracing for something, even in stillness.

He's used to being on. Always on display, always prepared. But now? Here? He's just Camden.

And I *like* him.

Probably more than I should.

5

Camden

We're talking about moss.

Not metaphorically.

Literal moss.

Apparently, there's a kind that glows faintly in caves up north, and Brent saw it once in a documentary and thought it was the coolest shit ever. I don't know how we got onto the subject—probably something about strange British nature or weird local facts—but somehow, it's fifteen minutes later and I'm sitting in the corner of my team's pub, trying not to smile like an idiot while a heavily tattooed American tells me about bioluminescence with the enthusiasm of a drunk history teacher.

And what's weirder is I'm relaxed. My shoulders aren't near my ears. My jaw's not clenched. My guard's still there—somewhere—but it's been shoved to the back seat by this calm, warm presence who keeps looking at me like I'm worth talking to, not for what I do on the pitch but just... for me.

It's dangerous.

He's easy. Not in the casual sense—but in the way he fills silence without pushing, jokes without jabbing, listens without making it feel like I'm under a microscope. Witty, chilled, confident, but not in that brash, look-at-me way that makes my skin crawl.

It's too easy.

I don't know him. That's rule one. No letting people in who haven't earned it.

But Brent's already sliding under my skin like he belongs there. And all it took was two meetings and a few too many text messages I looked forward to more than I do payday.

On top of that, he's attractive. Like, really fucking hot.

It tends to be smaller guys who expect me to throw them around and call me daddy or some shit who clamour for my attention. Brent's almost as tall as I am. Broad in the shoulders, lean through the waist. His T-shirt clings to muscle in a way that's completely unfair— but not in a poser kind of way. Just... natural. Like he actually uses his body for something instead of living in the gym mirror.

When he took off his hoodie earlier, I nearly swallowed my bloody tongue.

He's got a lip ring I'd kill to pull on and eyes that always seem amused by something I haven't said.

And I'd like to.

The thought slams into me like a kick to the ribs.

Shit.

I clear my throat and stand abruptly, knocking the underside of the table with my knee. "I've got to head off."

Brent blinks once. If he's surprised or put out, he doesn't show it. Just nods, still calm. "Yeah," he says. "Long day. I should probably head home too. I've got tomorrow off, and getting in bed before eleven sounds amazing. Gonna sleep like a log."

My brows pull together. "Wait—what time is it?"

He glances at his phone. "Quarter to eleven."

I blink. "How the hell...?"

Time does not just disappear on me. Not with people I barely know. Not when I'm this... me. But somehow, it's happened.

I shoot my teammates a nod on the way out. Rafi gives me a wave. Jules throws me a wink. Lachie—of course—bounces his bloody eyebrows like he's already halfway through composing a filthy group chat message.

Internally, I flip him off. Externally, I keep walking. He probably thinks I'm getting lucky.

If only.

I'm so tempted. My body is halfway to leaning in, pinning Brent against a wall in some quiet alley, my brain already composing headlines I'll regret. But then I remember—he's going to be working on me soon. Needles. Intimate skin. Long hours.

Talk about awkward.

Outside, I brace for that uncomfortable goodbye. The lingering too-long moment. The hand hovering in mid-air. Instead, Brent grins, warm and easy, and holds out his palm for a shake. No weirdness. No expectation.

"Had a good night," he says. "Shoot me a message when you want to chat more about the ink, if you want." Then he turns and walks away down the street like he hasn't just made my brain short-circuit and my chest ache in ways I don't have the training to deal with.

I watch him go. And fuck—I'm not ready to say goodbye.

"Brent," I call out, my voice low, uncertain, and not at all connected to the part of my brain that usually stops me from doing stupid shit.

He turns immediately, hands tucked into his pockets, smile soft around the edges, curiosity in his eyes. "Okay?"

Fuck.

"Yeah," I say quickly. "I was just...." Words vanish. Just gone. I have no idea what I'm doing. I am absolutely not about to say I'm not ready for the night to end. Jesus. "Nothing. Just... uhm... get home safe, yeah?"

His tongue dips out, brushing over that cursed lip ring, and I watch it happen in real time—helpless. He doesn't look away. That gaze of his is clear and steady, assessing without pressure. Calm. Open. Meanwhile, my heart's doing laps in my chest like it's training for the bloody Olympics.

That lip ring. It's going to be the death of me.

The silence stretches—too long. Too heavy. I can practically hear the sound of my own dignity crumbling. I pull myself together, or try to. My lips part, ready to mumble another awkward goodbye and retreat like the grown-arse man I'm not—

"I can show you those sketches properly if you want," he says suddenly. "Have a play with some of those changes you mentioned?"

I nod once, then again like my body's been possessed by that damn car insurance dog. Because everything in me is screaming *bad idea, walk away, rules, distance, control.* But none of it's stronger than the part of me that wants more.

His smile spreads, slow and brilliant. And fuck me dead, I am so screwed.

"You want to walk with me? Or your car...?"

"It's safe in the car park around back," I manage, voice slightly rough. "Macca, the owner, keeps it secure for players."

He nods. "Come on, then." He beckons, just a little gesture of his hand, and my feet?

Yeah, they move. Like he's gravity. Like I'm the tide.

We fall into step side by side, the pub's rowdy noise fading behind us. The air is cool, mist soft against the back of my neck. The path leads us past a few small shops—all closed up for the night, shutters down and glowing with the spill of distant streetlamps. The florist's window still has fairy lights blinking across a sign that says, "Back tomorrow, unless the plants kill me first." A bakery sits next door, the scent of something faintly sweet still clinging to the pavement.

We pass an alley that cuts behind the row—narrow and dark, leading to the other side of the block where there's an old mural half gone with age and probably a dozen foxes nesting in the bins.

The silence between us hums. Not awkward. Not exactly. It's tense. Thick.

Every step is heavy with awareness. Of the space between our arms. The brush of his shoulder. The fact that I can hear his breathing shift when I glance at him from the corner of my eye.

I cast him a look—half a glance, just to gauge. He swallows. His throat bobs. And then he goes and does it again. He plays with that fucking lip ring, and I might actually self-destruct.

The alley catches my eye—the narrow one, shadowed between the newsagents and the mural-stained wall. It's barely lit, tucked out of view from the main street, and before I know what the hell I'm doing, my hand is on Brent's wrist.

He looks over, surprised—but not alarmed.

He's still smiling, still following.

I tug him towards the mouth of the alley and press him back against the wall before I can talk myself out of it. He gasps—not shocked, more breathless—and his eyes flare wide. His back hits the brick, and he laughs under his breath, lips parted, gaze locked on me with something that looks a lot like yes.

"Well," he says, voice low and playful, "hello, Captain."

I freeze. Just for a second. Because fuck—I didn't plan this. Didn't think. I don't do this. Dragging someone into the dark like some walking cliché.

Brent's not just anyone, though. He's a guy I have to work with on my tattoo, someone whose voice has been living in my head since I met him. Someone who makes me want things I've trained myself not to want.

And here I am, pressing him to a wall like I know what I'm doing.

My heart's thudding loud enough that I can feel it in my throat. And now? Now I'm second-guessing every-thing. "Shit," I murmur, dropping my head for half a second. "Sorry, I don't usually drag... this isn't—"

He tilts his head, still smiling. "Camden."

My eyes lift.

"Breathe." That smile's still there, softening every-thing. His hand curls lightly around my wrist. "You're not dragging me. I came."

His words tug something loose in my chest. Still, I can't quite let the tension go. "I don't do this," I admit, voice gravelled and too honest. "I don't... react like this. I don't know you."

"Not yet," he says gently. "But you could."

That lands harder than I expect. Not pushy. Not smug. Just... possible. Then he moves and spins us.

I let him, too stunned to stop it.

My back hits the wall with a muted thump, and he steps in, close enough that his breath skims my jaw. One of his arms braces beside my head. The other curls just slightly at my waist.

"Okay?" he murmurs.

I nod.

Once.

Twice.

My feet shift instinctively, and he nudges one of his in between mine until I lower slightly, just enough to meet him where he is. I swallow thickly, awareness ricocheting through me like static.

Then he kisses me.

No hesitation. No nerves. He just takes it—the thing I wanted but was too scared to reach for. And I'm gone. Completely, utterly gone.

The moment his lips touch mine, everything else drops away. The noise from the street. The faint scent of bread from the bakery. The thrum of blood in my ears.

Gone.

All that's left is Brent—his warmth, his calm, and that wicked little lip ring that presses cold against my bottom lip before his tongue follows, hot and confident and so damn in control that my knees nearly buckle.

He kisses like he's done this a thousand times and knows exactly how to undo me with one tilt of his head, one subtle shift of pressure. My dick punches against the inside of my dress pants, sudden and sharp, and I grunt—low and rough—into his mouth.

He doesn't pull back. He doesn't even flinch. He just

deepens the kiss, a hand curling at my hip to steady me as if he knows I'm coming undone.

I don't let people take control. That's not who I am. Not off the pitch. Not in life. And definitely not in this.

But Brent doesn't ask. He takes. And I let him.

When he finally pulls back, I chase him without thinking—mouth following his like I'm starving for something I only just realised I've been missing. It's instinct and embarrassing as fuck, but I can't help it.

He pecks my lips once more, gentle, like sealing the moment. Then his voice, low and calm, breaks the tension. "Come on," he says. "Let's get off the street."

It's like a bucket of water to the chest. Right. We're outside. Still. Alley-adjacent.

Fuck.

"Yeah," I mutter, dragging in a breath. "Let's do that."

We fall into step again, walking quickly now. My head's a mess—buzzing, stunned, a little dazed. I half expect him to take a turn towards a flat or side street, but instead, he leads us towards Black Salt Ink.

The shop's shutter is halfway down, lights dimmed except for the one above the main station. He unlocks the door, pushes it open, and gestures me inside. It smells like antiseptic and ink. Familiar. Clean. Calming.

He flicks on another light and walks to the counter,

grabbing a portfolio and an unopened bottle of water, which he tosses to me without missing a beat.

I catch it by pure luck.

"Sit," he says, nodding at the station table.

I do—grateful, honestly, for something solid under me. My knees are still not okay. Across from me, he flips the portfolio open. Quiet. Professional. Like he didn't just kiss me like he wanted to take me apart in the street.

Christ.

Brent lays out the sketches, the ones he took photos of and sent me yesterday. His hands are steady, fingers stained faintly with ink even now. He doesn't say anything at first, just gives me a moment to look.

"These are what I've got so far," he says, sitting down across from me. "Based on what we talked about before. Obviously, I haven't had a chance to work in the notes you gave me tonight yet, but I'm glad we're on the same page about direction."

I nod slowly, scanning the bold shapes, the clean flow of lines. It's good. Really fucking good. Even before adjustments, it's already speaking to something in me.

"I like this," I murmur, tapping the one that mirrors the structure from my right arm. "This one flows better than the others."

He leans in a little, not crowding, just close enough to read the page beside me. "Yeah. I studied the photos that Tank took of your right piece. That's where I thought you'd lean. I'll tweak the elbow section, tighten the wrap, sharpen the direction down the forearm. Maybe bring in more negative space."

I lift my gaze. "I want it to feel like it belongs. Not like it's fighting the other side."

His lips twitch. "You and symmetry, huh?"

I take a long sip of the water he passed me. "I like balance. On the pitch and off it."

"Noted," he says easily.

I watch him as he scribbles a few things on a sticky note, head tilted, brow drawn in quiet focus. It's unfair, how this moment—just the two of us, a table between, pencil scratching paper—feels calmer than it should after what just happened in the alley.

It's centring. It grounds me.

I needed this. Talking about the sketch helps me find my footing again. Helps me be me again.

But still, I can't forget how he kissed me like he already knew exactly how I'd taste.

Brent grabs a fresh pencil and flips to a clean page in the sketchbook, posture loose but focused. His brow furrows slightly as he starts blocking out shapes—quick, light strokes, just roughing out ideas. He's quiet for a minute. There's just the soft drag of graphite filling the space between us.

I watch his hands. They're confident, efficient, with no hesitation. I don't know why that makes me feel calmer, but it does.

"You know," he says, not looking up, "the first person I ever inked was my best friend's older brother. I was seventeen. Probably shouldn't have even been holding a machine unsupervised, but Dutch—my mentor—had this hands-off, 'figure it out or fuck it up' approach to teaching."

I raise a brow, relaxing a little. "That sounds promising."

"Oh, it gets worse," he says, grinning. "This guy, Tyler, shows up all full of swagger, like 'Yeah, man, ink me up, no big deal.' Wants a tribal sun—because it was back in the day, and no one was making good decisions."

I snort despite myself.

Brent's smile widens. "I get maybe thirty seconds in and the machine stalls. Just dies in my hand. Tyler doesn't even flinch. He's halfway through telling me about a rave he's throwing in a barn, and I'm panicking, like 'This is it. I've ruined a man's spine, and my career's over before it started.'"

I let out a quiet laugh. "What did you do?"

"Faked it," he says proudly. "Made some vague excuse about switching needles and then spent the next ten minutes trying to fix the machine with my elbow covering the fresh linework so he wouldn't notice I'd botched the curve."

"And did he?"

"Not until two years later when he came in to get it covered up," Brent says, flicking his eyes up to me with a shameless grin. "Said it looked like a cartoon egg hatching."

I huff a low, amused breath. "Did you do the cover-up?"

"I did. Fuck knows why he let me, but he let me fix up my shitty design. Somehow, we're still friends. Mostly."

I shake my head, but the grin pulling at my mouth is harder to fight now.

There's something disarming about Brent, even when he's telling a story that should've had me walking out the door ten minutes ago. It's the way he owns it. The way he laughs at himself without pretending he's perfect. He doesn't try to impress me. He just is.

And that... that's dangerous as hell.

Because the more I sit here across from him—his long fingers dusted in graphite, his hair falling forward as he sketches, that faint smudge of ink on his cheek from earlier I hadn't noticed before—the more I feel my grip loosening.

The reasons I shouldn't want this blur at the edges.

The excuses I've clung to start crumbling. And that kiss? That stupid, perfect kiss? It's echoing too loud in my head.

It's not supposed to feel like this. It's not supposed to feel... right.

I push back from the chair so fast it scrapes against the floor. Brent startles, pencil still in hand, gaze snapping up to mine.

"Cam?"

"I can't—" My voice comes out rough. "I just need— Sorry. I need to go."

I'm already moving. Already ducking out into the reception like the building's on fire and I forgot how to breathe. Because if I stay one second longer, I'll fall harder. And I'm not ready for what that means.

Not yet.

Not with someone who might actually matter.

By the time I crawl into bed, my brain's still tangled in Brent. In his stupid lip ring. His voice. The way he'd looked at me with zero judgement, just patience and curiosity and a quiet kind of focus that shouldn't be as disarming as it is.

I'm exhausted, but sleep's clearly not on the cards—

not with my thoughts racing like they've just snorted a line of preseason adrenaline. So I do what I shouldn't. I reach for my phone. It's past midnight, but the screen lights up the second I touch it—and my stomach swoops.

There's a Messenger notification from Brent. My breath hitches. I tap it open.

A voice message that's over two minutes long.

I freeze. It's late, definitely too late for casual conversation and even for tattoo sketches or rugby updates or shared memes. My heart does a weird stumble. I press Play before I can think better of it.

It starts instantly.

A sharp breath. A low groan.

"Fuck—Camden..."

My cock twitches.

He's panting. The sound of slick skin on skin is unmistakable, and Jesus Christ, it's him—Brent. His voice, rough and breathless, wrapping around my name like a fucking prayer.

My balls pull tight. I lie here, stunned, heat pulsing under my skin, cock swelling fast beneath the sheets as the audio keeps going. He's not holding back. It's raw. Dirty. Him chasing release with my name wrecked on his tongue.

"God, you—" A ragged moan. *"—looked so fucking good tonight... Been thinking about your mouth all day..."*

I'm frozen, rooted to the mattress while my dick fights for space against the waistband of my boxers. Just as I reach down—just as my palm brushes the ache beneath my waistband—there's a scuffle in the audio. A muted curse. A bump.

"Oh fuck, no. Shit... shit—"

Then silence. The recording ends abruptly, and I almost drop my phone when it pings.

> Brent: Please don't listen to that.

> Brent: It wasn't meant to be listened to.

> Brent: Fuck.

> Brent: Please just delete it.

> Brent: Ignore me. I'm an idiot.

Another ping.

> Brent: I'm so sorry.

> Brent: Shit. Camden, seriously...

> Brent: I didn't mean to send that. Just... delete it, okay?

I stare at the messages, at the little timestamp, at the fact that it says he's still online with the cursor moving, probably mortified. Probably pacing his room, wondering if I'm going to ghost him or sue him or show up to slap him upside the head.

I don't know what to say. My cock's still hard. My body is still burning. But my head? My head is a mess.

Was that real? A mistake? Some kind of twisted test? I can't tell. I should respond. Say something. But I don't trust myself right now.

Instead, I lock the screen, turn off the lamp, and lie here—awake. Wanting and confused.

Jesus Christ. What the fuck just happened?

It's all too much, too fast. And holy hell, if this is what he sounds like when he's getting off alone, I'm in trouble.

6

Brent

TWO DAYS. THAT'S HOW LONG IT'S BEEN SINCE I kissed Camden Crawford against a brick wall like I had a goddamn death wish.

Two days since he kissed me back like he wanted to taste what made me tick.

Two days since we sat in the shop afterwards, pretending we weren't both completely wrecked—me sketching like I hadn't just kissed a man who could knock me flat with a single shoulder feint, and him watching me like I hadn't just blown through half his boundaries without a second thought.

And also—minor detail—two days since I accidentally sent him a voice message of me jacking off to the memory of said kiss.

Yeah. Fucking stellar move.

Here's how that went, in case you're imagining something sexy and cinematic: I got home, still buzzing. Should've had a cold shower. Should've done anything else. Instead, I got hard the second I walked through my flat door. All it took was remembering the sound he made when I pressed him to the wall. That soft, surprised inhale. That little grunt when I tugged his bottom lip.

So, naturally, I dropped onto my bed and reached for my phone. Innocent enough, right? Scroll through our message thread, get my rocks off like a normal, desperate idiot. What I didn't account for: I cannot, under any circumstance, multitask.

At some point during the proceedings—probably when I muttered his name like a depraved voicemail from hell—I must've hit Record.

Did I notice?

No. Because I was two seconds from coming and thought the slight vibration from my phone was some phantom pleasure wave from the gods.

It was not.

It was Messenger asking if I'd like to send my two-minute-and-twelve-second sexcapade to Camden Crawford. And with my fingers slicked in lube and my brain short-circuited, I didn't hit Delete. I hit Send.

Because clearly, I should never be allowed near technology during orgasm.

I think I made a choked, panicked dolphin noise. Then I fumbled to Unsend it like the coward I am, only to realise he'd already opened it.

What followed were a series of world-class humiliations:

Me: Please delete that.

Me: I meant to send it to... the void. Not you.

Me: Oh God. Camden. I'm so sorry.

Me: That wasn't for you. Obviously.

Me: Can we pretend I've never touched my dick?

Okay, those may not be the exact things I texted, but I can't look at them to remind myself. The whole thing is just too humiliating.

Needless to say, he did not respond.

For two full days, I sent a few more half-hearted apologies, even considered mailing him a bouquet of "I have no impulse control" flowers. Eventually, I stopped texting entirely. I'm now operating under the "ignore it until death claims you" school of coping.

Which brings me to now—sitting in the studio, two days deep into mortification, sketchpad in front of me, phone on silent like it might explode if I so much as breathe near it.

I'm not proud. I've handled humiliation better than I've handled this. But to be fair... humiliation never involved me moaning a man's name into a voice memo by accident.

I drag a hand down my face. Maybe he's forgotten. Maybe he's busy. Maybe he's moved to Antarctica. Whatever the reason, Camden's been radio silent since that night—and somehow, that's worse than any punch to the face I ever took wrangling with my brothers.

I lean back in my chair, staring at the sketch of his tattoo-in-progress. And yeah... I miss him. Even if he probably thinks I'm a walking cautionary tale about mixing lube and mobile devices. Even if I deserve it.

Still.

Goddamn.

I hope he texts back.

Camden Crawford, local rugby god, guardian of his inner sanctum, has ghosted me so hard I feel like I've been benched from his entire emotional league. Sure, I've been ghosted before. It comes with the territory of adulthood. Sometimes after a first date, sometimes after a night of sweaty limbs and bad decisions. I don't usually get sucker-punched by it.

And now, apparently, I'm the proud owner of a growing collection of unanswered messages, a dangerously overworked design sketch, and a complex emotional attachment to a man I've kissed once.

Awesome.

To top it off, Tank's last day was yesterday. He hugged me, said something vague and encouraging about "owning the space," and then buggered off to Canada like this place isn't held together with duct tape and good intentions.

So it's real now. It's mine.

Black Salt Ink is mine.

And while that's what I wanted—hell, what I worked for—it's also suddenly a lot. Bookings to manage. Equipment to maintain. A damn thermostat that seems to have two settings: surface of the sun or Arctic Circle. And apparently, I've already managed to screw it all up by running off one of the few high-profile clients we've got.

I moved here thinking this would be it. The place I put down roots. The life I build for myself instead of waiting for something back in the States to call me home. I miss my family—some days more than others—but this? *This* was supposed to be my next chapter.

Right now, though, it's hard not to wonder if I've made a mistake.

Still, I've never been a quitter. Not when I left home at eighteen, not when I apprenticed for a man who didn't believe in second chances, and not now. Especially not now.

So I suck in a breath, push my hair out of my face,

and get back to it. If Camden's ghosting me, then fine. I'll wait him out. Let him come to me.

Or at least... try. But still, Camden isn't just hot. He's a great canvas. The kind of guy who knows what he wants, respects the art, and isn't full of crap. I was genuinely excited to work with him. Still am.

But instead, I've been obsessively tweaking the sketch for his sleeve design like it's going to sprout legs and walk out the door without me. I've reworked the shading, cleaned up the linework, and adjusted the elbow flow three times, even though I know the first version was fine.

Carrie keeps throwing looks at me like I'm leaking emotional damage all over the front counter. And Flick? He's trying to bribe me into beer o'clock every twenty minutes. I don't have the heart to tell either of them I'm just... waiting.

Waiting for my phone to buzz.

Waiting for a grumpy message.

Waiting for someone who kissed me like he meant it, then walked away like it was a mistake.

And I hate that it stings. Because it wasn't even a real thing.

Right?

Right.

The day crawls. There's no client in the chair and no

distraction in sight. It's just me, a lukewarm coffee, and a mountain of intake files that somehow never shrinks no matter how many I go through. The shop is quiet, with Carrie humming at the front while Flick taps his foot to whatever's coming through his headphones.

It's the slow kind of day that drags every loose thought up to the surface. Which, of course, means I've spent far too long wondering if Camden's going to text back. Still nothing.

I'm flipping through appointment notes from two months ago, trying not to obsess over the sketch I've already reworked to death, when my phone rings.

I lunge for it like it's a lifeline—too quick, too hopeful—and end up juggling the thing as it nearly flies from my hand.

Flick snorts from his station, not even bothering to hide his laughter. "Smooth."

I shoot him a withering look, even as I answer the call and check the screen.

Cosmo.

I sigh. "Of course."

Cosmo is my youngest brother. The surprise child. The chaos child. My parents had four of us already—three boys and a girl—and then boom, surprise baby number five rolls in like a nuclear glitter bomb.

And they called him Cosmo.

They thought it was hilarious. He still thinks it is.

"Hey, little man," I say as I press the phone to my ear and drop back into the office chair.

"Yo," he says, voice too loud and full of unearned energy. "What's up, ink god?"

"I *will* hang up."

"You won't. I'm the only one keeping you from dying alone in your shop surrounded by empty Red Bull cans and crushed dreams."

I rub a hand over my face. "What do you want?"

"I'm just finishing exams. Thought I'd call my favourite brother."

"I'm the only brother who answers your calls."

"And yet... still the favourite."

I smile despite myself. And truthfully, I miss the shit out of him and the rest of my family.

We talk for a bit—him rambling about a paper he bullshitted his way through, an ice hockey team drama I only half understand, a guy he maybe kissed or maybe dreamt about, unclear—but eventually he pauses.

"You sound weird."

"Thanks?"

"No, like... not bad. Just off. You okay?"

I pause. And then—because apparently my mouth is running emotional updates without consulting me—I say, "I kissed someone."

Cosmo makes a long *ooooooohhh* sound, like I've just admitted to robbing a bank with a supermodel.

"I didn't mean to," I add.

"Wait, what? Was it, like, an accidental kiss? Did you trip and fall on their face?"

"No," I groan. "I mean I didn't plan it. It just happened. Heat of the moment. And now... I think I got ghosted."

He's quiet for a second, which for Cosmo is suspicious. "Damn," he says at last. "Was it, like, good?"

I close my eyes and lean my head back. "It was... a lot."

There's a beat of silence before he drops his wisdom, delivered with all the grace of someone who gets most of his life advice from memes and YouTube shorts. "Life is too short, man. Like, you remember that gorilla? The one in captivity for, like, twenty years? They released him back to the wild and he died in a day."

I frown. "What the hell—"

"Don't be the gorilla, Brent."

"What does that even mean?"

"You stay locked up in a zoo of your own overthinking, you're gonna miss the jungle. Or die in it. I dunno. Metaphors aren't my strength."

I'm laughing before I can stop myself, the sound catching in my chest. It's ridiculous. It's so Cosmo, and somehow it helps, even as a pang of homesickness squeezes inside my chest. "Thanks, philosopher child."

"Anytime. Just don't die in the wild, man."

"I'll try not to."

He hangs up with a cheery "Go make out with some-one!" and leaves me sitting here, smiling at my phone like a fool.

Don't be the gorilla.

Fuck.

Easier said than done.

After Cosmo's gone, I stare at the phone in my hand, thumb hovering over the thread of messages I have with Camden. The last one I sent was twelve hours ago. Maybe more. I scroll up, reread the one with the dumb flirty feather joke, and wince.

God, Brent, really?

Still... there's nothing aggressive. Nothing pushy. Just a guy trying to hold a thread between him and someone he maybe shouldn't have kissed. But definitely wanted to.

I tap out a new message. Professional. Neat.

Me: Hey—no pressure, but wanted to check in. Design's looking strong, and I'm happy to go over it whenever you're ready. Studio's quiet tonight if you want to pop by. If not, no worries. Just let me know what works.

I hesitate for a beat, then hit Send. The second I do, the bell over the door chimes. I glance up, already halfway to rolling my eyes because, of course, someone walks in with sixty seconds to spare before we lock the place—

Then I almost swallow my goddamn tongue.

Camden.

Big, broad-shouldered, and looking like someone just dared him to walk into traffic. His brows are drawn, his mouth in that tight line I now know means he's two seconds away from bolting. His hands are shoved into the pockets of his hoodie, his thick brown hair covered by a beanie, and he looks about as comfortable as a man wading through a minefield barefoot.

Flick glances over from his station, one brow already on the rise. Carrie pauses behind the desk, eyes flicking between us.

Camden's standing just inside the doorway, as if he'd been there—*waiting*—when the message came through. His hood's still up, shadowing his face, but I don't miss the tightness in his posture. Like he's still not sure if he should be here. Like he's halfway out the door even as he stands in it.

I clear my throat and force my voice to stay even despite my heart burning at inferno levels. "Hey. You, uh... you came."

He nods once. Short. Sharp. "You said it was quiet."

I blink. "I only just sent that," I say carefully.

He shrugs, eyes flicking around the shop but never quite meeting mine. "Figured you'd be here."

"I am."

Then I turn to Flick. "You and Carrie can head out. I've got it." Christy is already long gone—only working part-time at reception. The rest of the time we fend for ourselves.

Flick raises both eyebrows now, but he doesn't say anything. Just flicks his gaze between the two of us, grabs his bag, and offers me a low, amused "Night, boss."

"See ya," I mumble.

Carrie mouths, "Good luck," as she passes me and makes a clean exit.

The moment the door closes and the latch clicks, the silence drops like a curtain. It's thick and tense. I'd like to say it's thick with chemistry, but that's probably wishful thinking.

We stand here, awkwardly facing each other with all the grace of two teenagers at their first school dance. We both open our mouths at the same time.

"I—"

"You—"

I smile, trying to cut the tension. "You go."

Camden hesitates. His eyes flick towards the floor,

then back up to me. His mouth twitches—not a smile, not quite. And then he says, "I'm sorry."

I blink.

"About the other night," he adds quickly. "I shouldn't have left like that. I... I handled it badly."

My stomach sinks a little, just enough to feel it. I manage a quiet laugh. "You know *I* kissed *you*, right?"

He looks at me—really looks this time—but doesn't answer. He just shrugs one shoulder, almost helplessly.

I nod, trying to make this easy for him. Trying not to let my own disappointment show. "It's fine. You don't owe me anything."

"I didn't mean to disappear on you," he says, and it sounds like he's forcing the words through gravel.

"But you did."

"I know."

We stand here in this moment, too many things unsaid and one too many already out in the open. Then he clears his throat and shifts his weight. "I'd like to move forward with the sleeve."

Ah. Right. Of course.

My chest squeezes tight, but I give him the easiest smile I can muster. "Sure. I've actually been tweaking the designs. Want to take a look?"

He nods, stepping further into the studio, eyes flicking to the station we sat at last time. He heads that way without being told. Professional. Straight to busi-ness. I follow, pulling the sketchbook from the desk.

And that's it, then. The kiss is a memory. The goril-la's back in the cage. But if this is what he wants—distance, control, clean lines between what happened and what will—then I'll give it to him.

Even if I kind of hate it.

7

Camden

You'd think I'd have learned my lesson by now. Making out with a bloke in a dark alley near a public pub, with half the city's nightlife two pints away from pulling their phones out? *Yeah. Real subtle, Crawford.*

Sunday was my day off. It was supposed to be all peace and recovery. A long lie-in, stretch session, maybe a roast with the lads. Instead, I spent the whole fucking day wanting to deck myself. What didn't help was how goddamn hard I'd been after receiving his voice recording.

Every time I walked past a mirror, all I could think was *What the hell were you thinking?* And yes, before you ask: Did I spend the next two days systematically searching my own name for bullshit press? You're damn straight I did.

Every major rugby outlet. Every back-alley social media account with a blurry logo and too many numbers. Hell, I even checked the bloody *Daily Mail* comments section. Twice. And nothing. Not a single story. Not a grainy shot of a side-alley kiss or a headline accusing me of "getting cosy with a mystery man."

It should've been a relief. Instead, it made me feel worse.

Because what kind of person assumes the bloke they kissed—who drew up sketches for free, who talked moss and tattoos with me like I wasn't a total guarded arsehole —would run off and sell the story to the press?

Apparently, me. *That* kind of person is me.

And that's shit.

It's not logical. Not fair. Not even remotely who Brent's shown himself to be. But it's where my head went—thanks to years of paparazzi, fake stories, fans crossing boundaries, and one unforgettable "hot night with a rugby star" sold to the highest bidder six years ago by someone I'd trusted.

So yeah, it's messed me up. And that guilt is what leads me here. Not quite on my knees asking for forgiveness, but... close. Close enough that the words come out stiff and heavy in Brent's studio while he stands watching me like he's still bracing for a slow-motion car crash.

"I'm sorry," I say after my initial apology about disappearing on him. "About the other night. I handled it wrong."

His eyes widen and his cheeks flame red.

"Not about... uhm... I mean about not responding," I'm quick to say. "I came straight from training. Didn't want to leave it longer."

His expression shifts just slightly. It's still neutral, still holding back, but there's something softer behind his eyes, like he sees it—the effort, the reach.

He doesn't know I've been checking for a betrayal. He won't know. That part stays mine.

As does the other part—the one that can't stop thinking about his hands on me. About the way he took control of the kiss, the weight of his body, the lip ring dragging heat along my skin. Then the sound of his shuddering breaths when he panted my name in the recording.

I'm not here for that. I tell myself that, again and again.

I'm here because he's talented. His work's excellent. The designs are on point. I want the sleeve. The rest... is background noise I plan to ignore.

Mostly.

Hopefully.

Maybe.

Brent turns towards the workbench, flips open his sketchbook, and gently lays out the updated sleeve design.

And damn. It's good.

The structure's tighter—flowing up from the wrist and wrapping around the elbow in a way that feels intentional. Like it's always belonged on my skin. The negative space balances the bold blackwork perfectly, and the elements we'd discussed—sharp lines with symbolic symmetry—are woven in with more depth than I'd imagined.

"You've been busy," I murmur, leaning in to study the shading on the forearm section.

He shrugs casually. "Just fine-tuning. You already gave me a solid foundation to build on."

I glance up at him briefly. "It's really bloody good."

That earns a small smile—nothing smug, just... warm. He pulls a stool over, slides onto it with easy confidence. "So... you still feeling the clean lines through the upper shoulder, or want to soften it a bit?"

I swallow in relief that he's brushing past my awkward apology and isn't attempting to apologise again in the flesh, instead jumping to the artwork. "Stick with the clean. I don't want it to fade into abstract. Feels more like me this way."

He nods and makes a few notes. "You healed up from that hit in the Bristol match?"

"Mostly." I shift in the chair, stretching out my side. "I don't bounce back the way I used to."

"Ah, yes." He leans on the table with one elbow, mock-grave. "The tragedy of ageing. Sneaky shit that age thing, huh."

I grunt out a laugh. "Watch it. I've still got a few good years left." My shoulders lose some of their tension.

"That's the spirit." He grins. "To be fair, I get it. I twisted my knee last year crouched under a table to plug in a charger and limped for three days. I've accepted that I'm built for sketching and snack runs, not combat."

"Ever played anything properly?"

He tilts his head. "You mean beyond failed attempts at gym class? Nah. But my little brother plays ice hockey. I think I told you before. He thinks he's made of titanium."

I shake my head, amused despite myself. "At college?"

"Yeah. Just about to finish his second year. He's fast as hell, chirpy as shit. Scored some ridiculous goal the other week and sent me a clip like he was auditioning for the NHL."

"I watched a couple of games while I was in the

States," I admit, keeping it casual. "Weirdly addictive. Met a few players out there too—tough bastards."

Brent perks up. "Yeah?"

I nod but don't elaborate. I don't share all my business on a whim—not even with someone whose sketches feel like they belong under my skin.

Still, Brent doesn't push. He just rolls with the shift in conversation like it's nothing. "You probably saw more professional action in two games than I've seen in my entire life. I left the States long before my brother was at college."

I glance at him—at the way his T-shirt clings to the muscles across his shoulders, the way his forearms flex when he picks up the pencil again, easy and unselfconscious. He looks like someone who belongs on a pitch, or even a rink. Strong. Solid. Fit in a way that isn't about show. Just quiet, functional power.

And I really shouldn't be thinking that. Let alone saying it. So I just raise a brow. "Could've fooled me."

His mouth tilts into a half-smile. "Guess the ink's good camouflage."

I look away before I let myself stare longer than I already have. The moment stretches, comfortable now. Something in me relaxes further—not fully, not foolishly —but just enough to remember what it feels like to sit with someone and talk. Without worrying what's being dissected beneath the surface.

He flips another page and jots something down. "I've got a full backpiece scheduled to finish on Wednesday," he says. "Guy's a masochist—four hours in and swears he's fine while I'm the one needing a break. And then a couple of touch-ups Thursday."

"Sounds brutal."

"You'd be surprised how much people love their pain."

I glance down at the design again. "And after Thursday?"

"Open slate."

"Lucky you."

He grins. "Temporarily. What about you?"

"Game on Sunday. At home. Tough side."

His expression shifts—more serious, like he's mentally circling the date. "How you feeling about it?"

"We're third in the table. We need the win to stay in it. So... it's one of those games."

"Pressure?"

"Always."

He nods slowly. He doesn't offer advice. Doesn't say something trite like *You've got this*. Instead, he just sits with it and holds it like it's real. Somehow, that lands deeper than any encouragement could.

Brent scratches something into the margin of the sketch—just a note, maybe a measurement—and leans back in his chair. He stretches his arms behind his head, T-shirt pulling just slightly across his chest, revealing the ink along his biceps. It's unfair, really, how casually good he looks while talking about lines and elbow flow like it's nothing.

"You know," he says, voice easy, "I really don't know that much about rugby."

I glance up from the design. "Yeah?"

He shrugs. "Caught the odd match at the pub. I get the basics—big blokes, lots of shouting, a ball that bounces like it's got trauma. But the rest? Bit of a mystery."

A low laugh escapes me before I can stop it. "Not far off."

Brent grins like he's proud of himself, then gestures towards me. "You guys look terrifying, though. Watching a scrum's like watching a bear pit with rules."

"Not that many rules."

"That explains a lot."

I shake my head, but there's something about his tone —half curious, half teasing—that puts me at ease. Or maybe I just want to stay here longer, in this quiet pocket of normal. "It's the Gallagher Premiership," I say, keeping my voice steady. "Twelve clubs. Top four at the end of the season go through to play-offs. We're third right now, so every match matters."

"Right." He nods, considering that. "And Sunday's kind of a big deal, then?"

"Yeah. We're playing at home against Newcastle. They're currently top of the league. If we lose, we'll drop to fourth."

Brent hums, more thoughtful now. "Maybe I'll try and get to a match before the season's out. Could be fun."

I nod along, but then he adds, so casually it catches me off-guard, "Not sure I've got anyone to go with, though. Still settling in. New area and all that. Not exactly drowning in mates." He says it without hesitation or apology. Just a simple truth dropped between us like it doesn't cost him anything. It's so at odds with how I live —carefully, strategically, always guarding something.

And for some reason, it makes my chest go tight.

It's not pity. Not even empathy, exactly. It's... recognition. Familiarity. And then comes the thought—quick, quiet, and dangerous: *I could be his friend.*

The idea roots itself before I can stamp it out, because I don't need more friends. I've got Lachie, Jules... hell, even young Rafi, and the rest of the team. And my family. That's enough.

But Brent doesn't push. Doesn't ask for anything.

And I'm still thinking about that moment in the alley. About the way his hand curled around my hip. The way he kissed me like he wasn't afraid of all the things I didn't say.

And he didn't sell the story. Not even a whisper of it appeared online.

Yet, the voice in my head whispers again. That familiar, paranoid bastard. The one trained by years of mistrust and betrayal. It's always there, even when I want it quiet.

But I swallow the doubt, clamp my jaw, and before I can stop myself, I hear the words leave my mouth. "I could... probably get you a ticket."

Brent blinks, surprised. "Seriously?"

"Yeah." I force a shrug, keeping it casual. "Got a few for home matches. Player comp list. Doesn't cost me anything."

His expression shifts. A flash of something—genuine pleasure, maybe. Warmth. "Thanks. I mean, yeah. I'd like that," he says simply, like he means it.

I scratch the side of my jaw, not sure what to do with how easy that felt. "After the game, we'll probably head to the pub again. The same one. You're welcome to come, if you're interested."

There's a beat of silence before he says, "As friends?" His voice is calm and light with zero pressure. My pulse kicks up anyway, because the answer in my head is *No, not just friends.* I'd absolutely be up for his mouth on mine again. I've replayed it a hundred times. The weight of him. The way he tasted. The control he took without demanding it.

But that's not safe. Not smart. So I clear my throat. "Yeah. Friends."

Brent studies me for half a second longer before he nods. "Cool."

That word again. Like it's just that simple. Like he's okay with the space I've just drawn between us. And the worst part? He probably is. Because he's decent. Because he means it when he says he wants to go to a match. Because he tells the truth, even when it's a little raw.

And me? I'm still wondering how long I can keep pretending I'm not already halfway to wanting more.

There's a beat between us after I offer the ticket. A pause that could tip either way. Then Brent shifts in his seat, glancing over towards the compact fridge behind the reception counter. "You want a beer?"

I don't even think about it. "Yeah," I say, my voice coming out low and steady.

He gets up, walks over, and pulls two bottles from the fridge with an easy confidence that has no right being as distracting as it is. His movements are smooth and unhurried. He pops the caps on the edge of the counter—

of course he does—and brings one over, handing it to me by the neck.

"Cheers," he says, his voice soft but solid.

We clink bottles—just a light tap—and drink.

The beer's cold, just bitter enough to cut through the lingering tension in my chest. I lean back in the chair and glance around the shop for the first time tonight, really taking it in. The walls are painted a matte charcoal, clean but warm, with framed prints of in-progress linework and bold colour pieces lining the space like a gallery. The floor's polished concrete but softened with worn rugs near each station. Small potted plants sit near the front, by the tall windows, their green softened by dusk spilling in through the blinds. The lighting's warm, focused, like someone thought hard about how to make this place feel like more than just skin and ink.

"You planning to make any changes?" I ask, nodding towards the shop.

Brent leans back, resting his ankle on his opposite knee. "Not at the moment. Tank had good taste. I've got a six-month option to buy the place. I'm considering it, but I want to see how things go first."

Makes sense. Smart, even. I nod and take another sip. "You settling into Exeter okay?" I ask, kind of blowing my own mind right now as I'm being so damn social and inquisitive.

He hesitates—just a blink—then gives me a small smile. "Haven't explored too much yet. Been to North Devon once. Took a day trip to Instow and Westward Ho!"

"Good spots."

"Yeah, I liked the vibe. Quiet, scenic. But I wanted somewhere with a bit more population, more energy day to day. Exeter felt like a good middle ground. Enough hustle, but it doesn't feel like it's trying too hard."

I hum in agreement. "I get that."

He glances over, curious. "You been here long?"

"Nine years. I moved from the Midlands when I signed with the club full-time."

"Good move?"

"Best one I made, probably." I let my thumb roll over the condensation on the neck of the bottle. "Nothing against Walsall. The town did me proud growing up. Solid people. Just... bit rough around the edges these days."

Brent grins. "I think that's code for 'built character.'"

I chuckle under my breath. "That's what my mum says. Usually when I complain about the public transport."

We lapse into a moment of easy silence, the kind that settles without strain. Just two blokes in a quiet shop, beer in hand, and the buzz of the city tucked safely outside the windows.

There's something... comfortable here—too comfortable, truth be told. I know I shouldn't lean into it and shouldn't want more. But sitting across from him like this —his bare forearms inked and resting on the table, the curve of his smile soft and genuine—it's hard to remember why I built those walls in the first place.

8

Brent

I'm at the match. I probably shouldn't be. Not for any real reason, just for the simple fact that I'm a glutton for punishment. Camden came through with a ticket like it was no big thing, like it meant nothing more than an extra seat on the comp list.

And now here I am. Sitting in a row of hyped-up fans, sunscreen and beer thick in the air, pretending like I haven't been friend-zoned so hard I could be running the support group.

But it's fine. *Really.*

We've been texting every day since the shop. Every. Day.

Sometimes about his sleeve. Sometimes about the pub menu. Sometimes just random nonsense—memes, random hockey updates from my little brother, that video of the dog who can surf. I keep it casual. Chill. The kind of texting where I absolutely do not ask what his mouth tastes like again or whether he thought about me that night as much as I did him.

I've got a good seat. Right near the halfway line, a few rows up. The view's incredible. Packed crowd, fans waving flags, belting out chants with wild, proud energy. It's old-school. Concrete and iron. The kind of place that smells like history and meat pies.

Fifteen thousand people are crammed into this stadium. I googled the hell out of it earlier—Willow Park, home of the Exeter Seagulls, though officially it's named something corporate and dull now. The place is rough around the edges but alive in the way only proper local stadiums can be. Tight sightlines. Echoing noise. A hum beneath the crowd like we're all wired into something ancient and furious.

The sun's still out—for once. A rare warm day in late spring. The sky's a brilliant blue, just the edges kissed with haze. But the shadows are stretching longer now. The sun's already starting to dip, and the floodlights are coming on, one row at a time. They give everything a soft edge of gold and grit.

It's the second half, and it's brutal.

The score's tight. You can feel it in the air. Every hit lands with a collective wince from the crowd. Every call from the ref is met with either cheers or the kind of swearing that would make a sailor blush. The pace hasn't slowed since the kick-off—if anything, it's gotten faster, sharper.

I watch Camden—because of course I do. He's in the middle of the scrum like a force of nature, body low, shoulders locked in. The man moves like he's built from stone and fury. Sweat glistens across the back of his neck, dripping down arms already streaked with dirt and effort. Admittedly, I'm not close enough to see said sweat, but my imagination is pretty killer when it comes to imagining Camden hot and dripping. I also definitely did not google rugby rules obsessively just to understand what he does on the pitch.

Absolutely not.

But it is helpful to know that as a tighthead prop, he's the anchor of the scrum. The brute force. The quiet chaos. The one who makes sure the rest don't fall apart under pressure.

And he's damn good at it.

There's a moment where the opposing team breaks through—close to the line—and Camden gets low, plants his feet, and slams into the guy like a freight train. No hesitation. No flinch. Just clean, efficient violence.

The whole crowd roars. I do too. Not just because it was a good hit, but because it was him. My fingers curl tight around the beer in my hand, and I force myself to breathe. Just breathe. Because yeah, I'm in the friend zone, but if this is the view from there, it's still kind of amazing.

The final stretch of the match is pure chaos. There are maybe five minutes left on the clock, and everything is blood, noise, and sheer grit. The Seagulls are clinging to a narrow lead, but Newcastle is coming hard—desperate, frantic, throwing everything into one final push.

The guy next to me—an older fan with a scarf that's seen better decades—keeps shouting, "Hold the bloody line!" like he's coaching from the stands. His pint's half spilled down his shirt, and I'm 90 percent sure he doesn't notice.

I'm on my feet before I realise I've moved, shouting, watching Camden throw himself into the breakdown like a man possessed. He's relentless, tactical, every movement controlled strength. He clears a ruck with the kind of power that makes the crowd collectively *ooof*, then lurches up again, barking something to a teammate I can't hear.

And then, blessedly—finally—the whistle blows, and the stadium erupts.

Thousands of people become one deafening roar of celebration—flags waving, voices hoarse from yelling, cups of beer sloshing with careless joy. The guy next to me lets out a shout that's half war cry, half sob of relief, clutching his pint like it's the last one on earth.

I laugh, still half in disbelief, clapping along even though I'm not really part of it. Or at least I wasn't, until now.

"Bloody hell," the man says, turning to me with a grin that stretches to his ears. His face is flushed from sun and adrenaline, his white Seagulls jersey streaked with something that looks suspiciously like ketchup. "That last five minutes took years off my life."

"Same," I say, breathless, heart still hammering.

His mate—a shorter guy with mirrored sunglasses pushed onto his head and the most spectacular farmer's tan I've ever seen—leans over, eyeing me speculatively. "First game?"

"Yeah," I admit, wondering if it was my American accent or how much my inked skin, piercings, and black clothes make me stand out that has him asking. "First live one."

"Well, you picked a banger. That tighthead—Crawford—he's a wall. Don't know how he keeps getting back up."

My chest warms a little, pride sneaking in like a secret. "Yeah. He's something."

One of the guys beside me leans over, clearly catching my tone. "You a fan of his?"

"Yeah," I say, keeping it neutral. "Seen a few of his matches."

He nods, satisfied. "Solid player. Doesn't say much, but he gets the job done."

The men nod before turning back to the pitch where the players are still shaking hands, swarmed by kids and camera crews. I'm still on my feet, still scanning the field, still watching for one very specific figure in the middle of it all.

Camden moves with purpose, focused even in the aftermath. I catch glimpses of him—mud-streaked, jaw tight, his hair pushed back from his face, eyes scanning the crowd. For a moment, I wonder if he's looking for me.

Probably not.

Still, I fish my phone from my jacket and fire off the text:

> Me: Congrats, Captain. You earned that win. And I hope your offer still stands, because I could definitely go for a pint.

I hit Send before I can second-guess it.

Beside me, the older fan claps me on the back, hard enough to jostle my arm. "You'll be back for the next one, then?"

I grin. "Yeah. I think I might."

And I wait, phone in hand, eyes on the pitch, hoping.

THE PUB'S LOUDER THAN USUAL. DOORS ARE OPEN to the early-evening air, the buzz of victory still fresh in everyone's voices. There's singing in the corner, and someone's already spilled their pint before even reaching their table.

I get there early. Too early, I suspect, as I have no idea what Camden has to do after a game before he's able to leave. I grab a beer at the bar, thank the server with a smile that's probably too polite, and move to the side, trying not to look like I'm waiting for someone—even though, yeah, I absolutely am.

I nurse my drink. I check my phone even though there are no new messages. I pretend not to keep glancing at the door.

And then I see him.

Camden.

In a shirt and dark jeans that look sinfully hot, hair still damp from the showers, that same no-nonsense expression on his face that's probably sent grown men running. And he makes a beeline straight towards me. My chest does something it really shouldn't—a jump, a flicker—and I brace myself.

He stops in front of me, towering just enough to remind me how much space he takes up. There's not quite a scowl on his face, but it's close. That usual furrow between his brows remains. Except his eyes... his eyes aren't tense. They're... searching.

"You came," he says, voice low, already edging towards that familiar gravel.

"You invited me," I reply, trying for neutral but smiling anyway. "Didn't want to miss it."

"Good," he says simply, and that's that. No drama. No awkwardness. Just Camden, steady as I've come to expect, grounding the moment without even trying.

We fall into step together, the crowd jostling around us. He doesn't introduce me to anyone, but he doesn't not acknowledge me either. Some of the players offer nods, a few raised brows.

Lachie spots me and grins wide, nudging the guy next to him before calling out, "Oi, look who it is—Crawford's ink guy shows up and sticks around. Must be serious."

Camden lets out a quiet sigh, but it's more resigned than annoyed. I catch the barest flicker of a smile at the corner of his mouth. He also pointedly ignores his friend and leads me towards the back of the pub. Food's already coming out and being placed on the tables—burgers, chips, salad, and sharing platters like someone ordered for a rugby team. Because, well, they did.

We sit side by side in a booth, not too close, but close

enough that when he leans in to speak, I can smell the clean, sharp scent of whatever soap he used. His knee bumps mine under the table—accidentally, maybe—but he doesn't move it.

"You enjoy the match?" he asks, voice pitched lower now that the volume's dropped a bit in the back room.

"Yeah," I say, and maybe I'm a little too eager, because I hear the energy in my voice even before I can tone it down. "I mean, I've seen it on TV before, but in person? It's wild. The pace, the weight of it. You lot don't hold back."

He huffs a quiet laugh. "No point holding back."

I turn towards him a bit. "The scrum's more brutal than I thought. You're just in there, anchored, like... like the centre of a wheel or something. And that breakdown near the end—Jesus, that was tight."

His eyebrows lift, just a little. "You've been studying."

I grin. "Maybe. I might've googled some stuff."

His eyes flick over my face, and I can tell he's amused. But also maybe—just maybe—pleased.

"Say 'breakdown' again," he says, dry as anything.

I narrow my eyes. "You mocking me?"

"A bit," he admits, lips twitching. "But I'm impressed."

We lapse into another moment of quiet as another round of food arrives. Wings first. Something messy and beautiful. Camden reaches for one without ceremony, wipes his hand on a napkin, and glances sideways at me again, offering me a sort-of smile before he bites into the wing.

I follow suit, and before long, the back room fills slowly—teammates trickling in, laughter bouncing off the worn brick walls, the occasional thud of a heavy chair being dragged back. Someone's already raided the jukebox, and a low thrum of 2000s indie rock filters through the hum of conversation.

Plates of food keep arriving like magic. Hot dogs, wedges, onion rings the size of bracelets. It smells like grease and salt and glory.

Camden and I are still side by side—closer than before, if that's even possible. The booth seat's narrow, all of the tables packed, and eventually there's nowhere else for our thighs to go but flush against each other. His pants are warm, firm, and solid against mine, and he doesn't shift away.

God, help me.

Every movement he makes sends a pulse through my body—shoulders rolling under his shirt, exposing his sinful forearms from where he's rolled up the cuffs, as he reaches for another wing. His hand is close enough that if I moved two inches, I could touch the inside of his wrist. I don't.

But I want to.

It's hard not to feel the sheer size of him pressed this close. He's massive—built to hit, to hold, to command space like it's nothing. My mind shouldn't be going where it's going. Not with this whole *friends* thing. Not when I've been watching him push his body to the limit for eighty minutes under the sun. Not when he's already this raw, this open in a way I know costs him something.

But I do. Of course I do.

I want to know what he sounds like when he gives in. What it'd be like to take him apart slow and greedy. To get my hands on that thick, powerful body and feel it shake under me.

My fingers tighten around the neck of my beer bottle. God, I'd wreck him.

And now I'm thinking about Camden Crawford, professional hard-ass and resident mystery man, on his knees—eyes dark, that mouth parted, his hand on my thigh, letting go for me. Trusting me to take control.

My skin heats. I swallow hard.

Fuck, I'm so gone.

A hot prickle climbs the back of my neck. I shift slightly, trying to adjust without drawing attention to the very real, very inconvenient situation in my jeans.

Camden leans in slightly, glancing at me, brow furrowed. "You all right?" His voice is lower now, quieter than before, just for me. His thigh presses more firmly against mine as he turns.

I practically squeak my "Yeah."

He raises a brow, unimpressed. "You sure?"

I take a long pull from my beer and avoid direct eye contact like a guilty schoolboy. "Just hot. It's warm in here."

A half-smile tugs at the corner of his mouth. "Could've sworn you were cold earlier."

"I run complicated," I mutter into my bottle.

He chuckles—*chuckles*—and I'm dead. That sound is going to live in my head for days. I glance sideways and catch him watching me with something that might be amusement... or something else entirely.

But he doesn't say anything. Instead, he lets the moment sit there, heavy with things neither of us are quite saying. And even though I'm burning up and biting the inside of my cheek to stay focused on anything other than the feel of his thigh against mine, the low sound of his voice, or the fact that he still hasn't moved away...

I think I might be the happiest, horniest, most tortured man in Devon right now.

Time slips by without me noticing. Somewhere between half-hearted jokes and another round of drinks, the energy in the room softens. The match buzz fades to a low hum. The food's been picked over, plates messy with bones and fries, bottles and empty pint glasses lined up in chaotic clusters across the table that has eight of us squeezed around it. It's getting late now—maybe edging towards ten, maybe later—but no one's in a rush to leave.

The noise is softer too. Less roar, more rumble. That post-match glow still clings to everything, but in that slowed, satisfied way that comes after winning something hard-fought. There's laughter, shoulders pressed together, heads tipped back. Rugby guys, proud and bruised and loud.

Camden's still next to me, his thigh still pressed against mine. He hasn't moved away. Not once.

Lachie, with a cut on his brow and a twinkle in his eye that says he lives to cause problems, leans over with a mock-stern look. "Still here, Crawford? Thought you only stayed for an hour before doing your brooding-wolf-slips-off-into-the-shadows thing."

Camden makes a low noise, clearly unimpressed. "Piss off."

Another guy—lean and tattooed, clearly a winger by the looks of him—grins around his bottle. "Seriously, though. He's stayed all night. Write it down."

Lachie eyes me like I'm part of some cosmic puzzle. "You've got a hell of a pull, mate. Usually takes a full five pints and an emergency team strategy session to keep him this long."

"Maybe I'm just charming," I offer.

Lachie smirks. "I like this one." Then he glances back at Camden and, without missing a beat, says, "You should definitely come to the next match."

Camden tenses beside me. Just slightly. But instead of arguing or deflecting like I expect him to, he says nothing. He simply takes another sip of his beer, eyes flicking anywhere but mine.

I look at him, trying to read what that silence means. Does he want me there? Or is this just one of those "it's easier not to explain" things? Still, I did enjoy the game, and the buzz, and even the weird, live-wire thrill of watching him work like that.

So I grin. "Sure. I'm up for it."

Camden doesn't respond immediately, but I catch the corner of his mouth twitch, like he's not entirely mad about it.

Then his phone buzzes again.

And again.

And again.

He pulls it out with a huff. "Sorry. It's blowing up tonight."

Lachie leans over with zero shame. "It's his jerk-off group. They're probably swapping nudes."

I splutter mid-sip and cough-laugh so hard, I nearly snort beer out my nose. "Jesus."

Camden glares at him. "Piss. Off." But he's not angry. Not really. More like exasperated. The kind of reaction that only comes from years of enduring the same brand of chaos. He looks at me and waves his phone slightly. "It's not a jerk-off group."

"Oh?" I say, still laughing. "Disappointing."

Camden shoots me a look, but he's smirking now. "It's actually a chat group I've got with a bunch of queer athletes. We all met last year—photoshoot thing, article in *Queervolution*. Kept in touch after. It's... decent."

My brain halts.

Holy fuck.

My gaze snaps to him before I can help it, eyes wide, heart doing that stupid stutter again.

He notices. Of course he does. His expression shifts slightly, eyes narrowing like he's trying to work out exactly what I know—and whether it's a problem. "What?" he says, cautious but not sharp. "Didn't think I had friends?"

"No," I say quickly, lifting a hand. "No, it's just— That's... cool. I actually saw your name when I was looking up what a tighthead prop even does. One of the links mentioned an old interview. Some press crap too."

His jaw ticks once, barely. "Yeah," he says after a beat. "They had a field day back then."

"I noticed," I say, softer now. "But nothing in the last few years, which is kind of impressive." It seriously is no easy feat, staying out of the limelight, especially as an out player.

He shrugs, glancing away for a second. "I learned to keep my head down."

He doesn't elaborate, and I don't push. But he looks at me again, more searching than before. Like he's waiting for some hint of judgement, some flinch.

He won't find it.

Instead, I smile. "Still badass, being involved in that *Queervolution* article."

His eyes flick to mine, something unreadable there. The tension in his jaw loosens, just a little. Lachie, mercifully distracted by someone else's fries, turns his attention away, and Camden relaxes a bit beside me. Not fully —he's still Camden, after all—but the edge softens.

I don't ask for more. But I file it away, this new layer of him. One he didn't have to share but did anyway. Because Camden Crawford might be the quietest man in the room, but there's a hell of a lot going on underneath.

And somehow, he let me see it.

He's still scrolling through his phone, thumb scrolling with the kind of concentration that looks suspiciously like he's trying not to smile. His mouth twitches once—*once*—and that's when the thought creeps in.

Wait a second.

I'd skimmed that article when it came out. It was a big deal—queer athletes from different sports speaking out, showing up, challenging perceptions. I remembered the photoshoot. How could I not? Saw the buzz. I even remember thinking, *Holy shit, where were guys like this when I was coming out?*

But now that I think about it, why can't I remember seeing Camden's name? Or even his image? Sure, I probably hadn't been reading it for the journalism, but still. If I'd seen him, I would've remembered. Hell, he'd have been my late-night fantasy long before I knew his name, never mind kissed him in an alley.

Probably for the best I didn't, I think, trying to fight the smile tugging at my mouth.

And maybe it's that—maybe it's the feeling of knowing just a little more about him, or maybe it's the buzz of connection still humming between us—but it's time to test the waters.

I tip my head casually. "So... is the group chat called Love the Game?"

The effect is immediate. He stops scrolling. His head lifts slowly, eyes narrowing with a look that could freeze the surface of a lake in July. The air between us sharpens. "Excuse me?" The words have bite. Not loud, but lethal.

Oh shit.

Abort mission.

I lift both hands, one still holding my beer. "Wait, no —hold on. I'm not spying or anything. I swear."

His expression doesn't budge.

"I only asked," I say quickly, "because my brother's in a group chat. Similar vibe. Queer athletes. He's in college—plays ice hockey. I told you a bit about him. His name's Cosmo. He mentioned the group name once."

Camden stares at me, still frozen. A beat passes. Then another.

I start to wonder if I've just accidentally ended our friendship, potential sleeve work, and the chance of ever seeing him shirtless again, all in one well-meaning question.

And then, he unfreezes, eyes widening just enough to register shock. "Wait. Cosmo?"

I nod. "Yeah. Pain in my ass. Talks like he's got his own podcast, never stops moving, allergic to shirts."

Camden stares for half a second longer, then lets out a low breath that almost sounds like a laugh. "No shit," he mutters, almost to himself.

I grin, some of the unease in my gut unravelling. "You know him?"

He huffs—actually huffs—and shakes his head, the tension in his shoulders practically melting on the spot. "Yeah. He never shuts the fuck up in the chat. Always tagging people in memes at two in the morning."

"Sounds about right," I say. "Once sent me a playlist titled 'You'd Be Hotter with a Moustache.'"

Camden chuckles—a real one this time. Not quite full-bodied, but enough to make me feel like I've won something I didn't know I was competing for.

"Jesus," he says, scrubbing a hand down his face. "That kid's everywhere."

I laugh. "He's like glitter. Gets into everything and impossible to shake."

Camden looks at me again, and this time there's something different in his eyes. Not fully relaxed—he's too tightly wound for that. But there's less guard. Less steel. His voice, when he speaks again, is warmer than I've ever heard it. "Small fucking world."

"No kidding."

He shakes his head again, his smile staying in place. "Cosmo's your kid brother."

"For better or worse," I say with a shrug.

And in this moment, he feels closer. Like the wall's

still there, but the gate's cracked open just enough to see through. And damn, this version of Camden Crawford? Quietly amused, maybe even a little at ease? This version might be my new favourite addiction.

9

Camden

It's well past ten, and the pub's still humming, though there's less noise and more warmth. But that might be something to do with Brent's side being flush with mine. The back room's half cleared out, the energy dialled down from "victory riot" to "low-key satisfaction."

And my head's buzzing, but not from the pint.

Brent is Cosmo's brother.

Cosmo.

As in, the wild-card college hockey phenom who'd damn near stolen the show during that photoshoot last year. I remember the day vividly. We were all there for this "global queer athlete" piece. There were sprinters, more ice hockey players than I could shake a stick at, a football player—the proper British kind—who I've met up with a couple of times since, a retired cricketer who had zero time for anyone under the age of forty, and—of course—Cosmo.

That kid was a walking headline. Loud, charming, full of chaos and confidence, he spoke like a caffeinated sports commentator and acted like he was everyone's hype man. The moment he walked in, I remember thinking, *This kid's going to take over the world or spontaneously combust trying.*

He made half the room laugh, called the lighting guy "boss," tried to get people to do choreographed shoulder pops mid-shoot, and got himself added to the group chat before we'd even left the building.

And yeah, he's still in that chat. Still chaos incarnate. We've got Olympic hopefuls in there. Amateur cyclists. Quiet wrestlers. A lacrosse player who only responds in haikus. Somehow, I've turned into one of the old farts in the group—lurking more than contributing—but it's become something I value. A rare space where I don't have to be on.

Knowing Brent is connected to that—to them—loosens something tight inside my chest. Something I didn't realise had been clamped down all night.

Maybe I can trust him.

It's not just Cosmo's reputation that matters—it's how Brent talks about him. Pride without ego. Warmth without bragging. He isn't riding his brother's success; he's just in his corner. And I know what a big deal Cosmo is. I've seen the highlights online. Sure, he hypes himself, but he backs it up. The kid's got fire.

I catch myself smiling a little and turn towards Brent. We're still close—thighs brushing. Always touching, but never too much.

"Cosmo's... a character," I say, voice pitched low.

Brent snorts into his drink. "Understatement of the year."

"He keeps that chat alive, though. It's... good, having that group. Bit of everything in there. Good kids like Cosmo, and old bastards like me."

"You're not that old," Brent says, but he's grinning, like he knows full well I'm going to roll my eyes. I do.

Still, the tension that had been wound so tight in my chest since the whistle blew? Since walking into this pub with Brent already inside, waiting? It eases. It's not gone, but it's better.

I clear my throat. "He ever deal with the media? Fans?"

Brent leans back slightly, nursing what's left of his lager. "He's pretty protected at college. The school's good about that. Coaches, PR staff—his teammates have his back too. But as a family, we kind of made it our mission to look out for one another. Stay grounded. No bullshit."

I nod, quiet for a beat.

"I miss them, though," he says suddenly. His voice shifts—still open, but softer. "I don't regret moving here. Not for a second. But being that far away from them? Some days that's harder than I expected."

That hits somewhere deep. I glance at him, wondering if I have a right to ask, but the words are already on my tongue. "Think you'll ever go back? For good, I mean?"

He turns his head and looks right at me. I shouldn't be holding my breath, but I am. Like something in me is waiting. Bracing.

"I don't know," he says after a pause. "I've got no set plans. I've been here a long time. It's home now, in a weird way. Next year, I'll apply for British citizenship."

There's a flicker in his voice—not hesitation, exactly, but something softer beneath the surface. Like he's made peace with it. Like it still surprises him, calling another country home. Like part of him is still trying to mean it fully.

I blink. Something in me—something tangled and

tightly guarded—unravels a little. It's not just that he's staying. It's that he wants to. That this life, this place, is his. Even if sometimes, maybe, it still feels like he's got one foot somewhere else.

I look at him too long, and when I do, I realise the truth is catching up with me. We'd agreed on friends. Tentative. Unspoken. But I'm attracted to him. And not just casually, and definitely not in that one-night way I've come to tolerate when the mood and the stars align.

This is different.

This is slower, warmer. This is a smile I want to keep earning. A voice I want in my ear when I'm walking home.

And that shit right there? That's scary as fuck.

I'm still watching Brent. Still trying to process the whole potential British citizenship, that Cosmo's his brother, and that I might actually like this man in a way that has nothing to do with simple physical attraction when I hear my name.

Loudly.

Twice.

"Crawford!"

I twist in my seat to find a few of my teammates waving me over—one in particular swaying a little too enthusiastically for comfort. Fuck.

I sigh, then glance at Brent. "Sorry," I say, leaning in just enough to be heard. "Give me five?"

He nods, but I linger a second longer.

"And don't—" I hesitate, then throw subtlety out the window. "Don't go anywhere."

His brows rise, just for a beat... like he wasn't expecting that. But then that smile—*that smile*—breaks over his face. Confident. Warm. Easy in a way I'll never be.

"I won't," he says.

God, help me.

I step away and push through the back room towards the noise. The lads part a bit as I arrive, and I clock who the problem is immediately. Briggs. He's younger, just barely out of academy squad last season. Big, full of talent, and currently three pints past his limit. We've talked about keeping a low profile post-match. We always talk about it. But somehow, this guy's got the tact of a cymbal-playing monkey.

"Briggs," I growl, already regretting this, "what the fuck are you doing?"

"Caaaam," he sings, grinning wide and slinging an arm over my shoulders. "Captain. My capt'n. You're so serious tonight."

"That's because you're being a dickhead."

"Just celebratin'. Celebratin' third place!"

"We're not done, you twat," I mutter, dragging his arm off me. "Four more games. You do remember the calendar, yeah?"

He wobbles dramatically, then attempts a very unco-ordinated heel click. "I remember! I remember... that you never let me have any fun!"

I rub a hand down my face. "You're one beer away from me calling your mum."

He pauses, eyes wide. "You wouldn't."

"Try me."

Then, out of fucking nowhere, he wraps his arms around me like I'm a goddamn therapy dog and mumbles, "I wish I was you."

I blink. "What?"

He just hugs me harder, his face mashed into my shoulder.

"What the fuck does that mean?" I ask, trying to untangle his arms. But he stumbles sideways, and that's when I realise I'm going to have to get him out of here before he knocks over a table or someone decides to record him for a laugh. "Right," I mutter. "Home time, superstar."

Before I can call for backup, a voice speaks at my side. "Need a hand?"

It's Brent. Of course it is. And goddamn, he's already stepping in, wrapping one arm around Briggs's back, steadying him with surprising ease.

I glance at him, grateful. "You don't have to—"

"I know," he says simply. "But I've got brothers too. Trust me, I've done this routine."

We start hauling Briggs towards the back entrance. That's when Briggs turns his head and blinks at Brent, like he's just realised a whole new person is touching him. He stares hard, then slurs, "You're hot."

I damn near trip over my own feet.

Brent snorts but says nothing. He just keeps a firm grip on the guy.

My brain stutters. *Briggs is... queer?*

Is he?

He's never said anything. Never hinted. But also, the kid's private. Quiet. Intense when he's not three drinks deep.

Briggs mutters again, more to himself, "Men suck. But not the good kind of suck. Just the... the shitty, disappointing, leave-you-on-read kind of suck."

Brent bites back a laugh, while I'm busy trying to wrap my head around the fact that this is how I'm finding out about one of my teammates potentially being in the closet. In the middle of a pub, with the man I keep imagining naked keeping Briggs upright.

We make it to the exit, and I prop the door open as Brent guides Briggs into the cooling night air. I shake my head. "Jesus Christ."

Brent glances over. "You okay?"

"Yeah," I mutter. "Just... wasn't expecting that."

He doesn't say anything, just adjusts Briggs's weight slightly as we start guiding him towards the car park. We're halfway to my car when I catch the flash. It's fast, just one flick of white light in the periphery, but it hits me like a body blow.

My head snaps around. My gut tightens. My shoulders go high and hard. And then I see him across the lot, standing behind a parked van, phone in hand. Not even a long-lens camera, just a phone held high. Opportunistic. Feral.

Pap.

The bastard doesn't even flinch. Instead, he just lowers his phone like it's no big deal. But it is. I stop cold, one hand still wrapped around Briggs's upper arm. I want to deck the scumbag. God, I want to walk over there and lay him out with one swing. No warning. Just years of bottled-up rage behind a fist and a fractured screen.

But I can't.

Not because he doesn't deserve it, but because if I do —if I lose it now—I'll get fined by the club, maybe suspended, probably arrested. And that means more press. Exactly the thing I've been trying to avoid since I came out. Exactly what I can't let happen.

Behind me, Brent moves without a word, like he's already clocked the situation and read the temperature in my posture. He pulls a black baseball cap from his back pocket—something he must've shoved there earlier—and settles it on Briggs's messy head with surprising care. The drunk idiot barely reacts, but the shadow from the cap helps.

Then Brent steps up, tucks his arm more securely around Briggs's shoulders, and positions himself like a shield—a human barrier. There's no hesitation in his movements, just calm, capable action.

I get the car door open, and together, we manage to pour Briggs into the back seat without drawing more attention. He slumps over the second he hits the upholstery as dead weight. He's out cold.

I slide into the driver's seat and grip the steering wheel like it's the only thing anchoring me to the ground. My pulse is too high. My jaw aches from how tightly I'm clenching it. I don't look at Brent as he climbs in beside me. The air inside the car goes tight, tense, every muscle in my body humming like a wire about to snap.

I slam the door, start the ignition, and peel out of the car park with more speed than I should.

The first few minutes are silent. Just the sound of tyres rolling over slick tarmac, the rattle of bottles shifting in the boot, and Briggs's soft snoring in the back fill the space. The roads are mostly empty. It's late enough that the shops are dark, the streetlights casting long shadows across the estates as we drive past. A cat darts under a parked car. The clouds have rolled in, blanketing the sky in soft grey, the moon diffused and distant.

Brent tries to talk once. Just a quiet attempt to ease the mood. "Hey, so... earlier. That was—"

"Not now," I say, too quickly. Too harshly.

He falls quiet and doesn't push. He folds his hands in his lap and stares out the window, his profile outlined by the faint glow of passing lights. And now I feel like an arsehole. I know he was only trying to help. And he did help... without being asked, without drama. He just stepped in and made it better.

But my mind's spinning. That flash of light feels like a detonator, like the start of something I can't stop. I don't know what that pap caught. If Briggs was in the frame. If Brent was. If I was close enough to be headline-worthy.

If tomorrow the internet's going to see me in a quiet moment of vulnerability with a man I haven't figured out how to talk about yet—never mind explain. And what if Briggs gets dragged into it? What if that flash caught a half-mumbled confession with a recording and a team-mate mid-stumble, and suddenly I've failed him too?

Fifteen minutes of driving feels like a marathon. By the time we pull up outside Briggs's shared house, the guilt is layered thick beneath my skin. I sit in the car, engine idling. Brent hasn't said another word, and I can't blame him.

I exhale hard and finally look at him. He's already watching me. Quiet. Patient. But not hurt. Not angry. Just... waiting. And somehow, that makes it worse. Because I don't know what the hell to say to the man who helped me tonight—and who I might already be ruining this with.

Briggs stirs the moment we park. "Whuh...?" he mumbles, head lolling forwards as I cut the engine.

"Welcome back, sunshine," I mutter, climbing out.

Brent meets me at the other side, already helping ease the idiot upright and out of the car. Briggs manages to get his feet under him, though he's still wobbly, blinking like a man pulled from a deep and unfortunate dream.

We shuffle up to the front door with his weight slung between us. I pat him down one-handed, muttering under my breath until I find his keys in the back pocket of his jeans. Inside, the hallway's dim, the scent of something herbal and slightly stale lingering in the air.

"Briggs lives like a student," I grumble.

"I like that you say that like it's an insult," Brent says, still supporting the guy's weight. "Students are resourceful."

"Students can't hold their liquor."

Brent snorts. "True."

There's a shuffle at the top of the stairs. A figure appears—sleep-ruffled, T-shirt in hand, sleep shorts slung low on lean hips. He squints down at us, rubbing a hand through his messy hair.

"Shit," he mutters, clearly clocking the state of things. "Okay." He yanks the tee over his head and starts down the stairs, bare feet thudding softly on the carpet.

That's when I place him. "Kit," I say. "Right?"

He nods, already eyeing Briggs with the practiced exhaustion of someone who's seen this before. "What happened?"

I help shift Briggs a little higher, keeping him moving. "He's sloshed. Passed out for a while in the car. Snoring like an engine."

Kit sighs. "Brilliant. All right, can you get him to his room? First door on the right at the top. I'll grab a bucket, water, and paracetamol."

I nod, and Kit peels off towards the kitchen like a man on autopilot.

"Right then," Brent says gently, turning back to Briggs. "Let's go, champ. One foot at a time."

As we start the climb, Brent keeps up a calm, low stream of encouragement.

"That's it. Another step. There we go. You're nailing

this, mate."

I glance over. "You've done this before."

He grins, not looking away from the stairs. "First time I've ever lived alone. Before this, I always shared a house. Usually with people who couldn't hold their liquor. Or their dignity."

We finally reach the top, and I nudge open the bedroom door with my foot. It's surprisingly tidy in here. We steer Briggs to the bed and more or less pour him onto it. He groans and rolls over.

Kit appears with practiced timing, holding a glass of water, a blister pack of pills, and a plastic bin that's seen better days.

"Thanks," I say, stepping aside.

"I'll take it from here," Kit says with a sigh. "Again." He doesn't sound angry, just tired and used to it.

I nod towards Briggs. "Tell him I'll call tomorrow."

Kit gives me a tight smile. "Will do. Thanks for getting him home."

Brent and I slip out quietly, shutting the door behind us. Down the stairs, out the front, back to the car. And everything's heavy again. The pap flash replays in my mind like a warning siren. Briggs's drunken confession sits uneasily in my chest. My own mood, already a mine-field, just keeps dropping. I slide into the driver's seat and grip the wheel, my knuckles going white.

Brent doesn't speak at first. I think he knows better than to try. The drive is quiet.

Devon at night is low-lit and stretched out—long roads, soft glows from windows, hedges slipping by like silent sentinels. A few foxes dart out of view. The occasional porch light flickers in the misty air.

Brent glances at me a few times. I feel it. The question he wants to ask. The mood he wants to lift. He tries once. Says something—light, probably funny. I don't even catch all of it. My head's swimming too much.

I grunt some half-hearted reply, and he goes quiet again.

The silence thickens, and I hate that I've made it this way. What I should be doing is thanking him. He's helped twice tonight without flinching. Because he's been patient, and good, and exactly the kind of person you want at your side when things go sideways.

And yet here I am, gritting my teeth and shutting down. And all because the pap rattled me. Because Briggs might be struggling. Because I'm not just a captain or a prop or a public name—I'm a fuck-up when it comes to trusting people with my heart.

Because Brent... he's not like the others.

He's not a hook-up. He's not a fling. He's not even a harmless flirt. I'm interested. Big-time interested. And it's been weeks—not even two—not months, which is barely any time at all. But already, there's something about him—his steadiness, his wit, the way he sees me but doesn't push.

I want more. And that is the scariest fucking thing of all.

The quiet in the car is too much. I've driven longer distances in worse moods with less sleep and more injuries. But this? This silence? It grates.

Brent's beside me, watching the hedgerows blur past his window, lit by the rhythm of streetlamps and the warm glow of houses tucked behind stone walls and clipped hedges. We're back in the city now. The streets are tighter, the air heavier, yet still we don't speak.

I grip the wheel firmer. It doesn't help. I finally say, "I'll take you home."

He nods but still doesn't say anything. It shouldn't bother me—hell, I spend half my life wishing people would stop talking—but something about his silence feels... off. Wary. Weighed.

I glance over once. He's not brooding, exactly. But I can see him working through something. Lips pressed together, eyes distant, that little crease between his brows deeper than usual.

I know that look. He's debating.

Something in me twitches and tightens. "Spit it out," I mutter.

He turns, eyebrows raised. "What?"

"You're dying to say something. I've been a moody arsehole all night. Might as well let you get it over with."

His expression shifts, but not into the exasperated glare I was expecting. Not disappointment or frustration. No. He *smiles*. It's soft, even, practically bloody serene. How someone with a lip ring, an eyebrow piercing, and a constellation of hoops in one ear can look serene is beyond me, but somehow, he manages it.

Then, casually, like we're talking about nothing more than a cup of tea, he says, "I'm happy to go home with you."

I swerve slightly, correct immediately, and swallow hard. "Jesus," I mutter, hands re-tightening on the wheel.

"But not," he says, his grin growing, "if it's going to get us in a car wreck."

I breathe out, sharp and shaky. My shoulders still haven't unclenched. I should let it go. Should let him laugh it off and move on. But the question builds, hot and itchy under my skin.

I glance at him again. Not for long, but enough to catch that same calm, interested expression he's had since he first slid into the car, like nothing I've done tonight has put him off. "Why?"

Brent blinks. "Why what?"

"Why the hell are you giving me the time of day?"

He says nothing.

So I push on. "I've been a dick. Snapped at you. Ignored you. I'm grumpy. Moody. Complicated. And tonight—" My jaw tightens. "Tonight I've been fucking awful. So why?"

The car hums beneath us. Streetlights flash by in slow, golden intervals. Outside, everything's still. Quiet. Inside, I'm coiled so tightly I feel like I could snap. Then I glance his way again.

He looks at me like I'm not scaring him. Like I'm not pushing him away. Like none of what I've said has put so much as a dent in his certainty. And that smile's still there. Steady. Warm. No rush. No bullshit.

He shifts slightly in his seat, turns more towards me. His voice is low—not pitying, not soft, just real. "Because you showed up," he says. "Because you lead. Because you care about your teammates even when they're a drunken mess. Because you hauled one of them across a car park and into his house without complaint and, despite what you think, without real judgement. Because you didn't throw me under the bus for helping. Because you take the weight even when it's too heavy."

My throat closes.

He keeps going. "And yeah, you're grumpy. And guarded. And you've got moods like weather fronts. But you also stayed. You sat with me. You invited me. And you didn't have to."

He pauses before saying, "I like people who don't pretend. And I think you're not pretending. Even when you're being a bit of a prick."

I bark out a laugh that feels like a release valve cracking open. Then it hits me again—this bone-deep ache, because I don't see myself the way he does. I don't feel like someone worth the effort. I feel like a man who's constantly trying not to drown in the mess of his own overthinking. Who keeps people out because letting them in means getting hurt. Again.

But Brent? He doesn't flinch. He doesn't pull away. He just stays—with me, in this space that I don't let many people into—and that's what wrecks me most of all.

The quiet stretches, thick between us, until the road bends towards home and my building comes into view. I pull up out front, the engine humming low as the car idles, and suddenly it hits me. I brought him here. Home. With me.

And I've got no fucking clue what I'm meant to do next.

Brent unclicks his seatbelt like it's no big deal, like this is just what we do.

My pulse is in my throat.

Seriously, what the fuck am I supposed to do with him now?

I know what I want to do. Or rather, what I want him to do to me. Which—*Jesus*—isn't helping matters. I can barely think. My brain's stopped making useful thoughts and instead loops through vague flashes of skin, of that lip ring grazing across my neck, of his mouth opening against mine—

Get a grip.

But when I glance over at him, he's already out of the car, calm as anything. Cool air floods in when I open my door, and I scan the street automatically. My eyes do a sweep: down the road, across the opposite pavement, into the gaps between the buildings. No flashes. No shadows. Just the low hum of quiet streets and an occasional parked scooter.

Good. No press. Not tonight.

I nod towards the entrance. "Come on."

He falls in beside me, hands in his pockets like we're just two mates walking home after the pub. There's no tension, no awkwardness, just Brent—unshakably Brent.

At the front door, I fumble with my keys for half a second longer than necessary. My fingers feel clumsy. Everything feels a little too loud in my chest.

He leans in slightly, voice low. "Lead the way, Captain."

The way that word lands in my gut could be classified as an international incident. The door opens with a push and a soft creak, and we step into the entryway, our footsteps echoing lightly against the quiet.

Up the stairs to the second floor is my flat. I get the door open, and then I freeze. Because now we're here. Inside. Together. Just him and me and whatever the fuck is about to happen.

I turn to say something, maybe crack a joke, maybe tell him the bathroom's down the hall or that I've got nothing but protein bars and cold pizza in the fridge.

But I don't get the chance, because he's already moved.

He pushes the door shut behind us, then steps into my space, calm and sure, and suddenly I'm the one against the door, his body pinning me there, heat radiating between us like a living thing.

His hand lands on my chest—firm, grounding, warm. His gaze meets mine, and there's no teasing in it now. No smugness. Just clarity. Confidence and intention. "I've got you," he says, voice low and firm and so fucking certain it steals the air from my lungs.

I suck in a breath, and my whole body locks up. His hand slides lower, fingers brushing over the front of my jeans, and I swear to God, I almost fucking come. Just from that. From him. From the weight of his hand and the promise in his voice.

"I know exactly what you need," he whispers.

And holy crap on a cracker, he does. Somehow, this man I barely know—who's patient and cocky and kind and watching me like I'm something worth handling with care—has already read me like a book.

And fuck me, I want him to turn every page.

10

Brent

Camden's breath catches. His body tenses like a bow drawn tight, muscles straining under control he's clearly used to maintaining—on the pitch, in public, probably even in private.

But right now? Right now, I want to be the one he doesn't have to hold it together for.

His pupils are blown wide, gaze fixed on mine like he's trying to keep himself anchored, like if he moves, he might unravel completely.

Good. Because I'm here to catch him.

"Cam," I say, low and steady, my palm pressing just enough for him to feel it. "Let me."

His mouth opens slightly, like he might speak. Like he might argue.

I shake my head, just once, leaning in closer. "You think too much. I know why. I get it."

And I do. I've read the articles. The way the press chewed him up years ago and spat him out like a headline. I've seen what that kind of exposure does—what it takes. He's lived with that spotlight turned sharp and punishing for too long.

But this isn't the press. This isn't a story. This is me. And I'll earn every bit of his trust if that's what it takes.

I slide my hand up his chest again, feeling the rapid beat of his heart beneath my palm. "You don't have to hold it in with me," I murmur. "You don't have to do anything but let go. I've got you."

His throat bobs, and that breath he'd been holding shudders free. His fingers twitch at his sides, like he's not sure if he should grab me or push me off. So I move unhurriedly. Carefully but with purpose.

I sink slowly to my knees in front of him, palms dragging down the sides of his thighs as I go—claiming space, not asking for it.

Camden exhales sharply, one word tumbling out in a voice that's all grit and need. "Fuck." It sounds like it's been ripped out of him. Not performative. Not polished. Just raw.

I look up. He's staring down at me like he doesn't

know what hit him—chest rising fast, lips parted, a flush blooming up his throat. Every line of his body is drawn tight with restraint, with tension that hums under his skin like a current. His hands hover in the air—uncertain, twitching.

I wait and let him come to me.

And he does. One trembling hand finally lowers, threading into my hair like he's testing the reality of this moment. His grip is tentative, questioning. His thumb grazes my temple. "You sure?" he asks, voice quiet, wavering, like saying it out loud costs him.

I tilt my head and kiss the inside of his thigh once, deliberately slow. "Camden."

His breath hitches. His fingers tighten.

"I'm exactly where I want to be."

That hand stills. And this time, when he exhales, it's shaky—but it's surrender.

And it's beautiful.

I press my cheek against the front of his jeans and feel the strain there. Hard. Throbbing. Fuck, he's sexy like this. He's already trembling, and I haven't even touched him properly yet.

I kiss him through the denim. Once. Slow. Then again, right over the spot that makes him gasp. "Tell me if you want me to stop," I say against him. "But if you don't? I'm going to make you feel so fucking good that you'll forget what it felt like to hold back."

He doesn't speak, but his fingers contract in my hair, and that's all the answer I need.

A lamp burns low in the sitting room—thank fuck, because the last thing I want to do is risk moving him. If he gets a second to overthink, he might shut it all down. So I stay right here. Right in front of him. And when I finally undo his jeans and take him into my mouth, his head hits the door with a soft thunk, followed by a deep exhale that sounds suspiciously like trust.

He gives in—beautifully, entirely. And I know, without question, I've got him.

His hips jerk just slightly, instinctive, and then freeze again like he's afraid of doing something wrong. Of hurting me. Of losing control.

It hits me right in the chest—that restraint. That tight, aching grip on himself.

Even now, even with my hands on him, with my mouth on him, Camden's still holding on by his fingernails. That's not what I want. Not with me.

So I rest one hand on his hip, the other around the base of him, and lift my gaze to his. "Cam," I say softly, voice rough with heat and conviction, "you don't have to be careful. Not with me."

He doesn't say a word. But his hand slides deeper

into my hair, and when I take him again—slow and deep and steady—he makes a sound that's shattered.

The weight and heat of him fills my mouth, heavy and impossible to ignore. I move carefully, tasting him, learning every sound he makes in response. The catch of his breath. The whispered cursing. The breathless, almost disbelieving noise when I hollow my cheeks and go just that little bit deeper.

His legs widen, his back hits the door harder this time, and one hand thumps against the wall beside him.

I can feel it—him unravelling. Piece by piece, his control slips with every pass of my tongue, every pull of suction, every breath I steal from him and return with care. He tastes clean and heady, salt and skin and something wholly him.

I hum around him, and his whole body shudders.

"Fuck—Brent—" His voice is wrecked, like gravel and want and disbelief all rolled together.

I pull back just slightly to breathe, to stroke him with my hand, and look up. He's flushed. Eyes glazed. Mouth parted. A goddamn vision.

"You're all right," I whisper, lips brushing the head of him. "You're doing so fucking well."

That's all it takes.

His head drops back, jaw going slack, the long line of his throat on full display. The cords strain as he gasps, his hips pushing forwards in one instinctive, desperate motion—his whole body suddenly wound tight, coiled at the edge—

And then he breaks.

Not quietly. Not politely. It tears through him like a wave slamming into the shore—powerful, overwhelming, raw.

His body arches, a low, rough sound torn from his chest as pleasure shudders through him in deep, rolling pulses. I stay with him, my mouth and hand soft now, careful, coaxing him through every twitch, every after-shock. I can feel him unravel in my hands, feel how hard he worked to hold it together—and how completely he's stopped trying now.

It's beautiful, watching a man like him let go.

When he finally slumps, boneless and flushed, his breath comes hard and fast, each inhale shaky, like he's forgotten how to breathe without restraint. His hand slips from my hair and drifts down—slow, aimless—until his fingers find my jaw. His thumb brushes over my cheek like he's grounding himself. Like he can't quite believe any of this is real.

I press a kiss to the inside of his wrist. It's slow and intentional. A thank-you and a promise all in one.

He doesn't speak. He doesn't need to. Not when I can feel the tremble in his skin and the truth of it all in the weight of his body still leaning against the door—undone, unguarded, mine for the moment.

His eyes flutter open, glazed but locked on mine. "Holy fuck," he breathes.

I smile, still kneeling, my heart pounding. "You good?"

He huffs out a laugh, but it's breathless—more a sound of disbelief than amusement. "I'm not sure I remember my own name."

Carefully, I rise to my feet, placing a steadying hand on his chest as I go. He doesn't flinch. Doesn't stop me when I lean in and press a kiss to his lips—soft and brief. There's no heat in it, no push for more. Just contact. Just truth. Just... us, right now.

His eyes open slowly, and when they meet mine, I see the haze still lingering there—pleasure, yes, but also something quieter. Something that looks a lot like trust.

"I meant what I said," I murmur, letting my fingers rest lightly over his heart. "I've got you."

And I do.

Not just here in this moment, with his back against the door and the taste of him still on my tongue, but entirely. I've got his tension, his silence, his mess. I've got the parts of him he doesn't know how to share yet.

And when I say it—when I see how his expression shifts, like something inside him unclenches—I feel the truth of it settle in my chest with a kind of rightness I haven't felt in years.

He lets out a breath, slower this time. It's controlled, but there's something in the way he leans into my hand, just the barest shift of weight, that tells me everything I need to know.

He believes me—or maybe he's starting to. And fuck, if that doesn't mean everything. Every complicated, hard-earned piece of him.

He's still leaning against the door, lips parted, breathing slowly like he's trying to recalibrate the world. I take a step back, giving him space, even though every part of me wants to stay close. Not to start anything again, but just to stay near.

Camden exhales, drags a hand down his face, and clears his throat. "I could, uh... return the favour."

My heart does something funny at that—something low and aching. Not because I wouldn't love that, but because the way he says it sounds more like an obligation than a desire. Like he owes me something for letting go.

I shake my head. "Cam, what I did wasn't a favour."

His gaze flicks to mine, uncertain.

I soften my voice. "I wanted to. It was... honestly, it was my pleasure." A breath escapes me. "Literally and otherwise."

He huffs out something that might almost be a laugh, though it's tinged with discomfort.

"And yeah," I add with a self-deprecating grin, "I'm hard enough that a few strokes would probably end me right now, but that's not the point."

Camden shifts, eyes dipping as he tugs up his pants, putting himself back in order while very clearly avoiding my gaze.

"I don't want this to be some kind of transaction," I say gently. "I don't need anything back. I don't want out —I want in. Time. Connection. Something that isn't just about getting off."

That finally gets him to look at me. It's not quite shock in his eyes. More like wariness. Like the idea of someone sticking around without strings, without a hidden agenda, is so unfamiliar he doesn't quite know what to do with it.

I glance at the clock. "It's nearly eleven. You have training tomorrow?"

He shakes his head. "No. Recovery day."

Relief unfurls through my shoulders. "Good. Then how about we watch a movie?"

He frowns slightly, like he doesn't quite trust the suggestion.

"I'm serious," I say. "No tricks. Just your couch, a

stupid film, and me probably falling asleep with my head on your shoulder halfway through."

He studies me like he's trying to figure out what angle I'm working. But then something shifts—just a flicker—and he nods once. "All right."

He leads the way through the flat, moving a little stiffly, like the tension hasn't completely bled out of him yet. He heads to the kitchen while I hover near the sofa, trying not to stare at his arse as he walks—and mostly failing.

The space surprises me—not because it's flashy, but because it isn't. Warm lighting, books stacked on low shelves, mismatched cushions, an old Exeter Seagulls fleece draped over the back of a chair. It's not cold or staged—it's lived-in. Personal.

And somehow, it makes my chest go all stupid and soft.

I call out, "You making tea?"

"Yeah," he says, voice faint.

"Gross," I reply with a grin. "That's the most British thing about you."

He snorts.

"Honestly, I've tried. It tastes like boiled regret and lost hope. Ted Lasso absolutely nailed it."

His laugh carries from the kitchen—short, surprised, and real.

He returns a moment later with two mugs. He hands me one, and our fingers brush. I make sure of it. He doesn't pull away. Instead, he sits beside me, close enough that our legs touch. The tension's still there in his posture, but I rest my arm on the back of the sofa behind him—not touching, not forcing, just letting him feel the option of closeness without pressure.

"You good with something easy?" I ask, flicking through the streaming menu.

He nods. "Yeah. Easy sounds great."

I hit Play on something ridiculous and let the noise fill the space. The kind of movie that requires zero thought and rewards zero attention. My body's still buzzing with everything that happened—every sound he made, the way he melted for me—but I keep my touches light, occasional, never pushing.

Just enough to remind him I'm here. That I meant what I said. That he doesn't have to carry everything alone tonight.

He sips his tea. I sip mine, regretting every second of it. But I don't say a word. Because Camden's next to me on a sofa in his flat, his knee brushing mine, and for the first time all night, his shoulders have started to relax.

And I'll take that over tea-flavoured disappointment any day.

I don't know how long I've been out, but the first thing I register is a low voice and the soft press of a hand on my shoulder.

"Brent."

My eyes peel open slowly. Everything's dark, except for the low amber glow from a nearby lamp. The TV's gone quiet, the screen black. Camden is crouched beside the couch, looking at me, sleep-rumpled and steady.

My heart stumbles.

He's trying to get rid of me. That's my first, knee-jerk thought, and it stings. I sit up fast, blinking. "Sorry, I didn't mean to crash. I can grab a cab, no big deal—"

"No," he says firmly, cutting me off before I spiral. "I just didn't want to wake you too hard."

I pause, staring at him, brain still rebooting.

He stands and offers me his hand. "Come on," he says, quieter now. "You'll sleep better in bed."

For a second, my whole system malfunctions. My blood wakes up fast, and not just in my chest. My dick twitches, my pulse jumps, and the idea of his bed slams into me like a freight train. "Right," I say, clearing my throat. "Yeah. Sure."

He doesn't look at me while he leads the way, just

points to a half-open door off the hall. "Bathroom's through there. There's a new toothbrush on the sink."

When I step in, the light flicks on automatically. Everything is crisp and neutral—grey tiles, soft towels, a faint clean scent that might be eucalyptus. And sure enough, on the edge of the basin: a still-packaged toothbrush and a tiny cup with toothpaste already squeezed out.

He thought about this before waking me. The idea gives me stupid, swooping butterflies.

I wash my face, brush my teeth, and try to get my heart rate under control. No luck. When I step out again and pad quietly towards the bedroom in nothing but my boxer briefs, I hear the water running in what's clearly his en suite. Camden's showering. Probably needed to decompress—his version of resetting.

But my body isn't nearly as calm as my thoughts.

Just knowing he's behind that door, water sluicing over that strong, solid frame... the image is enough to punch my cock straight up against the tight cotton of my boxers. The head slips past the waistband, leaving nothing to the imagination.

I'm still standing in his bedroom, near the doorway, staring at the en suite door like an idiot, when the shower cuts off. A few heartbeats later, Camden appears.

Fuck me. He's in nothing but a towel. His hair is

damp, curling slightly at the ends, droplets of water still trailing down the thick column of his neck, his beard, and across his chest. He's massive—all over—built not like a model but like a fortress. No six-pack, just pure, necessary strength carved from years of brutal games and weight rooms and discipline.

And right now, he looks unsure. Vulnerable.

I don't let the moment pass. "I want you," I say, voice low and honest.

His eyes widen, breath hitching slightly. I glance down. He's hard, so fucking hard it makes my mouth go dry.

My gaze snaps back up. "How do you feel about being on your knees?"

For a beat, he's frozen. I brace for the brush-off. For the shutdown. For him to pull the wall back up and send me back to the couch. But instead... something in him melts. He exhales—one long, ragged breath—and the tension in his shoulders sags like he's just dropped ten pounds of weight.

His lips part. He doesn't say no. His eyes give me the answer first. And it's *yes*. Hell, it's *please*. And before his mouth even moves, I know he's going to let me take care of him again. And this time, it's not just physical. It's permission. It's trust. And that's the sexiest fucking thing I've ever seen.

He doesn't speak—not with words. But the way he looks at me, wide-eyed and flushed, tells me everything I need to know. He wants this. Wants me. Maybe not in a way he knows how to say yet, but it's there—clear as the hard line beneath that towel and the slight tremble in his fingers as he stands still, waiting.

I cross the space between us slowly, giving him every second to change his mind.

He doesn't.

My hand comes to his chest, warm and broad beneath my palm, and I feel his heart skip. His gaze doesn't leave mine, not even when I lean in and press our lips together.

The kiss is soft at first. Careful. But that doesn't last.

He groans against me—low and deep—and I take the invitation, tilting my head and kissing him harder. His mouth opens to mine like it's instinct. Like he's craving this, and Jesus, the way he melts into me makes my knees weak.

He tastes like mint and heat and something distinctly Camden. I wrap an arm around his waist and feel him lean in, big and solid and mine, just for now.

When I tug gently at the edge of the towel, he hesitates for only a moment before letting it fall to the floor. I draw back enough to look at him, just for a second. And fuck, he's glorious. Thick thighs, powerful chest, strength carved from years of battle on the pitch, but it's the vulnerability that knocks the breath from my lungs.

I lead him to the bed, easing him down until he's flat on his back, propped on his elbows, watching me with that uncertain hunger written all over him.

I strip, then climb onto the mattress slowly, kissing my way down his body. Every inch of him is mine to explore. My lips drag across the swell of his pecs, tongue tracing the lines of his tattoos. I pause at each design, already imagining how I'll connect them. How I'll help complete the story he wears on his skin.

He lets out a sound—half groan, half breath—when I mouth over one of the new patches of ink on his bicep.

"You've got no idea how much I've thought about doing your sleeve," I whisper, lips brushing his skin. "How much I want to mark you up in all the ways that matter."

He exhales sharply, hands twisting into the sheets.

I move lower. Across his stomach. Over the sharp plane of his hip. But when I reach his groin, I bypass his cock entirely.

He groans, head falling back, hips twitching. "Please... fuck, Brent—"

I smile into his thigh. "Not yet." I ease his legs open, and his breath stutters as I settle between them. I run my hands over his thighs, awed, possessive. I kiss his skin just above his knee, then drag my mouth higher.

When I reach the sensitive stretch behind his balls, he gasps—loud and unguarded—and I breathe him in. That's when I realise what he's done.

"You made yourself ready," I murmur against his skin, voice almost reverent.

His cheeks go pink. His eyes don't meet mine. His chest rises and falls like he's been running sprints. He stammers, "I-I didn't know if—"

I cut him off with a kiss to the inside of his thigh. "You're perfect."

He shakes his head once, eyes squeezed shut, like he doesn't believe it.

I kiss him again, lower this time. Then again. "You're so fucking beautiful, Camden. Strong. Sweet. And mine for tonight."

When I press open-mouthed kisses to his rim, he gasps—full-bodied, shaking—and his legs fall wider. "Fuck... Brent... I can't—"

"You can," I murmur. "You are."

I taste him—salt, skin, heat, and something intimate, something that's purely him. It's earthy and clean, almost electric, like the spark that catches on the back of your tongue right before lightning strikes. It's real and raw. I swear, I could drown in it.

I worship him, and he breaks. He's vocal—so damn vocal—and every breathy curse, every ragged moan, lights me up from the inside out. His voice wrecks me.

"Jesus—don't stop... please... oh my God—" His fingers twist into the sheets, knuckles white, hips jerking helplessly. He's undone. Alive under my mouth. And he gives it all to me—no shame, no holding back, just pure, desperate want.

And I swear, every sound he makes brings me this close to losing it. But not yet. I want to feel him fall apart again, and this time, I'll be right there—eyes open, mouth on him, heart full.

He nods before I even finish telling him I want him. That alone undoes me a little. The way Camden gives himself over—like he knows I'll handle him right—there's nothing casual about it. It's trust, and it's loud, even in silence.

I ask, "Back or knees?" and watch him freeze. His cheeks flush. He hesitates just long enough for me to know what this is: not uncertainty but exposure. A kind of shyness that doesn't match the way he arches into me when I touch him—but it's there, and I respect it.

I make the call. "Hands and knees."

He exhales like I've just given him permission to breathe again. Like the decision being made for him somehow lets the tension slip off his shoulders. He moves into position.

But before I reach for him, I pause. "Cam," I say quietly, brushing a hand over the curve of his back, "we should talk protection."

He glances back at me, flushed and a little dazed, but nods. "Yeah. Good idea."

"I'm negative," I say. "Tested a month ago. I can show you the results, if you want."

He hesitates for a second, then shakes his head. "I believe you."

I still and let the weight of that settle. "You trust me?"

He looks over his shoulder, cheeks pink, eyes dark with something more than arousal. "Yeah. I do."

I shift forwards, pressing a kiss to the space between his shoulders. "Okay. Then I'll ask—do you want me to wear one?"

His voice is low, breath catching. "No. I want... fuck, I want to feel you."

I swallow hard. My hands tighten where they rest on his hips. "You sure?"

He nods again. "Raw. I want all of you."

Jesus.

I let the words sink deep, settle under my skin, stoke something low and intense in my belly. And somehow, it's not just about the physical—it's about the gift he's giving me in this moment. That trust. That choice.

There's no rush. I ask for the lube, and he reaches back to hand it to me without a word. He's already trembling, open from my tongue, but I still take my time.

Two fingers. Slow and careful.

He gasps, hips twitching back towards me like he can't help it.

"You're doing so fucking well," I whisper, pressing kisses along his spine as I move. "Just breathe. Let me take care of you."

Then three fingers, stretching him wider. He moans, loud and unfiltered, and the sound lights me up from the inside. He's needy, desperate, pressing back against my hand with ragged little sounds. Noisy and breathy. It nearly knocks the air out of my lungs.

"Fuck, Camden," I groan. "You feel incredible."

"Please," he pants, voice wrecked. "Don't stop."

"I'm not going to stop." I kiss the base of his neck. "I'm going to fuck you so good you forget how to think."

He moans again, fingers curling tight in the sheets.

I keep him there, stretched and slick, trembling and waiting. And when I finally pull back, lining up behind him, I take a breath—because I already know, when I push inside, I'll lose every bit of control I have left.

"Please," he whispers, and it undoes me. "Please, I need you."

Jesus Christ. I have to stop. Just breathe. I press my forehead to his back, my dick nudging against his hole while I try not to come from just the sound of his voice. He's everything—soft and raw and wild and mine.

"Hands off your dick," I growl, and his fingers curl into the sheets instead.

He listens. God, he listens.

I line myself up again and push in, inch by inch. He's hot and tight, and it feels like I'm slipping into something I've been waiting for without realising it. Like the final piece clicks into place.

I freeze once I'm fully in—just for a second—because if I move, I'm done. And I need this to last. I need to give him more than just the rush of it.

When I start to move, it's careful at first. But I can hear it in his voice—he doesn't want careful. He wants to feel it. To stop thinking. And I can give him that. I want to.

"You want it hard?" I murmur, reaching the edge of my own control.

"Yes—fuck, yes."

So I give it to him.

Exactly what he needs.

Hard. Fast. Dirty.

Every thrust drives deeper, sharper, and he takes it—arching into each one with a gasp that curls in my gut like fire. He's gripping the sheets, muscles flexed, knees spread wide, and his back bows beautifully as I work into him.

"Jesus, Cam," I groan, hands tight on his hips. "You feel so fucking good—so tight. You're taking me like you were made for it."

He shudders at my words, breath catching. "Brent—oh fuck—"

Each time I hit that spot inside him, his voice cracks. It's a desperate, broken sound that's half shock, half pleasure. His thighs tremble beneath my hands. He's undone. But it's not the kind of wreckage that leaves someone undone. It's honest. Grounded. Present. He's here with me in every shake and gasp and curse.

And fuck if I don't want to burn this into memory.

"That's it," I growl. "You take me so well, baby. So perfect. Every inch."

He cries out again, voice dissolving into open-mouthed moans. I see the way his arms tremble, his head dropping forwards, sweat sliding down his neck. He's holding on. Barely.

I know the feeling. I'm getting close—tight in my gut, breath coming harder—and I need more. Need him. So I slow just long enough to slide my arm around his torso, pulling him upright. He comes easily, back flush to my chest, his body slick and hot beneath my hands. I wrap one arm around his waist to keep him grounded while the other finds his cock.

"Hold on," I whisper into the side of his throat, voice ragged as I pump him in time with each thrust. "You're not going anywhere."

His head tips back against my shoulder, exposing the arch of his neck. He's panting, groaning, completely lost to the rhythm. I drive harder now—deeper, chasing the edge.

"I've got you," I murmur again, voice catching. "Come for me, Cam. I want to feel you let go."

He moans, louder now, gasping as my hand works him and my hips snap against him with precision. His body jerks—and then he's gone.

He cries out, every muscle tensing before releasing all at once as he spills over my hand, ropes of cum painting his stomach and my fingers. His head lolls, lips parted, voice hoarse from the sheer force of it.

I keep going. Just a little longer. Just enough to push me over too—his heat, his voice, the way he gives himself to me finally tipping me past the brink.

I bury myself deep and freeze, trembling against his back as release rips through me like wildfire. The world narrows to him—his breath, his warmth, his strength—

and I stay there, chest to his spine, heart pounding so loud it echoes in my ears.

The air between us hums. And in the silence that follows, his hand finds mine, lacing our fingers together and grounding us both.

Neither of us says anything. We just stay like this. Breathing, linked, and settled in something that feels too big to name. As the last of the tension seeps from my body, I wonder—quiet and breathless—what the hell we've just started.

Whatever it is, I don't want to stop. I just hope, when morning comes, Camden doesn't start building those walls back up again.

11

Camden

I wake with my face pressed to warm skin and my arm flung across a solid chest. My leg is tangled with another—his—and there's a steady thrum of breath against my hair. Brent.

I blink slowly, my eyes adjusting to the soft morning light. It's quiet. Still. The hum of the city muffled by the thick windows and the stillness between us. I don't move.

His body is a furnace, his arm a heavy, secure band across my waist. I breathe him in—skin, sweat, something warm and clean beneath it all—and wait for the panic. Wait for the usual thud of regret to settle into my chest.

But it doesn't come.

Instead, I feel... safe. Grounded, even.

His cock is hard against my thigh, and the thought hits me like a freight train: I want to taste him. The idea itself stuns me. Not the wanting—I've wanted him from the moment he shook my hand and smiled like he knew what to do with someone like me —but the impulse, the intimacy, this isn't who I am. I don't do overnights. I don't do sleepy cuddling and soft thoughts about waking someone up with a blow job.

And yet... here I am, clinging to him like I've done it a hundred times before.

I'm so lost in my own head I don't even realise he's awake until he speaks, voice still rough with sleep. "You're thinking far too hard this morning."

I freeze. "Shit, sorry." I start to pull back, flustered.

But his arm tightens around me, dragging me even closer. "Nope. Stay put," he murmurs.

And fuck, I melt into him. "Morning," I croak, my throat dry, heart loud in my ears.

He shifts just enough to find my mouth and presses a kiss to it—soft, lazy, sweet. The kind of kiss that makes my toes curl and my chest go all warm and useless. It's not hungry. Not demanding. Just... affection, poured straight from him into me.

I'm a puddle of goddamn goo.

"Morning," he replies against my lips. He kisses me again—soft and unhurried—then rolls back enough to tuck a knuckle beneath my jaw. "What's the plan today?" he asks, his voice still husky with sleep but laced with curiosity.

I blink slowly, brain sluggish. "Uh... Sunday recovery. No training. You?"

He stretches with a low, satisfied noise. "I've got a client this afternoon. Few hours from now."

"Plenty of time for breakfast," I murmur, then wince. "Except I have, like, no breakfast food."

Brent stretches, his stomach letting out a quiet growl. "Okay, how about we go grab some breakfast? There's a place around the corner I saw yesterday—does a full English. Not sure if it's any good, though."

I go still. Out. In public. With him.

The panic is instant—tight and cold, latching on to my ribs before I can stop it. Not because I don't want to be seen with him, but because I do. And what that might mean. What it might look like.

Brent notices, because of course he does. His smile softens, and he immediately reroutes, casual as anything. "Or," he says, voice easy, "I can head out, grab something, and bring it back here."

I blink, caught off-guard by the pivot, and the fact that it came without judgement, without a pause. Just instinct and care.

Before I can speak, he shifts closer and presses a kiss to my temple. "It's okay," he says gently. "I get it."

I glance up at him—at those eyes that always seem to see more than I want to give away. He's not hurt. Not offended. Just... steady.

And somehow, in the quiet weight of that look, I believe him. He really *does* get it.

Before I can respond, his phone buzzes on the nightstand. Then again. And again.

He sighs. "That'll be the family group chat blowing up." He stretches to grab his jeans, completely naked as he steps out of bed. And I—Christ—I almost choke.

The morning sun is cutting through the blinds in long golden stripes, laying over the lines of his back, his broad shoulders, the dip of his spine. The faint sheen of sleep-warmed skin glows under it, and when he leans to dig his phone out of his jeans pocket, every muscle shifts in harmony. I'm not proud of the strangled noise I make.

He turns, grinning, and my gaze catches on the flash of metal through his nipple—how the hell did I miss that? —and then lower, at ink wrapped around his hips. And then lower still.

"Tony," he says, scrolling. "One of the twins. It's the family chat. He's trying to organise Fourth of July stuff already. Says I'm banned from bailing this year."

"You go back for it all the time?" I ask, surprised by how normal the question sounds.

"I try to every other year," he says, "which isn't

always possible. It's kind of a Parks tradition. BBQs, family chaos... all that good shit. Last year I skipped because of my schedule. I think they're holding it against me."

He smiles down at the message, and I watch it transform his whole face. It's unfair—how good-looking he is when he's like this. All unguarded and gorgeous, standing in my bedroom like he belongs.

I tear my gaze away before I embarrass myself further.

He tosses the phone back onto his jeans and pads over to the bed, slipping under the covers again like it's the most natural thing in the world. "So," he says, settling beside me, his tone light, "what's your breakfast order?"

And just like that, it's easy again. Quiet. Real. And even if I'm not sure what this is, we're finding a rhythm I'm not ready to give up just yet.

"I could definitely eat," I say, trying for nonchalant even though my heart's still pounding from watching him stand naked in morning light like some sort of sin incarnate. "Full English? Maybe something sweet. Whatever you bring back, I'll eat."

Brent arches an eyebrow, smug smile curving his lips. "That sounded dangerously close to innuendo."

"I'm not denying it." I smirk and nudge him with my knee. "Now go. Feed me, tattoo man."

He leans down and kisses me—another one of those soft, slow, almost reverent presses of lips that's way too much for a morning after. Way too much for something we've never actually named.

And then he's up, stretching, tugging his clothes back on, and disappearing out the door with a casual "Be back in twenty."

The flat is suddenly quiet without him, and I'm not sure I like that. I exhale and reach for my own phone, left on the bedside table and still plugged in from last night. The screen lights up with a few training reminders, a message from our media guy checking on Briggs after last night's debacle—honestly, I'm not even surprised he knows; Davey seems to know everything—and a couple of texts from Lachie—one of which is just a single rainbow emoji. Subtle.

I don't reply.

Instead, I open the Love the Game group chat, suddenly needing something familiar. It's still wild to me that I'm in this thing—a whole group of queer athletes from around the world, from all levels and all sports, trying to survive the chaos of sport and identity and media. It's not perfect, but it's a lifeline sometimes. The kind of thing I didn't know I needed until I had it.

Still, today, opening the chat feels... weird. Knowing Cosmo's in there. Cosmo Parks. Brent's baby brother. A kid I've shared more conversations with than I can count. Who's asked me for advice. Who I've offered encouragement to. Who's a damn good ice hockey player and a decent human to boot.

And now I've fucked his brother and am currently waiting on breakfast in bed with said brother. Not that I'm ever telling Cosmo that.

The last flurry of messages is from yesterday morning. Nothing to do with me—just the usual chatter.

> CONNOR:
> STILL THINK IT'S COMPLETE BOLLOCKS
> THEY CALL IT "SOCCER" OVER THERE. I
> REFUSE.
>
> FERRIS:
> SAYS THE GUY ACTUALLY FROM
> ENGLAND. YOU DON'T GET TO JUDGE.
>
> CONNOR:
> EXACTLY BECAUSE I'M FROM ENGLAND.
> IT'S FOOTBALL. END OF.
>
> COSMO:
> I'M JUST HERE FOR THE CHAOS. ALSO,
> SOMEONE PLEASE TELL ME IT'S OKAY TO
> FAKE AN INJURY AND BAIL TOMORROW.
>
> CONNOR:
> PERMISSION GRANTED. PULL A HAMMY.
> BE DRAMATIC.
>
> FERRIS:
> WOW. THE MORAL COMPASS IN THIS
> CHAT IS SO BROKEN.
>
> COSMO:
> THAT'S ON MY BROTHERS. THEY'RE THE
> WORST INFLUENCES.

COSMO:
ONE OF THEM SENT ME A VIDEO OF A
RACCOON STEALING A BOTTLE OF
WHISKEY THIS MORNING. SO LIKE...
MAYBE HE'S IMPROVING?

My lips twitch. It's a dumb throwaway line, but something about it punches me right in the chest.

One of them. That could be Brent.

I've read Cosmo's name in this chat a hundred times. Shared GIFs. Advice. Late-night rants. I've probably sent him stupid voice notes after away matches. I've even talked to him in the flesh.

And now I've kissed his brother senseless. Touched him everywhere. Let him touch me back.

The guilt shouldn't be this sharp. I didn't do anything wrong. Neither did Brent. But it still feels like I'm holding a secret in both hands and wondering when it'll spill.

I exhale, let the phone drop to the bed beside me, and scrub a hand over my face.

The flat smells faintly like Brent's skin, my muscles ache in the best way, and if I close my eyes, I can still feel the way his fingers traced every inch of me last night like he was memorising a map.

And yet... here I am. Spiralling.

I'm so good at that.

My phone buzzes.

Brent: Your full English is incoming.
Hope you're a beans guy, because I
wasn't sure if that's a universal thing or
a weird British rite of passage.

My heart jumps as I type back.

Me: Beans are good. But if you forgot
the hash browns, I'll never forgive you.

His reply is instant.

Brent: You wound me. I'd never forget
the hash browns.

And just like that, some of the weight in my chest lifts. Just a little.

I head to the kitchen to make a cuppa and Brent a coffee. His attempt at hiding his dislike for tea yesterday was pretty weak. The thought makes me smile that he drank it anyway.

The group chat dings again, the screen lighting up with a string of new messages from the Love the Game group. I tap it open, half distracted, until I see who it's from.

COSMO:
CAMDEN! YOU'VE BEEN LURKING—
STATUS SAYS YOU'RE ONLINE. DON'T
THINK WE DON'T SEE YOU. 👀

COSMO:
WHERE DO YOU LIVE AGAIN?

Before I can type a response, Connor jumps in.

CONNOR:
CAMDEN, DON'T DO IT. THE MAN ONCE
GOT A GUY'S POST CODE AND SHOWED
UP WITH HOMEMADE BANANA BREAD
AND A SIX-PACK.

COSMO:
AND HE ATE ALL OF IT, SO YOU'RE
WELCOME. ALSO, BANANA BREAD IS A
LOVE LANGUAGE.

BRAYDEN:
WHAT ISN'T A LOVE LANGUAGE IN YOUR
WORLD?

COSMO:
CHAOS. BUT LIKE, AFFECTIONATE
CHAOS.

I sigh and give in, thumbs flying across the screen.

ME:
EXETER.

Cosmo's response is immediate.

COSMO:
NO WAY.

COSMO:
MY BIG BROTHER JUST MOVED THERE A
FEW WEEKS AGO.

COSMO:
YOU TWO SHOULD TOTALLY MEET. HE'S
BEEN KIND OF A LONELY BASTARD
LATELY.

My eyebrows shoot up. *Oh no.*

> COSMO:
> ACTUALLY, HE'S BEEN TALKING ABOUT
> SOMEONE HE'S INTO...

> COSMO:
> THINKS IT'S UNREQUITED.

I jerk forwards a little.

> COSMO:
> MAYBE YOU COULD KEEP HIM COMPANY
> UNTIL HIS NEXT VISIT HOME. YOU COULD
> TOTALLY STEP UP AND BE THE BIG
> BROTHER HE NEVER HAD.

> COSMO:
> OBVIOUSLY YOU CAN'T KEEP HIM.
> WELL, UNLESS YOU DELVE INTO A
> WORLD OF INCEST.

I choke on nothing—just the idea of that message lodges in my throat like a brick. I slap the phone face-down on the kitchen counter and stare at it like it just insulted my entire bloodline.

Fuck my life. Cosmo is matchmaking me, right?

To Brent.

Without even knowing it's me.

Without knowing Brent already spent the night here. Without knowing Brent's cock was pressed to my leg this morning while I debated whether I had it in me to wake him up with a blow job.

> COSMO:
> HOLY SHIT. WE COULD BECOME
> BROTHERS. TOTALLY CALLING BEST MAN
> RIGHTS.

BRAYDEN:
MATE… THERE'S SOMETHING SERIOUSLY
WRONG WITH YOU.

I groan into my hands. My chest is on fire in equal parts embarrassment, awe, and pure disbelief. I peek at the phone again.

CONNOR:
CAMDEN? YOU OKAY, OR DID COSMO'S
MATCHMAKING FINALLY KILL YOU?

Honestly? Maybe. Because he's talking about *me*. I'm the crush. Shit, I am, right? The guy Brent thinks isn't interested. The guy Cosmo thinks could step in and be the "big brother he never had."

Holy. Fucking. Shit.

I set the phone down, my mind racing. The coincidence is almost too much, but the warmth building in my chest tells me it's real.

Just then, the intercom buzzes. I jolt like I've been caught doing something I shouldn't—because, in a way, I have. I press the button, and Brent's voice crackles through. "Hey, it's me."

I buzz him in, then unlock the door, picking my phone back up and staring at it like it might reach out and slap me.

Brent enters a few moments later, balancing a tray with two large containers. "Hope you're hungry," he says, kicking the door shut behind him.

I blink at him, still holding my phone like it might combust. "Uh... yeah. Just..." I show him the screen. "So, funny story."

His brows lift as he reads the messages, and then recognition flickers in his eyes. "Ah. Cosmo."

I nod slowly. "Yeah. Still hard to believe I know him."

Brent chuckles, clearly amused. "The universe really said 'plot twist,' huh?"

"Plot twist that ends in a mild heart attack." I sit on the stool at the breakfast bar. "He was literally matchmaking us without knowing it was us."

"Don't worry." Brent's voice is low and warm as he sets the coffee on the counter. "I won't say anything."

There's a pause. My throat feels thick, my heart climbing into it. "Yet," I say, barely more than a whisper.

Brent turns, really looking at me, and something flickers in his expression—quiet and unshakable. Hope, yeah. But also something steadier. Something that feels a lot like belief. Not just in the possibility of us, but in me. As though he's seeing all the parts I keep locked up and choosing to trust that I'll let them out when I'm ready.

And the fucked-up thing? I want to. I really want to.

So much has changed since yesterday. And not just the sex—though, Jesus, I still feel the echo of his body against mine, the way he gave it to me so good and so right that I still have to breathe through the memory or risk getting hard all over again.

But that's not it. Not the heart of it.

The real shift is how I'd been so sure—*so sure*—that I was done letting anyone in. I'd built the walls, reinforced them, lived in their shadow.

And now?

He's here. In my space. Unpacking food like it's the most natural thing in the world. And I'm sitting here wondering how the hell I went from guarded silence to saying "yet" like there's a future I'm even willing to imagine.

My chest tightens, nerves crawling across my skin. Maybe he sees it, maybe he just feels it, but Brent doesn't push. Doesn't ask questions. He just glides past my awkward moment with easy grace, peeling open the food containers and settling onto the stool next to me.

"Here you go," he says with a smirk. "Breakfast first. Existential spirals later."

It makes me laugh—quiet and short, but real. I shuffle beside him, our thighs bumping. I'm still buzzing from Cosmo's messages, still reeling, and still stunned. But maybe... just maybe I'm not dreading what comes next.

Maybe, for the first time in a long time, I'm kind of

looking forward to it. I don't even care if it makes me a fickle arsehole that all I needed was a good dicking to leave myself open for more. The ache is worth it.

12

Brent

MONDAYS AND TUESDAYS ARE MY OFFICIAL DAYS OFF, but I can pretty much pick and choose my hours. And with the way things have been going—and Thursdays being Camden's almost guaranteed day off—I'm kinda considering reworking my schedule to spend time with him.

That's if he wants to, which... considering both Monday and Tuesday ended with me tangled in his sheets after he called to say he was home, I'm hoping he's keen to spend more than a frantic few hours with me.

Every time we've hooked up, it's been a trembling balance of fun and intense—impressive really, the way he seesaws between the two so effortlessly. He'll have me laughing one minute, breathless the next, and completely unravelled by the time we're done.

But it's not just the sex.

It's the way he watches me when I'm talking, really listening. The way he keeps trying to hold back something warm behind those guarded eyes, like he's just waiting for the moment it all gets taken away. It makes me want to prove him wrong—over and over again.

I'm on my way to his flat now—he texted this morning asking if I was still free tonight, followed by "no pressure," as though I wasn't already half in love with the way he's started to pick up on my constant use of "no pressure" before doing something wildly vulnerable. Like asking to see me on a weekday.

I bring a couple of beers in my bag just in case, and when he opens the door, I'm hit again with that quiet warmth that somehow lingers in his space. His flat smells like whatever detergent he uses and something woodsy and clean. He looks freshly showered and already barefoot. My brain short-circuits a little, because it's such a small detail—but weirdly intimate.

"Hey," he says, stepping aside to let me in.

"Hey yourself." I grin, brushing past him. "You surviving your week so far?"

He groans. "Barely. The physio has me doing extra rotational work after training. Apparently, thirty-one means I'm made of glass."

I laugh. "You're the fittest piece of glass I've ever seen."

Camden rolls his eyes but his mouth twitches at the corners, and it feels like a small win. We head to the kitchen, and I hand over the beers, sliding onto a bar-stool while he grabs glasses.

"You'd think with how much you train, they'd let up a little," I say.

"Not with four games left in the season." He opens one beer and sets it in front of me, then leans against the counter with his. "We're still third in the table, but it's tight. Every game could change things."

"Do you still get that nervous energy before a match?"

Camden tilts his head. "Not nervous, exactly. More like... hyper-focused. Like everything else gets pushed to the background."

I nod, soaking it in. "So that's why you go quiet after a game? Recalibrating?"

"Partly." He shrugs, his voice softer now. "Also just... being around people all day takes it out of me. I love the lads, but I'm not wired for noise twenty-four-seven."

"Same," I say. "Which is hilarious considering I work in a tattoo shop with music blaring and clients oversharing."

That earns me a real laugh, deep and low, and something in my chest settles. We chat like that for a while—about training, teammates, the stress of press deadlines and social obligations. He asks about my shop, about my ambitions. I tell him more about the six-month buy-in window, and how I'm leaning towards taking the plunge.

"You'd be great," he says simply, as if it's a fact, not a compliment.

It catches me off-guard. I swallow around the sudden lump in my throat. "Thanks."

Later, we migrate to the couch, beers in hand. The television plays in the background, muted and forgotten. Our conversation slows into easy stretches of quiet and little touches—his knee brushing mine, the warmth of his arm just close enough to feel without crowding. He's softer like this, more himself.

A thought tugs at me, one I've been carrying since that night outside the pub. I glance over at him, tentative. "Hey... can I ask you something?"

His brow lifts, wary but open. "Sure."

"That teammate from the pub—Briggs?" I hesitate, then commit. "What he said... have you talked to him?"

Camden stills. The shift is subtle—shoulders tightening, mouth pressing into a thin line—but I feel it.

"I tried," he says eventually. "He brushed it off. Joked about being drunk. Said I must've misheard."

"But you didn't."

"No." His voice is quiet. "I didn't. And I've known him a while. He's never been... I don't know. Never given off anything. But lately... he's been off. Guarded."

He leans forwards, elbows on his knees, brow furrowed. "I'm worried about him. I don't know if it's a sexuality thing or something else entirely, but he's closing himself off. And if it is about that...." He shakes his head. "I hate that we still live in a world where it has to be this hard."

I nod slowly. "Yeah. I get that."

Camden looks over at me, and I offer a small smile.

"I came out in high school," I tell him. "Didn't have much of a choice. Got caught kissing my then-boyfriend behind the gym."

His mouth twitches in surprise.

"My folks were... cool about it. Loud, chaotic, weirdly supportive. My mom said something about knowing since I started designing Halloween costumes for all my siblings."

That earns a soft chuckle.

"And there's definitely something in the water back home. One of the twins is bi, the other's gay, and then there's Cosmo—out and proud, obviously."

Camden barks out a laugh. "Jesus. Your family sounds like a sitcom."

"You have no idea." I grin. "We could power our own Pride float."

He shakes his head, still smiling. "My parents aren't like that. I mean... they're good people. Supportive. But they're quiet. From the West Midlands. Reserved."

"They took it okay?"

He nods. "Better than I expected. I think... I think they knew before I did. Even with all the rugby, the size, the noise—my mum especially. She didn't say anything at the time, just made tea and asked if I wanted to talk. She's still like that. Quiet but solid."

I smile at that. "Sounds like you get your grumpy serenity from her."

He snorts, but I see the fondness in his eyes.

Camden's still smiling when he leans back, arm now slung over the back of the couch, his fingers absently brushing my shoulder. The gesture feels easy—comfortable—and I lean into it without overthinking.

He glances at me, then says, "My brother Joel's getting married in July."

"Oh yeah?" I recall him mentioning a wedding. That he's opening up to me sends a flutter of fondness in my gut.

"Yeah. July 1. He's younger—only by two years, but he acts like it's ten. He's been with Yasmin for three years now."

I catch the fondness in his tone. "You like her?"

"Love her. She's bossy as hell, but she keeps him grounded. Makes him happy. That's enough for me."

I nod, sipping my beer. "Family wedding. That'll be full-on."

"Oh yeah." He chuckles. "Whole family will be there. I'm heading back a couple of days before—see my folks, help out, survive the chaos."

"Will you be home for the week?"

"Short and sweet. I'm heading to the States for a work thing, then summer training kicks off in August. I'll get a few weeks off once I'm back."

I nod, lifting my glass. "Good timing." Question fills his gaze, so I explain, "I'm heading to see my family on the third."

He glances at me, curious. "Right, your July Fourth celebration."

"That's the one. Cosmo added his own special brand of guilt-tripping since I missed last year. Claimed it wouldn't be a real summer without my ugly face at the barbecue."

Camden chuckles. "Is the Fourth of July really such a big deal?"

"Oh, it's huge. Think fireworks, questionable potato salad, people crying over burnt hot dogs. Someone always tries to launch a bottle rocket off the roof. It's chaos."

He smirks. "That sounds terrifying."

"And yet deeply patriotic." I lean closer with a grin. "Also? Hot. Like, face-melting, shirt-sticking-to-your-back hot."

He shifts beside me, bumping his knee into mine. "So... basically a health hazard disguised as a national holiday."

"Exactly." I tip my head towards him. "You'd hate it."

He huffs out a laugh but doesn't deny it. "Probably."

The silence that follows isn't heavy. It's soft. Familiar in a way I didn't expect this soon.

He takes another sip of his beer, then murmurs, "It's been a while since I saw them. My family."

I don't push, just reach out and let my knuckles graze his. A quiet gesture. He doesn't pull away.

And somehow, the quiet that follows says more than anything we've managed all night.

I glance over at Camden, the quiet between us comfortable but buzzing just enough that I want to keep it going. We're sitting close—shoulders grazing now and then—but not touching otherwise. His hand curls loosely around his beer glass, thumb slowly tracing the condensation. The kind of detail I shouldn't find distracting, but here we are.

I shift, resting an elbow on the back of the sofa. "So what's the visit for? July, I mean. You've mentioned it, but...."

He glances over, eyes thoughtful. "I've got a work thing." He pauses, then adds, "The Seagulls arranged a little tour with three rugby teams in the States. It's all exhibition stuff—PR, awareness. No pressure, no league points."

My brows go up. "There are rugby teams back home?"

Camden chuckles. "Apparently. Mostly amateur, semi-pro setups. But they've got solid local followings, and there's been a push lately to grow the sport in North America."

"God, I've been gone too long. I thought football still ruled everything."

"It does," he says with a grin. "But rugby's making noise. Slow and steady."

I tilt my head. "Where're you playing?"

"Jacksonville. Tallahassee. Then the final game's in Atlanta."

I sit up straighter, heart skipping. "Wait. Jacksonville?"

Camden's head tilts. "Yeah?"

"My parents live in Habersham, near Savannah.

That's like what, two hours away?" I laugh under my breath. "That's where I grew up."

He blinks, then smiles slowly. "No shit?"

"No shit." I shake my head, still surprised. "I mean, damn. That's close. Too close for the universe not to be having a bit of fun."

He's watching me now—not guarded, not cautious. Just... curious. Warm.

"Think your folks would go to a game?" he asks.

"Oh, hell no." I grin. "My mom would bring a sunhat the size of a dinner table and spend the whole time complaining about heat stroke. And my dad would try to start a chant and get ejected from the stands for swearing at the ref."

Camden snorts, amused.

I hesitate a beat, then shrug, softer now. "Okay, fine. I'm full of shit. They'd absolutely love it. Especially if it was for you."

His head tilts, eyes narrowing slightly, but there's a flicker of something warmer behind them. "Yeah?"

I nod, quieter this time. "Yeah. You're... becoming important."

The corner of his mouth lifts, just enough to knock the breath from my chest. Camden's smile blooms fully then—rare, unguarded. "I kinda want to meet them."

It's playful, but the words echo louder than they

should. The smile drops from my lips a little, not because I'm not happy, but because that meant something. That hint of future. Of things mattering more than just right now.

"I think they'd like you," I say, quiet and honest.

Camden looks down at the bottle in his hand, that smile still tugging at one corner of his mouth, like he's trying not to let it settle too deep. Then he gives a gentle shrug. "Well, your brother already likes me. That's a start."

I snort. "Don't even. I'm still recovering from Cosmo trying to emotionally adopt you via group chat."

He smirks. "He said I was broody."

"You are broody."

"And you're nosy."

"Touché."

We lapse into a beat of silence that's not awkward at all, just soft and steady. The kind that makes you aware of how close someone is, of the shape of the air between you.

I shift again, this time a little closer, my hand brushing his thigh as I set my beer down. He doesn't move away. He just watches me with that thoughtful gaze of his—heavy-lidded, not quite smiling.

"You nervous about the US trip?" I ask, voice low.

Camden exhales slowly, then nods. "A bit. Not for

the games. It's more... just being visible again. Press stuff. Fan stuff. New crowds. New eyes."

"Old ghosts?"

"Some of those too."

I rest my hand over his. "You don't need the pep talk. But I believe in you."

His gaze drops to our hands, and for a second, I think he might pull away. Instead, he turns his palm and links our fingers. "Yeah?"

I nod. "Definitely. And I'll be back home for a bit, too, remember? Just for the week, but... maybe I'll catch one of those games if there's an overlap."

Camden lifts an eyebrow. "You'd come?"

"Habersham's two hours away from Jacksonville," I say with a shrug. "Seems like a waste not to. Besides..." I squeeze his fingers gently. "Wouldn't mind seeing you on the pitch again." Though truth be told, all being well, I'll be getting a ticket for his next home game.

His throat works as he swallows. "I'll send you the schedule."

Another moment of quiet, this one heavier, not with tension but with possibility. I can feel the weight of it, sitting here between us. An invitation neither of us quite knows how to voice yet, but it's there.

And neither of us is walking away.

Camden's still holding my hand when he says, "If you do come to a game... it means telling Cosmo."

I glance at him. "Yeah. I figured."

"He, uh... he might react."

I huff out a laugh. "Cam, my brother reacts to breakfast cereal. If I tell him I'm going to see you play, he'll be halfway to designing matching merch by lunch." I'm also kind of surprised he hasn't told his group chat he's heading to the US. Though to be fair, Camden guards his privacy so closely, am I really that surprised?

He raises a brow, intrigued. "Has he always been like that?"

"Oh yeah," I say, smiling despite myself. "I love the little chaos goblin, but he's got two speeds: sleep and obsessive enthusiasm. Yesterday, a parcel showed up at my flat from him."

Cam's mouth twitches. "Dare I ask?"

"A cuddly gorilla."

He blinks. "A... gorilla."

"Holding a banana," I clarify, fighting back a grin. "Big plush thing, smug as hell. No note. Just vibes."

Cam's laugh cracks the air. It's low and surprised, full-body, and it hits me square in the chest.

"And this wasn't random?" he asks, still chuckling.

"Not exactly." I shake my head, biting down my smile. "It was a callback to a very Cosmo brand of advice.

I was on the phone with him a few days ago—feeling like shit, convinced I'd messed everything up with you, actually—and he goes, 'Don't be the gorilla, man.'"

Camden stares, confused and amused. "What does that even mean?"

"Right?" I laugh. "So apparently, this gorilla got released from captivity and died like a day later in the wild. Completely metaphorical train wreck. Cosmo goes, 'Don't be that guy. Don't let fear keep you locked up just to die when you finally try to live.'"

Camden doesn't say anything right away. His expression shifts—open and serious, but softened. The hand not holding mine taps against his leg absently, like he's trying to process the sudden thud of weight behind the words.

"That's... kind of amazing."

"Kind of typical," I counter. "Cosmo hides his wisdom under layers of chaos and breakfast burritos, but when he lands one, it sticks."

Camden's still quiet, but he nods, and I can see the moment it settles into him—that idea. *Don't be the gorilla.*

"Sounds like he's good at calling people out," he murmurs.

"He is. In the most ridiculous way possible. But yeah."

He shifts closer, our shoulders brushing, and I can feel the warmth of him through his hoodie. "You gonna tell him about us?" he asks quietly.

I exhale, then nod. "Yeah. I want to. Cosmo, my family—they'd love you."

Camden doesn't look away, but something in his posture tenses just slightly.

"But," I add gently, "I also get that this... whatever it is... it's still early. No labels. No pressure. I don't want you feeling exposed before you're ready."

His brows pinch slightly. "You sure?"

"Positive." I nudge his knee with mine. "I'm not hiding you. I'm protecting what this is. Whatever we're building—it matters to me. And I want it to be ours before it becomes anyone else's."

He's quiet for a moment, then gives a slow, almost imperceptible nod. His fingers find the hem of my sleeve, tugging once. Not quite a thank-you, not quite a yes—but it says enough. So I lean in and press a kiss to his temple, quiet and unrushed.

And he lets me.

13

Camden

THE WHISTLE CUTS THROUGH THE DAMP AIR LIKE A blade. My ears are ringing—partly from the effort, partly from the dull roar of a disappointed away crowd. The scoreboard glows like an accusation: Gloucester 24 – Exeter 17.

Two losses in a row.

I stare up at the night sky, still heaving for breath. The floodlights bleach the drizzle into a slow silver fall. My lungs burn. My calves twitch. My chest tightens with something more than exertion.

A fumble.

My fumble.

It wasn't game-ending—at least, not alone—but it shifted momentum. Killed a surge. One second, I had the ball; the next, it bounced out of my grasp like a greased-up mistake, snatched by red jerseys and sprinted fifty yards upfield. They scored three plays later.

That was the beginning of the end. And I felt it as soon as it happened. Like something broke in the pit of my stomach.

I tug my gumshield out and shove it into my wrist guard, forcing myself to stay upright as the team moves off the pitch. Some of the lads keep their heads high. Others don't bother. There's a heaviness in the air that clings to every boot print on the sodden turf.

"Camden! A quick word?"

I'm barely three steps towards the tunnel before a mic is thrust at my chest. A reporter in waterproofs leans into me, teeth bared in what I guess is supposed to pass as a smile.

"Captain Crawford, any comment on what went wrong out there tonight?"

Wrong? I could write her a list. The breakdowns were sloppy. Kicks poorly placed. Our defence cracked twice in the second half. But it's my error—the fumble—they want blood for.

I wipe the rain from my brow, careful not to let it look like a flinch. "They were stronger at the breakdown. We made mistakes. I made mistakes. But we'll regroup. That's the job."

She tilts her head, like she smells blood. "Some

commentators are saying the team looks... flat. Unfocused. You've now dropped to fourth in the table. Play-off qualification is no longer in your hands. There's even talk about your captaincy being on the line. Thoughts?"

I stare at her. No blink. Just the hum of white noise in my ears. "Excuse me," I say, stepping away.

I hear her calling something after me—maybe a follow-up, maybe just my name. But I'm done.

Inside the tunnel, the floodlights fade behind me and the shadows stretch longer. Each footfall echoes off concrete. I brace my forearm against the wall, letting my head hang for a breath, then push forwards.

The locker room is quiet. Not silent—there's the hiss of showers, the occasional mutter, the crack of a boot being thrown into a kit bag. But it's missing the usual post-match rhythm: no jokes, no banter, no tension-breaking sarcasm.

Instead, the loss settles on us like wet clothes: clammy, suffocating, impossible to shrug off.

I sit, unlace my boots, and peel the sodden tape from my wrists. Across from me, Lachie's jaw is tight as he towel-dries his hair. He meets my eyes and gives a tiny nod. I nod back. It's the only communication that passes between us.

The scrape of a locker door slamming pulls my attention left—Jake and Marcus.

"Every bloody time," Jake mutters, loud enough for everyone to hear. "We lose structure because someone can't track their runner."

Marcus spins. "Are you talking about me?"

Jake shrugs. "If the shoe fits, mate."

Marcus takes a step forwards. "You calling me out after you dropped two balls in the first half?"

"Yeah, and I didn't cost us the match, did I?"

That's it.

I stand. "Enough."

Both of them look at me, startled.

"This isn't helping. This isn't who we are. We win together, and we lose together. Everyone made mistakes tonight."

Jake opens his mouth, but I don't give him the chance. "Everyone."

The air shifts, and Jake backs down. Marcus scowls but sits.

I breathe slowly. My voice is firm. "We've got two games left. One more loss and we're out of the running. I know that. You know that. But if we start imploding now, we're already done."

Silence.

Behind me, someone mutters, "We're already done anyway."

I don't turn to see who it is.

Instead, I lower onto the bench and lean forwards, elbows on knees. The ache in my shoulders spreads to my chest. I feel it. The captaincy—not the title but the weight. The sense that every dropped ball, every missed lineout, every angry teammate is another stone on my back.

I run a hand through my wet hair and glance towards the corner where Lachie's getting changed. He's quiet, focused, avoiding eye contact with everyone. That tells me more than anything.

He's angry. And worse, he's worried.

If we lose again next week, we won't even qualify for play-offs. It'll be the first time in five years. And I'm the one they'll blame. Because I'm thirty-one. Because I've got seventy-two caps and they think that makes me tired. Because when I fumbled that ball tonight, I looked human.

I stare down at my calloused palms, the blisters just beginning to reform beneath the tape.

The door to the physio room opens and Joyce steps out. He looks around, assesses the mood, and doesn't say a word, just nods once, slowly.

A couple of the lads head towards the showers. One or two don't bother. Just change and go, like they want to escape the stink of failure still clinging to the walls.

Lachie passes me, towel over one shoulder, kit bag in hand. He stops. "You good?" he asks quietly.

I nod and lie, "Yeah."

He slows as he reaches my bench, keeping his voice low—just for me. "You seeing Brent tonight?" he murmurs, gaze steady.

Things are still new between me and Brent, but I've told Lachie enough. He knows I've been spending a lot of time with him. That the last month has been a whirlwind of incredible sex, quiet nights, and—for the first time in a long time—me not feeling completely alone.

I hesitate. "Dunno. Maybe." It comes out gruff, but he doesn't push. He just nods, like he's handing me a small lifeline and hoping I'll take it.

"See you on the bus," he says, and keeps walking.

"Yeah."

He's gone, and I sit there a bit longer.

The room thins out. The silence gets louder. My thoughts crowd tighter in my chest.

The media will be waiting. Twitter—as hell no will I call it anything else—already has clips of my fumble, I'm sure. The armchair experts are probably dissecting my footwork. My grip. My age. My attitude. And none of them know me. Not really. But that doesn't mean their words won't stick.

By the time I get to the team bus, I'm the last one.

There are flashes everywhere. Cameras in my face. Microphones being waved like knives. The press are a pack of wolves tonight—hungry, loud, circling for blood. I keep my head down. Shoulders squared. I don't give them the soundbite they're aching for.

A reporter calls my name like we're mates. Another shouts something about leadership, about pressure. I hear my surname tossed out like it's up for auction.

I grit my teeth and keep moving.

The bus door hisses open, and I climb the steps, breath tight in my chest. I'm wet from the drizzle, collar clinging to the back of my neck, my kit bag dragging heavier than usual behind me. My fingers twitch with the need to punch something. Not someone—just... something solid. Something that'll crack.

Inside, the atmosphere is dead quiet. Heads are down. A few guys have their earbuds in. One or two scroll their phones with the thousand-yard stare of post-loss burnout. No one is joking. No one is even whispering. It's all just heavy silence, broken only by the dull thud of the doors closing behind me.

I spot an open seat midway back. Not beside anyone. Thank fuck. I slide into it and sag against the headrest, letting my body slump, knees spread wide, elbows braced on thighs.

I rub a hand down my face. We should've won the

game. Hell, we should've won both. But a couple of errors, a few missteps... and now we've gone from third in the league to fourth. One more screw-up and we'll be watching the play-offs from the couch.

And me? I fumbled the goddamn ball.

The same thoughts keep circling my mind, and I suspect they will continue to until we win the next game. We *have* to win it.

My jaw clenches as I drag my phone out of my pocket, half expecting silence there too. But there's a message.

> Brent: That looked like a brutal game.
> Hope you're holding up.

Just that.

No "chin up." No "you've got this." No hollow cheerleading bullshit.

It's... perfect. Exactly what I need. No noise. No pressure. Just him, checking in.

I stare at the words for a beat. Then my thumbs move.

> Me: Brutal's one word for it. Could've done with a few fewer fumbles. Namely mine.

The three dots appear.

> Brent: So you made a mistake.
> Happens. Anyone pointing fingers
> clearly doesn't play a contact sport for
> a living.

I huff out a laugh. It's barely a sound, more an exhale. I shift in the seat and rest my head back against the cold window.

> Me: Tell that to the tabloids.

That's the thing. There's no waiting for tomorrow's headline, not anymore. Everything is instant and splashed online for everyone to search up and read.

> Brent: Tabloids eat their own. Don't let
> them decide your worth. You're more
> than the headline they're hoping to
> print.

The knot in my chest loosens, just a little. His words don't try to fix anything. But they don't ignore it either. It's grounding.

But then the doubt creeps in—ugly, insidious.

I stare at the screen. I haven't told him yet how much I need to keep this separate from the rest of my life. From rugby. From the weight I carry on this bus every week. And I start to wonder...

Is this the distraction they're talking about?

Is Brent the reason I fumbled that ball?

No.

No, fuck that.

This isn't about him.

But the thought lingers. Quiet. Dangerous. Shadowed and unspoken.

I lock the phone and tuck it away.

Outside, the lights blur into long, streaking lines across the windows. Inside, the silence remains heavy and tight. I feel every missed pass like a bruise beneath my ribs. Every misstep like a fracture I can't reset. And deep down, beneath all the adrenaline and self-reproach, there's something colder. More uncertain. Not about the game, but about me.

About who I am when I'm not winning.

And whether I deserve someone like Brent if I can't even hold my own on the pitch.

Because if I can't lead this team, if I can't be the captain they need... what the hell am I even doing? And what happens when he realises I'm not as solid as I pretend to be?

THE BUS PULLS INTO THE STADIUM PARKING LOT, THE engine's hum fading as the vehicle comes to a stop. I stand, slinging my bag over my shoulder, and make my way down the aisle. The atmosphere is heavy; no one speaks. As I step off the bus, I offer a quiet "Goodnight" to the group, but it's met with silence. Unsurprisingly, no one is up for drinks—not that I'd go anyway.

Coach catches my eye as I head towards my car. He gives me a nod, and I approach him.

"Rough game," he says.

I nod, not trusting myself to speak without letting frustration seep into my voice.

"We'll review the footage tomorrow," he continues. "Get some rest."

"Will do," I reply, then turn towards the car park.

I stop walking when I see him—Brent, leaning against the hood of my car like he belongs there.

My breath catches. Not just because he looks good—*he always looks good*—but because I wasn't expecting him. And even though a part of me wants to bury my face in his neck and breathe him in, another part instantly flinches, scanning the shadows. My eyes flick over the dark edges of the lot, half expecting a camera lens to catch the moment and spin it into something ugly.

He sees the way I pause. Maybe he even sees the way I look around, and it kills me that I'm doing that in the first place.

He doesn't move, just says softly, "Hey."

"Hey," I murmur, too gruff. My voice is always like

this when I'm wiped, but tonight it's got more gravel than usual.

He straightens slowly, hands in his jacket pockets. "I didn't want to just show up at your place."

I nod, grateful for the respect even as I war with myself. Brent being here is both the best thing that could happen and the worst idea I can entertain. I shouldn't let him in—not after a game like this. Not when the headlines are already questioning my leadership, my focus. Not when I'm not even sure who I am without the wins.

But I'm so fucking tired.

Not just physically. Deep in my bones, I ache with something heavier than exhaustion. I want him. Want his steadiness, his warmth, his quiet refusal to let me spiral alone. And it makes no sense. We've only known each other properly for a month—but that month has cracked something open in me.

And that's the scariest part of all.

"I'm tired," I say. It's not rejection, not really. It's a shield I hope he can read through.

He just smiles a little. "That's okay."

"I don't mean...." I pause, unsure how to explain that I want him close but am afraid to need it. "It's just been a shit night."

"I know." He steps forward—just a fraction of space, but it's enough to feel the warmth of his body. Close but not crowding. "So let me be there. Not to fix it. Just to... be."

And fuck, there it is again. The way he gets me.

I want to kiss him. My body leans into the idea, but I don't trust the dark corners of this car park. I don't trust the shadows not to have eyes. So instead, I breathe out a shaky "Yeah. Okay."

His eyes soften. "I'll follow you home."

I nod and unlock the car, but my mind's a mess of static. I slide into the driver's seat and grip the wheel, staring straight ahead for a few seconds before starting the engine.

What am I doing? Letting him in like this. Letting him see me when I'm stripped bare. No pitch to dominate, no game plan to follow. Just me. Tired. Uncertain. Wanting.

And wanting... isn't something I let myself feel often.

But Brent? He makes me feel it all. And maybe that's the point. Maybe tonight, letting him in is the only thing keeping me from closing the door again—not just on him, but on this possibility we've somehow built together.

So I pull out of the lot, glancing in the mirror to see his headlights right behind me.

Still following. Still choosing me.

14

Brent

I ALMOST DIDN'T COME.

After watching the match—hell, after watching *him* —I nearly turned around three times before even making it to the car. Camden didn't look like he needed company when the final whistle blew. He looked like a man carrying too much weight and bracing for more. But I knew if I'd asked outright whether he wanted to see me tonight, he'd have said no. The man doesn't ask for help, not even when he's on fire.

So I didn't ask.

Now I'm following him up the stairs to his flat, the echo of his keys in the lock louder than either of us. He's quiet, his shoulders drawn tight and his gaze flicking once behind us before we step inside. I catch it—the assessing glance, the flicker of nerves, the subtle check for cameras or wandering eyes.

It makes sense. He's the captain of a top-tier team under a microscope. The last thing he needs is some press snapping photos of him with a bloke in tow, sensationalising his personal life when it's the game that should be centre stage.

And I'm okay with that. Really. Because what he needs tonight is some damn TLC.

As soon as we're inside, I set about running him a bath. He shoots me a look, part surprised, part bemused. He's not used to being looked after. I can see it in the way he lingers near the doorway, not quite sure what to do with himself. Still, when I hand him a beer and gesture for him to sit, he obeys—barely masking a tired smile. I take it as a win.

"I was gonna throw the ref through a wall," I say lightly, crouching to fiddle with the water temperature.

Cam snorts softly behind me. "Get in line."

The bath fills slowly, steam curling into the small space. I sit nearby, giving him room without making him feel alone. We talk about the game— something I hadn't expected him to want to do. But I think he needs to vent. Needs someone who won't tell him to move on or shake it off. Someone who'll just... listen.

When he gets to the part about the post-match press conference, though, his words falter.

"They asked about distractions," he says finally, voice low.

My stomach tightens. "Distractions?"

He nods, not quite meeting my eye.

I sit back against the wall and take a slow breath. "You mean me?"

Cam's silence says enough.

Fuck.

I should tell him I'll back off. That I get it. That rugby's his life, and I'd never want to jeopardise it. But I don't say any of that. Because while I do get it... also, fuck that. I like him. I want him. Not just in my bed but in my life. And I'm not going to let a few shitty headlines or his own internal doubts scare me off.

Still. Now isn't the time to say any of that either.

He needs calm, comfort, something easy. So I say, "You want a top-up on that beer, Captain?"

And his shoulders finally relax, just a little. Enough to remind me that while the night didn't start the way I wanted, I'm exactly where I need to be.

I test the water with my hand and nod. Perfect— steamy but not scalding. I glance back over my shoulder to where Camden leans against the doorframe, still cradling the beer I handed him, eyes distant.

"You are good with baths, right?" I ask, maybe a little late.

His answer is a half-assed grunt. "I've had worse ideas."

That's a yes for him. I take it.

When he steps fully into the bathroom, I grab one of the fluffier towels from the linen cupboard—he's not one to treat himself, but I am—and place it near the radiator to warm. I light one of the subtle candles I spotted on his shelf. Not floral, not sweet. Just a clean, cedarwood thing that smells like calm.

By the time I join him, he's already sinking into the water with a long-drawn-out sigh that makes something twist in my chest. He needs this. Not just the bath but the care. The pause. A soft moment in the middle of a very loud week.

"I feel like a bloody pensioner," he mutters.

"You're a pensioner who took four tackles and played all eighty minutes," I reply, grabbing the washcloth and soaking it. "You've earned this."

"Shouldn't you be, I don't know, tattooing someone or sketching a phoenix mid-flight across someone's ribcage?"

I hum. "Probably. But I'd rather be here."

He doesn't say anything, but his eyes flicker—just briefly—and something unspoken passes between us.

I kneel at the side of the bath, drag the wet cloth gently over his shoulder, then down one thick arm, watching the tension slowly ease from his posture. He doesn't stop me when I move to the other, just watches. Quiet. Maybe even a little curious.

The bruises are a patchwork of purples and yellows, blooming on his ribs and hip. A particularly gnarly one above his knee makes me wince. "Fuck," I murmur. "How're you walking?"

He shrugs like it's nothing. "Occupational hazard."

"Still," I say, running the cloth down his sternum now. "Doesn't mean you don't deserve someone taking care of you."

His mouth opens like he might argue, but then he closes it again. I take that as another win.

I let my fingers glide a little lower, circling lazily over the flat of his chest, then teasing gently at one nipple. It tightens under the cloth, and his abs flex beneath the surface of the water.

"Thought this was about TLC," he mutters, but there's no heat in it. His voice is quieter now, rougher and less certain.

"It is," I say softly. "But that doesn't mean you can't enjoy it."

His gaze flickers, jaw tightening. There's resistance—but no real desire to stop me. I keep going. Gentle circles.

The other nipple now. His breathing changes, and I'm aware of every sharp inhale, every faint shift in his hips under the water.

My hand moves lower, the cloth slipping aside, and I wrap my fingers around his cock—slow and unhurried. He's semihard already, the water lapping softly against his stomach as he lifts his head and meets my eyes.

"Brent...."

"I know," I whisper. "You're tired. You don't need to do anything. Let me take care of you."

His jaw clenches, but he doesn't argue. Doesn't push me away. He just leans his head back against the tub and exhales hard.

I stroke him slowly. A steady rhythm. Not chasing anything. Not demanding a reaction. Just coaxing pleasure from the stress-clenched body in front of me. His cock swells in my hand, thick and heavy now, twitching slightly under the water.

Camden's groans are low and guttural, a sound that punches heat straight to my gut. His legs shift—parting just enough—and I adjust, kneeling in closer, letting the water slosh against the sides of the bath.

I mumble to him, the words spilling out as my hand continues its slow rhythm. "You're gorgeous like this... soft and wrecked and letting go."

"Shut up," he grits out, but his hips buck into my hand, and I know he doesn't mean it.

"Let go for me, Cam," I murmur, dipping my forehead briefly against his damp knee. "You don't always have to hold it all in."

He whimpers—actually whimpers—and it makes me slow down.

"Brent... please."

I almost come just from that.

The edge flirts with us, dances around us. I back off, then bring him close again, over and over, watching him unravel bit by bit until his hand is gripping the side of the tub like he'll snap the porcelain in two.

His eyes are dark now, fevered. His chest is heaving. And I can tell—he's right there. But he won't come unless I tell him to.

So I do.

"Now," I whisper, voice gravelly. "I've got you."

He comes with a shudder, hips jerking, water sloshing over the sides. I hold him through it, slow and steady, until his body slumps back, boneless and trembling.

There's a long silence.

I brush the cloth down his stomach, cleaning him gently, even as his eyes flutter closed and his throat works around a swallow.

"I fucking hate how good that was," he mutters eventually.

I smile. "Then we're even."

He opens one eye. "For what?"

"For how fucking hard you make it not to fall for you."

He doesn't respond, but he doesn't look away either. And that silence? It says enough for now.

The water has barely settled before it sloshes violently to one side, slapping the edge of the tub and cascading onto the floor.

"Cam—"

I barely get his name out before a strong, wet hand fists the front of my shirt and yanks me forwards. My knees slam into the bathmat, and then I'm crashing into a very large, very naked man, the fabric of my tee soaking instantly as I tumble halfway over the edge. Camden's grin is feral, his eyes lit with something wild and determined.

"You asshole," I gasp, breathless with laughter. The sound barely makes it past my lips before his mouth crashes into mine.

The kiss is nothing like the slow, teasing brushes we've shared before.

It's not polite.

It's not sweet.

It's possession.

And I fucking melt.

His lips are hot and wet and demanding, slanting over mine with an urgency that makes my heart stutter. One hand cradles the back of my head, the other braced against the side of the tub, trapping me between the slick slide of his chest and the porcelain edge. His tongue brushes against mine, and I open for him without hesitation—eager, hungry, lost.

The kiss deepens.

Our tongues stroke, swirl, collide. There's nothing shy about the way we come together now—just hunger and the kind of trust that creeps up without warning. My fingers find his hair, curling tight, and he groans into my mouth like it does something to him. Like it matters.

And maybe it does.

Because this—this mess of wet skin, open mouths, unspoken heat—isn't just a kiss. It's a surrender. A claim. It's him saying *I'm here*, and me saying *I feel it too*.

I slide closer despite the ridiculous squeeze of two grown men trying to fit into a tub clearly built for one. My jeans dig into my knees, but I don't give a damn. His cock presses against my hip, mine trapped painfully behind denim, but it's the kiss I'm drowning in.

It's slow now—aching, thorough. Our mouths learn each other's rhythms, our breathing syncs, and every drag of his lips over mine sends heat coiling low in my belly. His teeth scrape my lower lip, and I gasp, hips twitching before I even realise I've moved.

His hand trails down to my jaw, tilting my face just enough to change the angle. The next slide of his tongue against mine is softer and lingers, and I swear I feel it down to my fucking toes.

When we finally pull apart, we don't go far. Our foreheads rest together, breath mingling. My pulse is thunderous in my ears. His eyes search mine like he's looking for the edge of a cliff he already knows he'll jump off.

And me?

I've already jumped.

***

CAMDEN TASTES LIKE MINT AND MORNING HEAT, and it takes everything in me not to drag him back to bed. He leans into the kiss—one of many—his mouth lingering just long enough for it to toe the line between affectionate and filthy.

"Brent," he warns, voice low and already breathless, "you're gonna make me late."

I grin and kiss the corner of his mouth. "Then you should've left five minutes ago, Captain."

He rolls his eyes but kisses me again anyway. One hand slides around my waist like he's trying to memorise the shape of me, and then he pulls back with a soft, reluctant groan.

He looks better today. Less tight around the eyes. There's colour in his cheeks again, and the heaviness he carried yesterday seems to have eased, if only slightly. It's a look that makes my chest squeeze, because I know what it took to get him here—and I know how fragile it still is.

"Meeting should be short," he says, adjusting his bag on his shoulder. "Few admin things and some reflection."

"Text me after?" I ask, already knowing he will.

He nods, then jogs down the steps. I watch him go, still a little dazed that this—whatever it is—is actually happening.

It's only when I go back inside that I spot it: his gameplay folder, sitting neatly on the side table near the door.

Shit.

I grab my phone and shoot him a message.

> Me: You forgot your stuff. Folder on the table.

> Me: Stay where you are. I'm bringing it down. Also, you owe me another kiss.

I grab the folder and rush down, my boots thudding

on the stairs. When I round the corner of the building, Camden's already by his car, grinning at me through the window.

I jog up to the driver's side and lean down to hand him the folder through the open window. "Your brain still in bed or just distracted by my stellar goodbye technique?"

"Shut up," he mutters, but there's a smile tugging at his mouth.

I lean in, kiss him again—short and sweet this time—and then step back with a wink. "Go. Be important. We'll talk later."

He nods, eyes lingering for a second longer than necessary, then pulls away down the street.

I'm back at the studio an hour later, prepping for a full day. Carrie's already here, elbow-deep organising stock, the usual playlist humming in the background. I'm half focused on prepping my station when the bell above the door rings.

I glance up, expecting my midday appointment—but it's a man I don't recognise. Older, well-dressed, clean-cut, and with no visible tattoos.

"Hey there," I say, polite but guarded. "Can I help you?"

He smiles and offers his hand. "You the owner?"

"I run the place," I say, shaking it cautiously. "Brent."

He nods slowly, gaze flicking across the shop walls. "Lovely work. Thought I'd come in, see what kind of stuff you do. You the artist?"

"One of them. You looking for something?"

He shrugs, lingering by the reception desk. "Just curious, I guess. Always been interested in tattooing. Never quite got the nerve."

I nod, still not entirely at ease. "Well, I'm happy to show you some portfolios if you're thinking about it."

We chat for a moment—surface-level stuff. Then he asks, casual as anything, "Ever inked anyone famous?"

Alarm bells clang in my skull. "Can't talk about clients," I say evenly. "Privacy's part of the deal."

He nods like he gets it, then leans in slightly. "Not even Camden Crawford?"

My spine goes ramrod straight. "What?" I ask, too flatly.

"I mean," he continues, smile still easy, "are you his artist? Or his boyfriend? Or both?" He laughs lightly. "Do you always sleep with clients or just the famous ones?"

I blink. "You need to leave."

He raises a brow, surprised by the sharpness in my voice. "I'm just asking—"

"Get out," I snap. "Now."

Carrie pokes her head out from the back. "Everything okay?"

"No," I say. "This guy needs to go."

She takes one look at the man and steps forwards, voice hard. "You heard him. Out. We don't tolerate harassment here."

One of our regulars—a mountain of a guy with sleeves from wrist to neck—steps into the reception area just in time to loom effectively. The guy finally gets the message and slinks out, muttering something under his breath.

As the door shuts behind him, I sag against the counter, heart pounding.

Carrie watches me, eyebrows drawn. "That... was definitely a journalist, yeah?"

"Yeah," I rasp. "Or some shit-stirring fan trying to sell a story."

She places a hand on my shoulder. "Camden okay with being public?"

"No," I murmur, throat tight. "He's not. And I think I just screwed everything up."

The studio feels too quiet after that.

Even with Carrie murmuring to a client who came in thirty minutes ago at her station and the hum of machines being cleaned, there's something off-kilter about the air. I try to shake it. Try to pretend that bastard hadn't shown up, hadn't looked me in the eye and asked if I usually fuck my clients. As if Camden is some conquest, some goddamn feather in my cap.

I scrub a hand down my face and unlock my phone again.

Still nothing from Cam.

I tried to call him five minutes ago. It rang out. That could mean a dozen things—he's in his meeting, he's in the locker room, he's ignoring calls. None of them sit right. Not after that stunt.

I type a message fast.

> Me: Hey. Tried to call. Please call me when you can.

I hesitate, then keep typing.

> Me: Just a heads-up, someone came by the shop asking questions. About you. About us. I told him to fuck off, but I think he might be press. He dropped your name.

I don't hit Send right away. I read it through twice. My thumb hovers. Then I send it.

Fuck.

There's a sting behind my eyes I'm not proud of. A mix of fury and shame and fear, all tangled into a pit that's taken up residence in my chest. I don't do this. I don't let people in easily, not in ways that matter. And now someone's trying to weaponise it.

I glance towards the hallway where my next client is due in ten minutes.

Carrie steps out from her station and gives me a look that says she knows I'm not okay. I offer a faint smile—reassuring, or maybe just resigned—and return to the reception desk. I've got a few sketches I can run through, some linework options I need to prep.

My hands move, but my head's not in it.

So I do the only thing I can: I flick off silent mode and set my phone faceup beside my sketchpad. Against every instinct, against every professional bone in my body, I keep it there. Open. Ready.

Because if Camden calls, I'll drop everything. Because he needs to know before someone else twists this into something it's not. Because he deserves to hear it from me. Because—

Because I fucking care.

And I don't know if that makes this better or worse. But I do know I'm not backing down. Not from this.

Not from him.

15

Camden

THE SKY'S THREATENING RAIN AS WE EXIT THE stadium, that sticky-grey kind of afternoon where the clouds feel too close, pressing down on everything. Lachie's beside me, muttering something about the footage we just watched, but I'm not really listening. My brain's still spinning with every fumble, every missed opportunity—and yeah, every comment Coach made with that strained I'm-not-blaming-you-but tone.

I tug my mobile out, my brows pulling low when I see missed calls and a couple of text messages. My phone's been on silent, and I know better than to check it during game tape replays. I thumb over the screen. It's Brent.

Brent: Hey. Tried to call. Please call me when you can.

Another one right beneath it:

> Brent: Just a heads-up, someone came by the shop asking questions. About you. About us. I told him to fuck off, but I think he might be press. He dropped your name.

I stop walking, and my stomach clenches—tight and cold. *Fucking hell.* I stand there alone, clouds thick overhead, thumb hovering over Brent's name.

"Cam?" Lachie calls out to me. When we make eye contact, his whole body shifts. "Something wrong?"

I shake my head once, shallow. "Just... give me a minute."

He nods and doesn't push, just keeps going towards the cars. I lower my phone, jaw tight, heart hammering hard enough to make my ribs ache.

I'm pissed.

Not at Brent. Not even close. At the situation. At the press. At whoever the hell that bastard was walking into Brent's studio, sniffing around like it was his right. Brent doesn't deserve that. He doesn't deserve being put in the crosshairs because of me. Because we're... whatever this is. And I sure as hell don't want him regretting it.

The thought makes something raw crack open in my chest.

I look down at the phone again, debating what to say.

What to do. I don't know if this is the beginning of something getting worse—or if it's the moment when I finally have to decide how far I'm willing to go to protect this thing we've barely begun.

But one thing's clear: This isn't Brent's fault, and I won't let him carry it like it is.

I hit Call before I can second-guess it, taking the final few steps towards my car. The phone barely rings once before Brent picks up.

"Cam?" His voice is tight. Worried. "Fuck. Thank you for calling. Are you okay?"

The squeeze in my gut intensifies. "I'm fine." It's a lie. Sort of. I'm angry. Frustrated. Tired. But not at him.

He exhales, the sound thick with relief. "I didn't want to text too much in case you hadn't seen it yet. I just... when he said your name—"

"Yeah," I say, dragging a hand through my hair. "I read it."

"I swear, I didn't invite that guy in. I thought he was just interested in the studio. He was... friendly, at first. Curious. I should've caught on sooner."

"I'm not mad at you."

Silence on the other end. Then, cautiously, he says, "You're not?"

"No." I let out a breath and lean against the car. "I'm

pissed off, yeah. But not at you. You didn't put my name in his mouth. You didn't send him."

Brent's quiet for a beat. I hear the faint rustle of movement on his end—maybe him sitting down, or pacing.

"I just didn't want you to be blindsided," he says finally, voice softer. "I know how much privacy means to you."

I close my eyes. That. Right there. That's what makes all this harder.

"I don't even know what I'm more angry about," I mutter. "That the guy came sniffing, or that I let myself think maybe... maybe we'd get away with it. That I could have something for myself without it being turned into a fucking headline."

Brent doesn't say anything at first. When he does, it's careful. "You still can. Have something, I mean."

I laugh, but there's no humour in it. "Can I?"

"I think so." His voice is steady now. "But I won't pretend it's going to be easy. If you want me to back off—"

"No." My answer is instant. Too fast. Too raw. I bite down on the next breath. "I don't want that."

There's a pause.

"You sure?"

"Yeah." I open my eyes and stare up at the grey sky.

"I don't want to give them another piece of me. But you? You're not the problem. You're the thing that's made the last few weeks... better."

Brent's inhale is sharp. "Cam...."

"I'm not saying I'm ready to do interviews or hold your hand on a red carpet," I add quickly. "But I'm not walking away."

There's a sound I can't quite name—a cross between a sigh and a quiet, relieved laugh.

"Good," Brent murmurs. "Because I'm not going anywhere."

After letting him know I'll stop by later and saying goodbye, I tuck my phone back into my pocket but feel every word from Brent like it's been etched into my ribs.

"What's going on?" Lachie's still watching me—not nosy, just genuinely concerned.

I exhale hard, scrubbing a hand through my hair. "Just spoke to Brent. Some dickhead showed up at his shop asking questions. About me. Us."

Lachie's eyebrows lift. "Press?"

"Probably." I kick a pebble with the side of my boot, sending it skittering across the asphalt. "Said he told him to piss off. But still."

There's a silence as I open the back door and throw my folder on the seat. The tension hangs between us, and then Lachie bobs his head.

"Look, I know you're spun out, but..." He hesitates, and I brace. "Do you think it's true? What they said in the press?"

My gut twists. "About what?"

"You being distracted. Slipping. Not hungry enough." He pauses. "Since meeting him."

I stop walking. "We're not dating," I snap, too fast, too sharp.

Lachie blinks at me once, then snorts. "Sure you're not."

I glare at him, but he just throws me a look like I'm the idiot in this conversation. Because I probably am.

He shrugs. "Look, I'm not here to judge. But I've known you a long time, and yeah, yesterday wasn't your best performance—but it wasn't anyone's. We've all been off. The loss wasn't on you."

I nod slowly. My mouth is dry, the pressure in my chest mounting. "I just... I can't afford for them to be right."

"About what?"

"That I've lost my edge. That I'm soft now. That I can't lead this team."

"Mate." Lachie shakes his head. "You've led this team through worse. Through season slumps, injuries, new signings, losing half the backline to international duty. One average match doesn't erase that."

I stare at him.

"And Brent?" he goes on. "He make you happy?"

The answer's there before I can even think. "Yeah. He does."

"Then you've got to trust that. Trust yourself. You've never been one to check out mentally just because you've got something good going off the pitch. And if you are happier? Lighter?" He smirks. "Maybe that's a bloody good thing."

I let out a breath. "I do still want to be here. Want to play. Train. Lead. I like the way Brent makes me feel—like I can breathe—but it doesn't make me want this any less."

Lachie nods. "Then maybe it's not a distraction. Maybe it's just new. And yeah, the media might sniff around, but you've got us. You've got this team. We're not bailing."

Something in me steadies.

He claps me on the shoulder. "Just don't let the bastards win. On or off the pitch." He winks at me and backs away to his Range Rover.

The air doesn't feel quite so suffocating. My mind's still racing, sure, but beneath it all is something calmer. Not just guilt or nerves, but hope, and that's something worth holding on to.

By the time I get to Brent's, the storm inside me has finally quieted.

I've already been home. I walked into my flat, and the first thing I noticed was the faint scent of him still clinging to my sheets—soap and spice and whatever he uses in his hair. It hit me like a punch to the chest. Not in a bad way, just... grounding. I'd stood there in the middle of the room for a minute longer than necessary, letting it settle. Letting *him* settle.

Then I cleaned. Nothing big—just tidied a few things, folded some laundry, wiped down the kitchen counters. Domestic shit. But it helped. Something about the rhythm of it is therapeutic. Something about the order.

I spoke to Mum too. Told her I was fine. We didn't talk long—just enough for her to hear my voice and for me to hear hers. It reminded me who I am. Where I come from. What I've already coped with. A couple of shit headlines and a nosy stranger? That's not enough to knock me over. So yeah, I'm more composed now.

And when Brent opens the door, looking like he's caught between greeting me and bracing for a punch, that steadiness doesn't falter.

He's tense, jaw set, eyes flicking over my shoulder

like he's making sure no one's followed me. He steps back almost immediately, staying behind the door—keeping himself hidden from the street view.

My chest tugs. He's protecting me. That's what this is.

"I've been checking socials," he says quickly, voice low and tight. "Nothing's come up. Not yet. But if it does —if that guy sells something or twists it—"

"Brent," I say, and I don't mean to cut him off, but I do.

His mouth clamps shut, like he's preparing to be told off or brushed off. So I do the only thing I can think of. I step forwards, grab his face in both hands, and kiss him.

No words. No warning. Just lips and breath and the warm press of him against me.

He stills for half a second—just one heartbeat—and then melts into it. His hands find my hips, holding me like I might disappear, and the kiss shifts, grows, deepens. It's not frantic or heated. It's not about sex.

It's about grounding.

About him.

About me.

About us.

I pull back, just a little, our foreheads brushing. He's breathing hard. So am I. But his eyes are soft now. Open.

"I'm okay," I tell him. "You didn't do anything wrong."

He swallows, Adam's apple bobbing against the side of my thumb.

"You didn't do anything wrong," I say again. "I'm here because I want to be."

He nods, slow and uncertain, like he doesn't quite trust it. But I do.

I step inside, closing the door behind me, and when his hand finds mine a second later, I don't let go. Not this time. Not when I've finally decided to stop running from something that feels this real.

We don't move right away. There's something about standing in the quiet warmth of Brent's flat—our hands still linked, his chest brushing mine with every breath—that makes it hard to break the moment. But he gives a small smile and tugs gently, guiding me further inside like I belong.

He lets go only long enough to flip the deadbolt behind me, then trails into the kitchen, asking over his shoulder, "Want a drink? I've got beer, juice, or that sparkling elderflower stuff you said tasted like posh lemonade."

I huff out a laugh, toe off my trainers, and wander in behind him. "You mean the one I said I'd only drink if I was wearing a cashmere jumper and had a golden retriever named Winston?"

"That's the one." He grins, reaching into the fridge. "Beer's good."

He hands me one, grabs one for himself, and nods towards the sofa. We settle there with our knees nearly touching, the air between us lighter than it was even five minutes ago. Still fragile, but no longer fraying at the edges.

We fall into that kind of silence that's not empty—just full of things neither of us is quite ready to say aloud.

Brent turns his beer bottle in his hand, thumb skating the condensation. "So, I was gonna tell you earlier, but..." He gives a little shrug. "I looked at your States tour schedule you sent."

My brows lift.

He doesn't quite meet my gaze. "I'll definitely be there," Brent says, quietly now. "That week. The same time as you. It overlaps."

I stare at him, warmth blooming low in my gut. "You going to come to the game for sure?"

He shrugs, casual—but I catch the flicker of something more in his eyes. "Well, if the offers still there and you want me to come, and if there are still tickets left."

"Right." I try to match his nonchalance, but my

mouth twitches into something dangerously close to a smile. "No pressure, but I think I can swing tickets for you and your folks if you really think they'll be interested."

"Yeah?" He leans back and relaxes when I nod. "Wouldn't want to distract you from all the important ball fumbling you've got lined up."

I roll my eyes and throw a cushion at him. He dodges easily, grinning, and I shake my head, but I don't deny the flush of warmth at the thought of him sitting in the crowd. Of him watching me play.

Not because he has to. Because he wants to. Because he's already looked at the schedule. That kind of consideration... it does something to me. Not flashy, not loud, just... solid. Intentional.

"You don't have to," I say, quieter now. "Come to the game, I mean."

"I know," he replies, voice matching mine in tone. "But I want to."

The words settle like something soft and heavy in my chest. I take a long breath, anchoring myself in the moment. Brent is here, beer in hand, every fibre of him still a little on edge from the press bullshit earlier—but still here. Still steady.

I don't know what this thing is we're building. We haven't defined it and haven't tried to. But I know how it feels, and I know I don't want it to stop.

Brent sets his bottle on the table, turning to me with that bright gaze of his—softened now, edges gone quiet. "You eaten?"

My stomach tightens. I shake my head, though I'm not really thinking about food.

He arches a brow. "You want me to cook something? Or maybe... shower first?"

There's nothing loaded in the question. Nothing obvious. Just that calm, smooth tone he always uses, like he's offering me a hand instead of a trap. But the way his eyes dip—slow, warm—the curve of his mouth barely lifting? Yeah. I know where this is going.

And fuck, I want it to go there.

Still, I play it cool, the corner of my mouth tugging up. "Pretty sure I don't stink. No training today."

"Mm," he hums, pushing off the couch and standing in front of me. He looks down, eyes skimming over me like I'm something he wants to unwrap slowly. "Still. Hot water. Steam. My hands on your skin."

My breath catches.

He grins, but it's not cocky. It's quiet. Earnest. "Could be nice."

The lump in my throat is stupidly large for how simple the words are. I nod, and he leans in to press a kiss to the corner of my mouth. Just there—soft and warm and nothing like the urgency that usually lights me up.

This is something else, gentle and intimate.

God help me, it makes my chest ache.

I follow him to the bathroom without a word, but my pulse drums in my ears like it's trying to tell me something I'm not ready to hear. The room fills with the sound of running water. I lean against the doorframe as he adjusts the temperature.

When he turns, steam curling behind him, he holds out a hand. "Come on, Captain. Let me take care of you."

And fuck, I let him.

I step close and his hands go to my shirt, fingers brushing over my abs as he lifts the hem and pulls it up and off. I'm big. I know I am. Broad through the chest, heavy through the thighs. Most of the time I feel like a tank—intimidating, powerful, built to hit and be hit.

But the way he looks at me makes me feel good. Not for what I can do. Not for what I am on the pitch. Just for being me.

He trails his fingers down my torso, tracing the lines of old bruises and the fresh ones from yesterday. His touch is reverent. Gentle. He undoes my belt with the kind of calm focus that makes my breath catch. Then my jeans. Then my briefs.

By the time I step under the water, my skin's already burning for him—and he hasn't even kissed me again yet.

I turn, water pouring down my back, but before I can say anything, he's stepping in behind me, fully naked, and sliding his arms around my waist.

And just like that, I melt. All that tension I didn't realise I'd been holding? Gone.

His lips press to my shoulder. "Let me look after you."

I nod, voice gone somewhere I can't reach. My chest cracks wide open as he takes the cloth and soap, lathers up, and begins to wash me—slow, deliberate strokes over my chest, down my ribs, across my stomach. His hands glide over me like I'm something precious, not someone who's spent a decade being told to toughen the fuck up.

And every time he touches me, I believe him a little more.

That I deserve this.

That I can want this.

That I can have it.

The soap-slick cloth circles my chest, then glides down my belly. My abs flex without permission. His fingers follow, taking their time, brushing lower, slower, until his knuckles graze my cock. It's already heavy, semi-hard just from the way he touches me.

"You always like taking care of people?" I manage, voice hoarse.

He grins against my shoulder. "Only the ones who pretend they don't need it."

His hand closes around me—not tight, not rushed, just warm, firm, achingly sure. I brace a hand on the wall, legs already starting to tremble. "Fuck."

Brent kisses down my spine, water beading across my skin. He takes his time, like he's got nowhere else to be. Like he's been waiting to do this properly. My cock pulses in his grip. He strokes once, then again, letting the slickness build while he sinks lower, trailing kisses down the curve of my back.

When his hands part me, I jolt. "Brent—"

"Let me," he murmurs, already kneeling in the shallow pool of water around our feet.

The next thing I feel is the heat of his breath, the shocking softness of his tongue flicking across my rim. My thighs twitch. My hand slams flat against the tile.

"Oh fuck—"

He groans like he fucking means it, tongue lapping, then circling with practiced ease. Every time he presses in deeper, I swear I could cry. The way he holds me open, the care he takes—it's not filthy, it's worship. I've never had anyone eat me out like they were starving. Like the sounds I make are their favourite song.

All while his other hand strokes me—slow, wet, rhythmic.

"Brent… fuck… you don't have to—"

"Wanna," he growls, tongue pushing in just enough to make my knees buckle.

I can't stay upright. I lean into the wall, letting my weight fall forwards, giving him all of me.

Because I want this.

Because I trust him.

And when he strokes me again—tightening just slightly, twisting at the head—I lose whatever scraps of composure I had left. Every nerve ending lights up, and I don't just feel good—I feel known.

He knows exactly how to touch me. How to work me up and keep me there, toes curling, teeth gritted, desperate and dangling on the edge.

I moan, loud and rough. "Fuck—don't stop—"

He doesn't.

I shudder through the tension, hips jerking, and then I'm gasping his name as I come hard, heat pulsing through me in waves.

Brent doesn't let go until I've ridden it out, until I'm slumping forwards, forehead resting on the cool tile, heart hammering.

There's silence for a beat. Then I feel his mouth press a kiss to the base of my spine.

Gentle.

Grateful.

Real.

When I turn, his eyes are still dark with want, but his touch is firm as he helps me shift, holding me like I'm something worth catching.

"Jesus," I mutter, chest heaving.

He smiles, brushing water from my brow. "You good?"

I nod, unable to speak. Because yeah, I'm good. I'm more than good.

I'm fucking his.

16
Brent

THE PHOTO OF ME LEANING INSIDE CAM'S CAR AND kissing him has been printed in a couple of less reputable tabloids and pages on social media. Cam told me there were some of the same paps hanging around the stadium after training, but since he's not given them anything to photograph, let alone a usable quote, interest seems to have dwindled.

Thank fuck.

I've got no issue with the spotlight—I can handle a camera flash without flinching—but I'd much prefer not to be reduced to clickbait. Especially if I'm being painted as the reason Captain Camden Crawford's been "off his game."

Which... I'm not. (And if I am, it's in a "he's well laid and emotionally supported" kind of way.)

It's been a weird week. Good weird. Cam's opened up more. I've slept over a few nights. We've had real, actual conversations about things like future games and summer plans. We've even gone grocery shopping together like a couple of domestic boyfriends. (He takes cereal choices very seriously.)

So yeah. Things are progressing.

And now comes the fun part: telling my family.

Cam had been quiet at first when I'd brought it up. Understandable. He's a private guy, and after the media bullshit, he'd looked like he wanted to crawl into a hole anytime someone even mentioned the word *relationship*. But when I reminded him that my family were *not* the media—and also not entirely unfamiliar with him—he'd relented.

I think what pushed him over the edge was the idea that if anything *did* leak further, the last thing either of us wanted was for my family to hear it from a gossip site. It was about respect, about not letting strangers shape the narrative before we had a chance to speak for ourselves. He nodded slowly after that, even mentioned that he'd probably have to do the same soon with his folks, and though I didn't press him, the fact that he said it out loud felt like something quietly significant. Like he was starting to believe that this—*we*—might be worth acknowledging beyond just the walls of his flat.

Which is why we're here now: sprawled on his couch two nights before his next match, our knees brushing, the TV playing something neither of us are watching, and my hand hovering over my phone like it's about to explode.

Cam eyes me from beneath his lashes. "You're gonna regret this."

"I already do."

He hides his face in the throw pillow. "Cosmo is going to be unhinged."

"That's the problem. I know."

That Cosmo previously attempted to play matchmaker when he realised Cam lived in Exeter... yeah, you can imagine. Not only did he blow up Cam's phone in their Love the Game group, but later that day, he sent me a meme that said "when your gaydar and Cupid have a threesome" and then another of a clown putting on makeup—captioned "me trying to act normal after setting up my brother with his future husband."

I'd ignored it all. Especially since, at the time, Cam had already been on the edge of overwhelmed. And I definitely hadn't told Cosmo that the guy he was shipping me with was the same guy I briefly mentioned had kissed me before ghosting me. And I definitely didn't tell him I'd already been getting hot and dirty with him either.

So now? Now, it's chaos just waiting to happen.

I shoot Cosmo a text.

Me: Hey. Got a sec?

His response comes in milliseconds.

Cosmo: Is someone dying? Am *I* dying?? Why do you sound ominous?

I groan and scrub a hand down my face.

Cam, lounging on the other end of the sofa, raises a brow. "He's going to combust."

"Yep."

I hit Call.

He picks up on the second ring, breathless and dramatic as ever. "What's wrong? Is it Mum? Is it you? Are you dying? Did you finally get that bad tattoo you always threatened me with in college?"

"Jesus, Cos. No one's dying."

He exhales—loudly. "Then what is it? You're being weird. You never ask to call. This has 'emotional reveal' energy all over it. If you tell me you adopted a duck, I swear to God—"

"I'm seeing someone."

Silence. One full beat of it before he all but shouts, "Oh my God."

On the couch, Cam stiffens slightly. I give him a tiny, reassuring glance.

"Is this a good oh-my-God or a 'should I hang up' oh-my-God?" I ask. Honestly, at this point, I'm looking for any excuse to end this call.

"It's a 'why are you keeping secrets from me, you bastard' oh-my-God," Cosmo blurts. "Who is it? Do I know them? Is it serious? Are they hot? It's serious, isn't it. Oh my God. Who is it?"

I roll my eyes. He knows I'm in England, yet he asks if he knows them. Technically, he does, but I swear Cosmo takes drama queen to a whole new level. I hesitate. "You've met him, technically."

A pause. Then Cosmo gasps. Loudly. "It's not—wait. No. It's not Camden Crawford. As in Camden 'stealth-sexy' Crawford? Exeter rugby guy? Tall, hot, and emotionally mysterious? That Camden?"

Cam groans. I shoot him an apologetic look.

Cosmo continues, breathless: "Are you kidding me? I knew there'd be chemistry. When I met him last year, I was like—yep. Big quiet vibes. Needs someone with excellent eyebrows and horizontal energy. Which, hello, that's you."

"Cosmo," I say slowly, "he's literally here."

There's a beat before the asshole cackles. "Oh my

God. I knew it. I knew it! *I* fixed you up, didn't I? I told you he was hot and broody and obviously your type."

I glance at Cam, who's shaking his head like he regrets everything about this moment.

I sigh. "Actually... we met about a month ago."

Cosmo goes silent. Suspiciously silent. "*Wait. What?*"

"I was already seeing him when you went full chaos matchmaker. We just didn't say anything. I'll be working on a sleeve for him next month."

Cosmo lets out an offended gasp so sharp I instinctively check the phone's volume. "*Excuse* me? Are you saying my matchmaking had nothing to do with this? Nothing? I feel betrayed, Brent. I gifted you a destiny, and you just... sidestepped it?"

"I didn't sidestep it," I say, trying not to laugh. "You just came in halfway through."

"You're telling me," he huffs, "that you, on your own, bagged Camden Crawford without my expert meddling? I call blasphemy."

Cam snorts under his breath. I glare at the ceiling.

"And just so we're clear," Cosmo continues, "I still get to be best man. Dibs. You heard it. It's binding."

"We're not getting married."

"Not with that attitude," he says primly. Then in the

background, there's a muffled voice. "Ugh. Gotta go, my group just got called. We're doing goat yoga."

"Of course you are."

"Say hi to Camden for me! Don't let him ghost you or get emotional constipation. And tell him I want photos."

The line goes dead before I can respond. I lower the phone slowly.

Cam raises an eyebrow. "Goat yoga?"

I nod. "It's best if you don't ask."

He chuckles softly, shaking his head again. "Your family's terrifying."

"Terrifyingly lovable," I correct, already regretting everything that just happened. And still kind of smiling anyway.

He leans in and kisses me. It's short and sweet, but still enough to get my dick interested. Before I can cling on to him and reposition myself on his thighs, he chuckles and shakes his head. "I've got an early start."

I bob my head, already knowing that over the next couple of days, he needs to be rested and focused for his next game. "No worries." I peck his lips and lift my ass off the couch. His hand on my thigh stops me. "Okay?" I tilt my head and roam my gaze over his face.

A tentative, almost hesitant smile tilts his lips. "You don't have to go."

My heart flips over a little. It's not like I haven't stayed over before, but him needing an early night and plenty of sleep means he wants me here for me, not just for company, right?

I nod, the corner of my mouth tugging up. "Then I'll stay."

The smile he gives in return isn't flashy or wide—it's small, quiet, honest. One of my favourites.

He squeezes my thigh before rising and stretching with a grunt, his T-shirt lifting just enough to tease a slice of skin at his waist. "You coming?"

I stand, following him down the hallway, flicking off the lights behind us. By the time I reach the bedroom, he's already toeing off his joggers and tossing his shirt in the general direction of the hamper. The lamps are on, casting a soft golden hue over everything, and he moves like someone who's bone-deep tired.

"Want anything before bed?" I ask, pausing near the en suite. "Tea? Neck rub? Interpretive dance?"

He huffs a quiet laugh. "No dance. But I wouldn't say no to the neck rub."

"Filed away for future use," I promise.

We brush our teeth together, bumping elbows over the sink like we've done it a hundred times before, and somehow that domesticity just about kills me. I'm half convinced I'll combust if he reaches for me now—but he doesn't. He finishes up, gives me a lazy smile in the mirror, then heads back to the bed.

I flick off the bathroom light and join him. The mattress dips under my weight as I slide in behind him, and he's already pulling the duvet up when I do something that makes both of us still. I snuggle in. Not kind of. Not subtly. Like, full-on spooning.

Cam stiffens for a moment like I've short-circuited him, then huffs out an incredulous breath. "You're the little one."

"I'm the limpet now," I mutter, already arranging myself around the solid curve of his back. "Ssh. Accept it."

He laughs again, breathier this time, but doesn't push me away, doesn't make a joke. He just... settles. I loop my arm around his middle and nudge my nose against the back of his neck, the neck rub he wanted forgotten. His hair smells like that cedar shampoo I swiped last week and never gave back. He sighs into the pillow—deep and slow—and it tugs at something behind my ribs.

"Cam?"

"Mm?"

"Just ignore my dick. It's excited about proximity. Doesn't mean I'm making a move."

His chest stutters with another laugh. "You know that doesn't help, right?"

"Still felt like the mature thing to say." I press a kiss to his shoulder. "Even though I absolutely am hard. It's a biological rebellion."

He squeezes the arm I have wrapped around his waist, his thumb brushing the underside of my wrist. "It's fine," he murmurs. "I like this."

That this isn't about sex makes my heart pull tight. I don't say anything for a bit—I just hold him. I've always been a snuggler. Don't let the tattoos or the lip ring fool you—I'm a touch-deprived softie with a cling complex. And this? Holding him like this? Feeling him relax into me, hearing the way his breathing slows?

Yeah. I'm fucked.

He shuffles back just a little, nestling deeper into the cradle of my body, and I nearly lose my mind with how sweet the gesture is.

"I'm glad you're here," he says after a while, voice barely above a whisper.

I rest my cheek against his shoulder blade. "Me too."

And I mean it. All of it. Every complicated, terrifying, amazing bit.

The room goes quiet again, nothing but the soft hum of the night outside and the occasional creak of the floorboards as the house settles around us. I feel him start to drift, the weight of sleep tugging him under. I don't follow right away.

I stay awake a little longer, just breathing him in. Anchoring myself in the steady rhythm of his body. Because right now—wrapped around the man who makes me feel like more than I've ever let myself hope for—I don't want to sleep.

I just want to feel this.

And hold on.

***

It's the second half, and the Seagulls are down.

The crowd at Exeter's home ground is loud, tense, and vibrating with anticipation that feels more like dread. I've been to games before—watched them live and on-screen—but nothing compares to this. To watching him.

Camden Crawford is in the thick of it. He's a fucking wall—tighthead, set in the scrum like he's born for it. The way he braces and drives, the way his legs and shoulders align like a machine, it's a thing of beauty. Controlled aggression. Power in motion. It should be poetry.

But today, there's a crack in the rhythm. A strain just beneath the surface. And I feel it in my chest.

Wolverhampton is all teeth and precision. They're playing fast, hard, mean. And they've got more than momentum on their side—they've got the lead. It's only by a few points, but in a match like this, a few points might as well be a cliff's edge.

I flinch as another tackle smashes down near the sideline. Cam's already back on his feet, barking orders, hauling a teammate upright by the shirt. His voice doesn't carry this far, but I can see it in his posture—pure command. But there's a stiffness to his movements, something wound too tight.

Then it happens.

The pass is fast, the kind of whip-quick throw you only risk when the pressure's mounting. Cam's already pivoting—he sees the opening—but the ball goes wide.

Lachie's the one who takes it. He's out on the wing, faster than he looks, already sidestepping when—

Crack.

It's the kind of sound that stills a crowd. A clean, brutal tackle—but too high, too late. Lachie's legs scissor mid-air before he slams into the turf.

And he doesn't get up.

The moment stretches, unnaturally so. Players start

to crowd, trainers rush from the sidelines. The ref's whistle is piercing, but all I can see is Cam.

He stops dead.

Then explodes.

Cam's across the field in seconds. He's screaming—I can't hear him, but the fury is in every part of his body. It takes three teammates to hold him back from going after the player who hit Lachie. The guy's already getting a red card, walking off to jeers, but it's not enough. Not for Cam.

Not when it's his best mate lying on the pitch, quiet and still.

The stadium has dropped into a strange silence, that holding-your-breath kind of tension. Lachie still hasn't moved. The medics are kneeling beside him now, and I catch the flash of a stretcher coming onto the field.

I don't even realise I'm standing until someone next to me gasps.

Cam's still fuming, his fists clenching at his sides, his chest rising and falling like he's just run a sprint uphill. His teammates are talking to him—one of the flankers with a hand on his shoulder—but he doesn't even look away from Lachie until they lift him carefully onto the stretcher.

My heart's thudding so hard it aches, because I know that look on Cam's face. It's not just rage. It's fear.

Fuck. I have no idea what to do. They just play on, right, even though a player's been taken off? I have zero clue. All I know is that I like Lachie, and he's clearly seriously injured. Then there's Cam, who looks ready to tear off someone's head.

As far as I'm aware, Lachie isn't married or dating, but maybe he has family here who are looking out for him. Even if I leave my seat, it's not like I'm going to get any information. I'm nobody to Lachie. It doesn't matter that I want to be there for him since his best friend can't be.

Indecision wars inside me. The game's yet to restart, and while fans around me have started to take their seats, I remain standing, staring at Cam.

Around me, people are murmuring in confusion, some loudly voicing their opinions.

"Definitely deserves the red, that. Disgusting hit—"

"Was clean. Just bad luck, mate. Happens."

"Did you see his leg? That angle wasn't natural."

The woman next to me grips her partner's arm, whispering, "He's not moving much, is he?"

My heart kicks hard against my ribs. I swallow past the dry lump in my throat and stay standing even though most fans are sitting again. The match hasn't resumed, but players are slowly drifting back into position. Officials are speaking quietly near the sidelines. Cam's crouched beside Lachie's stretcher now, a hand pressed to his friend's shoulder. The medics are speaking low and fast.

And then Cam's eyes find mine. The roar of the stadium dulls. He doesn't say anything, mouth anything. He doesn't have to. His expression is pinched with frustration, worry, barely leashed fury—and something else.

A silent ask.

He wants me to check on Lachie. Because he can't.

I nod once, sharp and sure, and start clumsily making my way out of the aisle. "'Scuse me. Sorry. Sorry." I shuffle past knees and beers and whispered questions, then hit the steps. I don't run, but I walk fast, heart thundering in my chest. By the time I reach the edge of the seating area, I see Cam talking to someone just beyond the sideline rope—an assistant coach maybe, or med staff. He's already setting things in motion, even while the ref confers with a guy in a blazer holding a clipboard.

I scan the stadium interior for signs. Somewhere, there has to be access to the team zones. I spot a steel security door marked with STAFF ONLY above it and jog that way. My boots thud against the concrete. My palms are sweaty.

Two security guards stand at the entrance, one on either side, earpieces in, built like fridges.

Shit.

I approach the guy on the left. He's mid-forties and tough-looking. He doesn't blink as I slow down.

"I need to get through," I say, trying to keep my tone even but urgent. "I'm, uh... I'm Lachie's brother."

His brow lifts. "You are?"

Shit. Come on, Brent. Think. "Half-brother," I say. "Different dads. He took Mum's last name."

He squints at me. "You American?"

"Yeah. Long story." I push a hand through my hair, trying to look distressed. "Look, please. I'm only here for a bit. I just need to make sure he's okay. He's all I've got over here."

The guard doesn't soften.

"You've got ID?"

"Not with his name on it," I say, too quickly. "Please—"

"Sorry, mate. No one through without clearance."

I stare at him, mouth parting, but I already know I'm not getting past. My shoulders sag. I glance around, trying to recalibrate, think of another lie that could work, or better yet, someone I could text. Cam's the only name that comes to mind.

"Okay," I mutter, already backing away, hands raised in surrender. "Okay. Thanks anyway."

The man nods once, already watching the next approaching body behind me. I retreat to the corner of the corridor and pull out my phone, cursing under my breath. My heart's hammering. I tap out a message to Cam—short, direct.

> Me: Blocked at the entrance. Told them I was Lachie's brother. Didn't fly.

I hesitate, then add:

> Me: Let me know if I can try anything else. Just want to make sure he's okay.

Phone gripped in my hand, I glance back at the security door. There has to be a better way.

Obviously, I know Cam can't respond. He's on the pitch. Focused. Doing what he does best—what he has to do. Still, I had to let him know I tried. That I'd be there if I could. I tuck my phone back into my jacket pocket and exhale hard, already scanning for another angle—literally and metaphorically.

That's when the ridiculous idea hits me.

What if I pretend to faint? Maybe hyperventilate? Something that'll get security flustered enough to leave a gap I can bolt through. I'm already mentally rehearsing how dramatic I'll need to be when the heavy door creaks open behind the guard.

A woman in an Exeter Seagulls tracksuit steps out. She's mid-thirties maybe, quick on her feet, purposeful in her movements. Her eyes land on me like she's been searching. "Brent?" she asks, already reaching into her pocket.

"Yeah." I nod fast, hope flaring in my chest like someone just cracked a window open.

"Come with me." She hands over a lanyard with a plastic pass. It reads: TEMP ACCESS: MEDICAL STAFF. The guard doesn't even blink, just steps aside like I suddenly belong.

"I'm Ellie," she says. "One of the physios. Camden sent for you."

The relief whooshes out of me so fast I nearly stumble. "He did?"

She gives a tight nod. "Asked that I collect you to support Lachie."

I follow her down a narrow corridor without question, legs already moving before I've caught up with my thoughts. "Shit, is it bad?" I ask, trying to keep my voice steady.

Ellie doesn't answer right away.

"Someone in the crowd mentioned his leg," I push gently, unable to help it.

She shakes her head. "There's nothing wrong with his leg."

That surprises me. "Then...?"

"He blacked out," she says bluntly. "Hit the ground

hard. Breathing's stable now, but he wasn't responsive at first."

My stomach flips.

"They're putting him in the ambulance. Cam wants you there until we can get his emergency contact here."

"Who's that?"

"His brother. Lives in Manchester. He's on his way, but it'll take a few hours."

I glance sideways at her. "Can I ride with him?"

Ellie's mouth lifts slightly, a bit of warmth breaking through the professional façade. "Cam refused to play on unless Coach Pritchard promised to get you in the ambulance with Lachie."

My heart does a weird twist at that. "He what?"

"He nearly clocked one of the Wolverhampton locks when they kept chirping during the delay. Coach had to pull him aside. Told him he needed to keep his head. Cam said—and I quote—'Not unless Brent gets in that ambulance.'"

I blink hard, throat tight.

"Coach relented. So... here you are."

"Right," I say quietly. "Okay."

We round a final corner, and suddenly we're at an exit. The corridor bursts into motion—sharp with urgency. The back doors of an ambulance hang open, and a paramedic is adjusting the stretcher's locks.

Lachie's already inside, unconscious or just groggy, it's hard to tell. He looks pale, face slightly drawn. A white band is around his wrist. I step up just as Ellie gives the paramedic a nod.

Another man stands at the side of the ambulance, also in Exeter kit. Stocky, greying at the temples, concern etched deep on his face.

"This is Brent," Ellie tells him. "Cam's approved him to ride along."

The man gives me a nod of recognition. "Pritchard," he says. "Head coach. You've got a calm head?"

"I've got a steady one," I say, stepping into the ambulance without needing to be asked twice. "And I'm not going anywhere."

"Good." He claps the side of the van once. "Take this and text me with updates." He passes me a card, which reveals a cell number.

I nod as the paramedics keep moving around me. One gives me a sanitising wipe and some instructions about staying out of the way. I settle on the bench beside Lachie and grip the side rail as the ambulance jolts to life.

I glance down at the man beside me—Cam's best friend, unconscious, hurt, and probably scaring the shit out of the whole team. I don't know him well, but I know this: If it were Cam on this stretcher, I'd want someone beside him. Someone calm. Someone who gave a shit.

So I lean forwards, rest my forearms on my knees, and say softly, "All right, Lachie. You've scared the hell out of everyone. Time to wake up and start with your inappropriate questions."

His chest rises and falls steadily.

That'll do for now.

17

Camden

THE MUD'S DRIED STIFF ON MY SHINS BY THE TIME I strip off my kit. My ears are still ringing with the crowd, the referee's whistle, the dull roar of everything the moment Lachie hit the ground. My right eye's almost swollen shut, but none of it matters.

I toss my jersey into the laundry bin, tug on my Exeter track pants, and ignore the sting as the waistband grazes a new bruise above my hip. I don't care. All I care about is Lachie.

I check my phone again, even though I've already read Brent's last message twice.

Brent: He's at the hospital. Stable. Awake. Concussed. They're running scans. I'm with him.

Thank fuck for Brent.

I didn't hesitate. The second I saw Lachie go down, I wanted to run with him to the hospital. But the match wasn't over, and he'd have gutted me if I'd walked off and left the boys short. I demanded Brent go instead, because I trust him. More than I want to admit.

Whether Coach Pritchard was surprised by that demand or not, I couldn't say. He didn't argue, just nodded once and made it happen. Even before I'd asked, Brent had been leaving the stands—just from one pleading look from me—and racing to Lachie's side. The man has no family nearby. Just me. And today, I wasn't enough.

I drag a hand through my damp hair, already starting to dry in stiff tufts. Around me, the locker room's quieter than normal. The adrenaline's wearing off, and every-one's in that raw, uneasy space that follows a game like this one. No one wants to say it, but we all saw it happen. The hit was late, dangerous, and Lachie didn't get up.

"I've had word from Brent," I say, voice gravelly as I zip up my jacket. The room tilts slightly. I press a hand to the bench to steady myself.

A few of the boys glance over.

"They've taken him in for tests. He's awake. Concussed, but no spinal trauma. They're still doing scans, but he seems lucid." I don't add that Brent told me he wasn't talking. There's something apparently going on with his throat. It's scary as fuck, but all I can focus on is him being awake.

A few shoulders drop. One of the rookies—Lewis, I think—lets out a shaky breath and mutters a "Fuckin' hell."

"Good he had someone with him," Rafi adds, tying his boots with more force than necessary.

I nod. "Yeah. Brent went with him. I asked."

Another silence settles. I don't offer an explanation. I don't owe one. Brent might not be part of the team, but today, he was exactly who Lachie needed.

"I'm heading to the hospital now," I add, pushing off the bench. "Coach says we've got recovery sessions tomorrow, but they're optional. I'll check in once I've seen him."

Jules claps me on the back as I pass. "Tell him we're thinking of him."

"Tell him we'll bring beer if he's stuck there overnight," someone else says, earning a dry laugh from a few others.

I don't smile. Not yet. Not until I see Lachie for myself.

I grab my keys and phone and head for the exit, every

muscle in my body aching, but only one thought cutting through the rest: *Get to the hospital.*

THE HOSPITAL'S ENTRANCE IS CHAOS. CAMERAS flash the second I walk up to the front entrance from the car park. Shouts follow—reporters calling my name, others yelling Lachie's, asking for updates, demanding statements. My cap's low, my hoodie up, but it doesn't matter. They know who I am. They always fucking know.

I push through the glass doors, jaw clenched, heart hammering, and find Brent waiting inside. The moment I'm through, the doors close behind me with a soft whoosh, shutting out the reporters and the noise. Brent's eyes meet mine, his expression tense, worried, and then he's in my arms.

Or maybe I'm in his.

I clutch him tightly, burying my face against his neck, and his arms come around me like a vice. My ribs scream, as does my cheekbone. I wince, sucking in a breath.

"Shit," Brent mutters, pulling back just enough to study me. "Your face. Your ribs too?"

"I'm fine," I rasp. "Lachie?"

He doesn't hesitate. "Still being seen. Your coach is here. He's with the doctors now. They're waiting for some results, but they've stabilised him. He's not alone."

I nod, breathing just a little easier, even as my chest still feels cracked open. "Thank you," I say, voice rough. "For being here."

He frowns like it's a ridiculous thing to thank him for. "Of course I'm here."

He reaches for my hand, lacing our fingers together without hesitation, and leads me towards the lifts. We pass a nurse station. A few eyes flick up. Maybe they recognise me. Maybe they're just clocking my bruised face. Either way, I don't care. I've got one priority, and he's up on the fifth floor.

"How's the team?" Brent asks gently as we step into the lift.

"We lost."

He flinches slightly, and then his thumb strokes mine. "Sorry, baby."

The word hits me in the sternum. I look down at him. His face is tired, soft with concern, and the affection behind that endearment threatens to gut me. I squeeze his hand but don't say anything. I can't.

The lift starts to rise, a soft whir filling the silence. The moment we're alone, with no windows and no watching eyes, I reach for him again. I tug him in by the hoodie, wrapping my arms around his waist and pressing my face to his shoulder. I just need to breathe him in. Something grounding. Something that reminds me the world outside this moment isn't everything.

He holds me like he gets it. Like he knows I need it without him needing to say anything. His fingers drift up my spine. One of them catches in my hair and lingers there, slow and steady.

Neither of us speak.

When the lift dings, we don't move right away. When we do, I keep his hand in mine, unwilling to let go.

The fifth floor smells like disinfectant and nerves.

We round a corner, our footsteps echoing on the polished floor, and I clock Coach Pritchard immediately. He's standing just outside one of the private rooms, arms folded, face pale beneath his usual tan. A doctor is speaking to him in low tones—serious ones. Brent slows beside me, and I tighten my grip on his hand for just a second before letting go.

Coach spots me the moment the doctor steps away. "Crawford," he says, voice low and worn, like it's been run through a shredder. His gaze flicks to Brent but doesn't linger. "You made it."

"Yeah," I croak. "How is he?"

The doctor, a man in his late fifties with salt-and-pepper hair and a grave expression, turns to me. "You're one of the teammates, yes?"

"I'm his best mate," I say. "And I'm his medical proxy if family can't be reached."

He nods. "We've contacted his brother. He's en route. He should be here within a few hours."

"What's the situation?" I ask, pulse thudding in my throat.

The doctor's mouth presses into a thin line. "Lachlan sustained blunt force trauma to the laryngeal area. From the footage we reviewed and the description your coach provided, he was tackled during the breakdown. The Wolverhampton number 5 drove into him at an awkward angle—his forearm caught Lachlan high and hard across the throat. The impact jarred the trachea and caused acute swelling around the vocal cords."

My blood runs cold.

"He's breathing on his own," the doctor continues quickly, likely seeing my reaction, "but the swelling is significant. It's partially obstructing his airway, and any further inflammation could make it worse. We've got him on oxygen for now, but we're prepping him for surgery within the hour."

"What kind of surgery?" Brent asks beside me, voice tight.

The doctor doesn't flinch. "A tracheal decompression

and possible surgical repair of a fractured thyroid carti-lage. We won't know the full extent until we're in there."

"Will he...?" I stop, struggling to shape the question.

"Will he talk again?" Brent says gently, finishing it for me.

The doctor sighs, nodding slowly. "We hope so. But trauma like this can cause long-term issues. His voice might change. There may be strain, or permanent hoarseness, depending on scar tissue and nerve involvement."

I stare at the door behind him like I might punch through it.

Coach's hand lands on my shoulder—not heavy, but solid. "He's in good hands, son."

I nod mutely.

"He hasn't said anything since it happened," Brent murmurs. "I noticed it in the ambulance. He was trying to speak, but...."

"He likely couldn't," the doctor confirms. "The trauma to the cords—combined with the swelling—makes it nearly impossible to project any volume. He's been communicating with hand squeezes and nods."

"Jesus," I mutter, dragging a hand down my face. "He was just—I passed him the damn ball."

"It's not your fault," Coach says. His voice is clipped and angry. "It was a hard hit. The ref didn't call it malicious, but I've already filed a report for the disciplinary panel."

I exhale slowly, rage simmering just beneath my skin. But right now, anger won't help Lachie. Being here will. "Can I see him?" I ask.

The doctor nods. "Just for a minute. We're getting him prepped now." He gestures towards the door and then heads down the corridor, iPad in hand.

Brent steps aside, letting me pass, and I swear I feel his hand brush mine again. A silent reassurance. I glance back once—he's watching me. Tense. Steady. Present.

Then I push into the room.

The soft beep of machines greets me as I step through the hospital room door. The blinds are drawn, casting a dim bluish hue across the room, but I can still see Lachie clearly—propped up slightly in bed, pale, bruised, his left eye swollen and the side of his neck heavily bandaged.

But he's awake.

And he grins the moment he sees me.

That familiar crooked smile doesn't quite reach his eyes, but it still sends a wave of relief through my chest.

I force a smile back, stepping closer, ignoring the chair and perching carefully on the edge of his bed. I don't say anything at first, just take him in. Every little shift of his fingers looks like it takes effort. He raises his brows a fraction and gestures weakly towards my face, then grimaces in a way that's half concern, half *you should see the other guy.*

"Yeah, yeah," I murmur. "Looks worse than it is."

He mimics a small jab with his hand and raises a brow again.

I huff a breath through my nose, trying not to laugh. "No, I didn't get in a fight, arsehole. Just a well-placed boot in the scrum. You're not the only one who got wrecked today."

He taps his chest gently, then gives a thumbs-down.

I understand. He wants to know about the game.

"We lost," I say quietly.

His face falls.

I nod. "Yeah. Not our best. But it was already slipping before... before that tackle."

He looks away for a second, his jaw twitching.

"They're saying it's your larynx," I tell him softly, watching his reaction. "Got crushed a bit in the collision. They don't think it'll be permanent, but it's compressing your airway. Makes it hard to speak. They'll get you fixed right up in surgery."

He raises his hand, fingers pinching together in a small, tight motion.

Yeah. Small odds. He knows.

"But you're here," I say. "You're breathing. You'll get through this."

Lachie's throat works as he swallows. It looks like it hurts. His eyes flick up to mine and narrow slightly—his version of *don't bullshit me*.

I let out a breath and scrub my face. "All right. I'm fucking terrified, okay? But I'm also really fucking relieved. And you"—I point a finger at him—"scared the shit out of all of us."

He closes his eyes for a beat, then lifts his hand, palm up, in a silent apology.

I shake my head. "Don't. You don't apologise for that. That wasn't on you. And we're going to sort it. I'll help however I can. I promise."

He nods faintly, eyes softening. And I realise, looking at him—this battered, quiet, stubborn bastard of a best mate—that no matter what the future holds, we'll figure it out together.

Even if it's without rugby for a while.

Even if it means learning how to speak again.

Even if all we've got for now are glances and the occasional crooked grin.

It's enough. He's here. That's what matters.

BRENT DRIVES MY CAR HOME. I'M TOO EXHAUSTED TO argue, too fried to focus on anything but the way his hand steadies the wheel and the soft thrum of the engine beneath us. The whole drive, I texted, made calls—checking in with Coach, confirming updates with the team, sending messages I don't even remember writing. We didn't leave the hospital until Lachie was out of surgery and his brother arrived. I hadn't realised how much I'd been holding everything together until Brent was quietly there, never asking for anything, just present. Solid. Reassuring.

I don't know what I would've done without him.

All I can think about is Lachie and his recovery. Everything can change in an instant.

I've always known this. Rugby's part of my bones, my blood, but I've seen more injuries—both minor and brutal—than I can count. This one hit different. It hit home. Lachie's not just a teammate—he's my best mate, my anchor on the pitch. Seeing him unconscious on the grass... it'll haunt me.

I'm relieved there's just one game left. We've still got to show up and give it everything, but I can't wait for the season to be over. I'm done. Tapped out. I'll do what needs to be done for the squad, for the fans, but after that?

I need rest.

His brother said he's taking him back to Manchester for recovery. It'll piss Lachie off—he hates being told what to do—but it's the right call. Their family's there. They lost their mum a few years back, and they've never had anything to do with their dad since they were kids. It's not just about having someone to help him—it's about being somewhere that still feels like home.

I sigh as we pull into the car park outside my flat. Brent turns off the ignition, glancing over. "You okay?" he asks quietly.

I nod, dragging a hand down my face. "Getting there."

Inside, I dump my bag near the door and kick off my trainers. Brent follows with less fanfare, slipping his keys and phone onto the counter. He says nothing when I sag down onto the couch and press my hands into my eyes.

A minute passes.

Then another.

He sits next to me, thigh against mine, and just lets me breathe.

Eventually, I check my phone again. A message from my brother lights up the screen.

> Joel: Heard about the game. And Lachie. You all right?

My fingers hover. Then I type back a quick reply.

> Me: Getting there. Thanks. Listen, do you mind if I bring someone to the wedding?

No sooner do I send it than I lower the phone and glance at Brent. "Hey," I murmur. "You free a couple of nights before you fly out? My brother's wedding... it's the night before you leave. Would you wanna come with me? As my... plus-one."

His face lights up like I just told him he won the bloody lottery. "Yeah," he says instantly. "Of course. I'll wear something fancy. But not too fancy. Because, you know, I'm still me."

Despite everything—the fatigue, the bruises, the emotional sledgehammer that was today—I smile.

Brent watches me quietly for a moment, then reaches over, fingers curling gently around mine. His thumb strokes over the back of my hand, grounding. "You really okay?" he asks softly, not pushing—just present.

I nod once. Then again. "Yeah," I say, voice hoarse. "Or... I will be."

"That's enough," he murmurs. "You don't have to be more than that tonight."

I look down at our hands. Mine's bigger, rougher. But it's his that feels stronger somehow. Steadier. Holding me together in ways I didn't realise I needed. "Thanks for being there. Today. With Lachie."

He leans over and presses a kiss to my temple. "You'd have done the same."

I snort. "I'd have decked the security guard."

Brent chuckles against my skin. "I nearly did. He definitely thought I was trying to stage a pitch invasion."

We fall into silence again, but it's a comfortable one. One where I can close my eyes, just for a second, and let the day fall away.

Eventually, Brent shifts, pulling me gently until I'm tucked against his side. He rubs slow circles on my back, his lips at my temple again.

"I'll look good in the wedding photos," he says quietly, and I can hear the grin in his voice.

"God help me," I murmur, but I press closer anyway, letting his warmth bleed into my skin.

Brent doesn't hesitate when he kisses me again. "You sure you're okay with bringing me along to something like that?"

"You're the first person I want beside me," I say, quiet but certain.

That gets me one of his smiles—the kind that reaches all the way to his eyes; it's warm and real. It slides under my ribs and settles there, making my chest ache in the best way.

"I'll charm the hell out of your family," he whispers,

lips brushing against my hair. "Cosmo will probably cry and tell me I've upgraded your entire existence."

I huff out a laugh.

We fall quiet for a while after that, my eyelids drooping. This closeness, this quiet comfort is enough to settle my worried heart, my overthinking, and maybe even a little of my soul.

A small smile curves my lips as I feel myself drifting off to sleep.

18

Brent

I was warned about the Crawford family.

Correction: I was warned about the sheer size of the Crawford family.

Cam gave me a heads-up on the drive over—his brother's wedding would be "decent-sized," which, I've come to learn, is British for *prepare to be swarmed by three generations of people who'll call you "love" and insist on feeding you.*

Still, nothing prepared me for walking into a venue already buzzing with cousins, aunties, and uncles—and being hugged by a woman I'm 87 percent sure is not entirely convinced I'm not a bodyguard.

I must look like one. The suit's sharp, black, well-fitted—thank you, Mom, for insisting I buy one—and paired with my visible tattoos, I'm aware I stand out like an ex-military stripper. But Joel's grin when he sees me is wide and genuine, and when he pulls me in for a hug and says, "You've got your hands full with my brother, haven't you?" I know I'm good.

Cam's family are... honestly, the kindest swarm I've ever met. Loud and warm, they're the sort who don't let you stand awkwardly alone for longer than three seconds. Tasha, the bride, wraps me in a hug that smells like expensive perfume and hairspray and whispers, "He never brings anyone. You must be special."

Cam hears her and mutters, "Jesus Christ," under his breath but doesn't deny it. And that alone makes my chest feel too full.

The ceremony goes off without a hitch. Tasha looks stunning. Joel's practically vibrating with joy. Camden, in a dark navy suit and a tie that matches the flowers, stands up beside his brother like the proudest best man alive. And when he catches my eye during the vows, I swear I see a softness there that's just for me.

By the time we hit the reception, I've had enough champagne to remember I can in fact speak to strangers, and Cam's hand finds mine under the table. No one's making a fuss. No cameras. No scrutiny. Just a room full of people who love fiercely and laugh loud.

It's informal enough that I've gotten away with unbuttoning my jacket and rolling my sleeves. Cam, sitting beside me, still looks immaculate—even if I keep catching him giving me that look. The one that makes my brain short-circuit and my pants feel too tight.

But now it's speech time, and all eyes shift to the front.

Cam clears his throat. "Right, well," he begins, gripping a pint in one hand and a few crumpled notes in the other. "For those of you who don't know me... you're lucky. I'm Camden, Joel's younger brother. Which means, by rights, I'm funnier, better looking, and slightly more traumatised from being forced to watch him lip-sync to Westlife for most of his formative years."

The room bursts out laughing. Joel groans into his hands. Tasha cackles.

"But in all seriousness," Cam continues, tone softening, "Joel has always been there for me. Through school, through rugby, through every injury, heartbreak, and hangover. He's the one who taught me how to throw a proper punch and how to tie a tie—though clearly, I forgot that part today."

He tugs his own knot loose to laughter.

"And Tasha..." He looks at her with open affection. "You've made him happier than I've ever seen him. You've made him less of a grump. You've even convinced him to start using a calendar. Miracles do happen."

Laughter again.

"I'm lucky to have grown up with a brother like Joel. And I'm lucky to call you my sister now, Tash."

There's a warm hush.

Cam lifts his glass. "To Joel and Tasha—may your days be full of laughter, your nights full of cuddles, and your Netflix queue eternally synced."

The toast goes up with cheers. Joel's trying not to cry. Cam sits back down, and I take his hand beneath the table, giving it a squeeze.

"That was... genuinely good," I murmur, impressed.

He nudges my shoulder. "Thought you might be grading me."

"I am," I tease. "You're currently top of the class."

He leans in. "Want to celebrate later?"

"Oh, I definitely do."

His smirk could level a city.

And in this moment—this perfect, golden-lit, champagne-soft moment—I think maybe, just maybe, I've found exactly what I came to the UK looking for.

Home. In a tattoo shop. In a rugby pitch. In him.

The speeches are over. The desserts come and quickly vanish like they were never real. And now... now comes the dancing.

Which, apparently, Cam has been waiting for.

The music kicks in—something upbeat and retro, maybe Earth, Wind & Fire or something equally disco—

and I make the mistake of thinking he'll stay seated for at least one song.

He does not.

"Let's go," he says, already tugging at my hand.

I blink. "Wait, what?"

"Dance floor. Come on."

"But I've only had four glasses of—"

"Exactly," he says, hauling me up with a shit-eating grin. "Perfect amount of coordination with none of the self-consciousness."

And he's right. About all of it.

The second we're on the floor, Cam becomes a menace in human form. A tall, overconfident, rugby-playing menace with rhythm I wasn't prepared for. He's not even trying to be sexy. He's just... having fun. Fully committed to every hip thrust and overexaggerated arm move. The man looks like a cross between a backup dancer for a boyband reunion tour and a dad who peaked in 2003—and somehow it works.

I'm doubled over laughing before the chorus even hits. "Cam, what the hell are you doing?"

He wiggles his eyebrows. "Bringing sexy back."

"Pretty sure that's illegal in at least four counties."

"You love it," he says.

And he's right again. But it's not just Cam tearing it up. His family? Oh, they're bringing it.

There's an aunt—Nessa, I think—who's doing a dead-serious cha-cha with a man I'm fairly sure isn't her husband. And on the far side of the floor, Cam's cousin Gracie is doing the worm in a dress that absolutely wasn't designed for floor-based activity. She pulls it off anyway. To cheers. And possibly a pulled hamstring.

A cluster of small children are rotating in a sugar-fuelled circle of doom nearby, led by an enthusiastic uncle who's somehow managed to affix glowsticks to his ears.

I lose Cam for half a second when he gets swept into a line dance next to an older lady who insists he's "too pretty to be single" and that she's got a granddaughter "built like a pin-up and a certified beautician."

Cam just laughs and points at me across the room. "Taken."

The lady gasps. "Well, damn. Lucky him."

I waggle my fingers.

"Flirt," Cam mouths.

"You love it," I mouth back.

We dance through three more songs, one dangerously close to a mosh pit, before I finally grab him by the collar and drag him off the floor.

"Hydration," I say.

Cam's sweaty, pink-cheeked, breathless, and still

smirking. "You just want to make out behind the marquee."

I sip my drink. "No comment."

"You totally do."

"Still no comment."

"You're very predictable."

"Says the man who just did the Macarena and made it look like foreplay."

He leans in, brushing his mouth against mine, voice warm and low. "You're welcome."

Jesus Christ.

We break apart just as Tasha strolls over, make-up slightly smudged and heels dangling from one hand. "You two are disgusting. And adorable. But mostly disgusting."

Cam raises his glass. "It's a gift."

Joel appears behind her, grabbing her waist. "They're in their honeymoon phase. Let 'em have it."

"You've been married four hours," I point out.

Joel shrugs. "Time flies when you're already perfect."

Tasha snorts. "You're sleeping on the couch tonight."

They bicker lovingly for a moment before wandering off again, and Cam turns back to me, all warmth and mischief. "You good?" he asks.

I glance around at the dance floor, the lights, the

people—this riot of laughter and colour and comfort. Then I look back at him.

And yeah. I'm good.

I nod, tugging him in by the front of his shirt. "The best."

We don't make out behind the marquee.

Not yet anyway.

But that look in Cam's eyes says we will.

The song shifts. The drums fade, a gentle piano kicks in, and before I can process the transition, Cam tugs me onto the dance floor and pulls me in close. He gives no warning, no words—just strong arms around my waist and the slow sway of his body inviting mine to follow.

I stumble for a beat—not because I mind, but because I've never slow danced before.

Not once.

But Cam makes it easy. He always does.

His hand spreads firm and warm across my lower back, the other clasping mine with surprising gentleness for someone who could probably throw me across the room if he wanted to. My other arm hooks instinctively around his shoulder. He's taller than me, so broad, and his chest is solid heat against mine. It's like dancing with a furnace wrapped in a tailored waistcoat and the scent of cedar and spice.

I breathe it—him—in, letting myself settle into the

rhythm. We're just swaying a little, side to side, but it doesn't matter. I'm moving with Camden fucking Crawford in the middle of a wedding reception, and nobody's staring. Or if they are, I don't care.

"Still with me?" he murmurs against the top of my ear.

I smile into his shoulder. "Barely. But yeah. You're an excellent dance partner for a first-timer."

His laugh is a rumble in his chest. "You're not so bad yourself."

The music curls around us, soft and sweeping. There are lights strung up around the garden, casting everything in a warm gold. Kids run past barefoot, a grandad spins one of the bridesmaids like he's in a Fred Astaire film, and somewhere across the lawn, someone's grandmother is telling a group of cousins about her fourth marriage.

It's perfect. Odd, hilarious, chaotic—but perfect.

Cam presses his forehead to mine, his smile lingering for a breath longer before his expression softens and the movement between us slows. The music fades into the background, replaced by the hum of conversation and clinking glasses. His hand slides up my back, fingers splayed over my shoulder blade like he's grounding himself there.

He exhales, quiet but weighted, and says, "He would've loved this."

I tilt my head just slightly, brushing my nose against his. "Who?"

"Lachie."

My chest tightens instantly, the joy in my blood settling into something quieter. "Yeah," I say, voice low. "He would've."

Cam's gaze dips for a second, his arms staying firmly around me.

I nod, letting the shift in mood settle between us as I keep close. "How's he doing?"

Cam's lips press together. "Healing, slowly. He's still not talking. I sent him some photos earlier—got a few texts back. Short ones."

A pause. Then, almost guiltily, he adds, "I think he's... struggling."

My fingers tighten slightly at the back of Cam's neck. "It's only been three weeks. He's allowed to be."

Cam nods, but there's a heaviness in the gesture. I can see how much it's still sitting with him. "His brother's looking after him. Said they'll reassess things with his specialists soon. But he's obviously not coming to the States now. He was meant to be there with us."

My heart aches for both of them—for Lachie, for

Cam who's spent half the season leaning on a teammate now stuck watching from the sidelines. I press a kiss to his cheek. "He'll get there. And you're doing right by him."

Cam tries to smile, but there's a shadow in his eyes. "I just... hate not being there. But his brother's doing good by him. Still—feels wrong, y'know?"

I squeeze his hand, tucking my chin against his shoulder. "I get it. But you're allowed to live your life, too, Cam. You didn't abandon him. He knows that."

He's quiet for a beat. Then he whispers, "I just want him okay."

"We both do."

The song shifts again, but we don't stop moving. I don't think either of us wants to.

He finally speaks again. "You're flying out tomorrow, right?"

"Yep. Heathrow, midday check-in." I frown a little. "You know that. You're the one driving me."

Cam shrugs, and there's this flicker of something in his eyes—like nerves, or maybe anticipation. His grip on my hand shifts slightly, firmer, warmer. "Just making sure," he says, but his voice is quieter now. He looks away, his gaze skimming the string lights above us and the blur of motion on the dance floor. Then, after a long beat, he says, "I've always wondered what an authentic Fourth of July celebration is like."

My heart stutters, confused for half a second. "Okay...?"

He knows what getting back to the States for the holiday means to me—being with my family, the food, the noise, the ridiculous number of flag-themed desserts my cousin Julia insists on baking every year.

Cam clears his throat, nervous now, like he's working himself up to something. Then he looks right at me, eyes steady. "I was thinking..." His thumb brushes the inside of my wrist. "Maybe I could fly out tomorrow. With you. Ahead of the team. See what Independence Day is really all about for myself."

For a second, I just blink. Like my brain's still booting up. "You'd do that?" I manage eventually, barely a whisper. "You want to?"

He nods, jaw tight, but there's something hopeful in his eyes. "Yeah. I mean... as long as I'm at the hotel in Jacksonville by the time the team flies in, I'm good. Cleared it with Coach already."

It hits me all at once—what he's saying, what it means. He's not just tagging along. He's choosing to spend those days with me. With my family. He's taking time—precious time, right before his Southeastern US tour—to come be a part of my life in a way I didn't expect he ever would.

My chest goes tight, and something warm and wide

blooms in my gut. "Cam," I say, a little breathless, "that's... that's a big deal."

His mouth lifts at one corner, soft and lopsided. "You're a big deal."

Jesus Christ.

I stare at him, stunned, for a beat too long before a laugh bursts out of me, unexpected and full of feeling. "You're seriously going to eat three kinds of barbecue, meet every single one of my siblings—including having to deal with Cosmo—and survive an inquisition from my mom?"

He grins now. "I've played international rugby. I think I can handle a few of your relatives."

"You have no idea what you're getting into."

"Nope." He leans in, our foreheads brushing, voice warm against my skin. "But I want to find out. With you."

And that's it. That's the moment I know I'm completely, ridiculously, head-over-everything for this man.

I slide my arms tighter around him, bury my face in the side of his neck, and breathe him in like he's the thing that's been keeping me grounded all night. "Fuck yes," I mumble. "Come home with me, Camden Crawford. Let's blow some shit up in the name of freedom."

He laughs—rich and real—and pulls me in even closer.

"Deal."

WE SURVIVE OUR LONG-ASS FLIGHT FROM HEATHROW to Atlanta, though "survive" is generous. I think Cam might've threatened a gate agent with death-by-scrum when we almost missed our connection. But hey, we made it. He even upgraded me to business class so I wouldn't be flying solo in economy. Talk about spoiled. And yeah, fine, I may have gotten a little misty-eyed at the gesture, though I blamed it on cabin pressure.

By the time we land in Savannah, it's late on the third. The air hits us the second we step outside—thick and sticky with Southern heat even at night—and I swear Cam makes a sound somewhere between a grunt and a "what the fuck."

Tony's already at the pick-up zone, leaning against his bright yellow Jeep like he's been plucked straight out of a Banana Ball infomercial. He spots us and takes off at a jog, a blur of yellow and wild energy. Before I can even drop my suitcase, he's got me in a full-body hug that lifts me half off the ground.

"Three years, you asshole," he says, voice thick. "Three freakin' years."

I laugh, clinging just as hard. "You're the one who moved to the circus."

He pulls back, eyes a little glassy, though he's quick to wipe at one. "Yeah, yeah. Shut up. I missed you."

"Missed you too."

Only then does he turn to Cam, who's hovering like he's not sure if he should look polite or protective.

Tony grins wide, clapping eyes on him. "You're even taller than Brent said. Love that for you. You a hugger or a handshake guy?"

Cam blinks. "Uh, whichever keeps you from tackling me."

Tony grins wider. "Oh, buddy." And before Cam can say another word, he's yanked into a hug too. Cam stiffens for half a second, but to his credit, he doesn't flinch. Much.

"You're all right," Tony declares, pulling back. "Strong silent type. Total upgrade from Brent's ex in high school who collected swords."

Cam side-eyes me. I shrug. "It was a phase."

Tony just throws our bags in the trunk like nothing's changed—and in the best way, maybe nothing has.

On the drive back to the house, Cam keeps glancing out the window like he's trying to orient himself via humidity and pine trees. Tony, meanwhile, launches into a full-blown Banana Ball explanation before Cam can ask. Which he doesn't. He looks confused enough just by the name.

"It's like baseball," Tony says, hands flying everywhere. "But if baseball had a baby with a circus and then raised it on a steady diet of TikTok and chaos."

Cam blinks. "I... don't know what that means."

Tony looks offended. "Mate. There's dancing. Uniforms are optional. We do backflips mid-play. Sometimes we play in kilts."

Cam turns slowly in his seat to look at me. "Is this a real sport?"

I snort. "Sadly, yes. And he's not bad at it."

"'Not bad'? I'm a fuckin' legend," Tony says.

Cam's trying so hard not to laugh I can see the vein in his neck bulging.

Then Tony, curious now, glances back at him. "So, what about you? I've watched rugby. Still don't get the rules. You a linebacker or something?"

Cam's lips twitch. "I'm a tighthead prop."

Tony blinks. "I don't know what that is, but it sounds like something dangerous and vaguely illegal."

Cam just shrugs like it's no big deal. "I anchor the scrum. Keep the line steady. Push against a wall of men trying to crush me. Hit hard. Take hits harder."

Tony's mouth hangs open. "That's badass. Wait, you do that on purpose and without a helmet or pads?"

Cam nods.

Tony turns to me, stunned. "Your boyfriend is terrifying."

I blink. Cam's gaze slides towards me, just as my own flicks to him. There's a beat. A pause just long enough for both of us to register the word neither of us has dared say out loud.

Boyfriend.

Cam's jaw ticks like he's considering saying something, but then—

He just shrugs. Easy. Casual. "Good," he mutters.

My mouth twitches. "Yeah," I say, playing it cool even as something warm and wobbly flares in my chest. "I know."

Tony, oblivious, whistles low. "Terrifying and hot. Well done, bro."

We both ignore that one. But neither of us corrects him. And maybe that says more than anything else.

Tony shakes his head and mutters something about needing to start lifting weights again. Cam just grins quietly and watches the road.

I settle back in my seat, warmth curling in my chest. I'm the only brother who didn't get into sports—barely made it through school sports, if I'm honest. But my parents never gave me shit about it. They supported every creative outlet I threw myself into. Tattooing. Drawing. Even that brief period where I thought I'd become a magician.

Still, I know my mom—especially—would love if I moved back. I feel it in the way she lingers on every FaceTime. The way she always asks if I'm eating enough. If the flat's warm enough. If I'm lonely.

Maybe I was. For a while. But with Cam beside me, arm brushing mine in the back seat, that ache doesn't sting so sharply anymore. He glances at me as Tony launches into another wild story, and I see the corner of his mouth lift—just slightly.

And honestly, under the warm, late-night Georgia sky, I think... maybe we're both exactly where we're meant to be.

19

Camden

The smell of grilled corn and smoked ribs hits me before I even make it out the back door.

It's hot—hotter than anything I've felt in a while. Georgia doesn't just do heat; it does full-body sauna. The air clings to my skin the second I step outside, a wet blanket of humidity wrapping around my limbs. I'm in a T-shirt and shorts, but I'm already rethinking both. My trainers stick faintly to the deck, and I don't even want to know what the pavement feels like.

Brent's standing just ahead of me, barefoot and smiling like he's never been more at home in his life.

And maybe he hasn't. Not in a long time, at least.

There's a speaker tucked under a shaded pergola blasting a mix of funk and country and something that might be bluegrass. The pool glints like polished glass, half full of his extended family—some swimming, some lounging, some half wrestling on inflatable floats. A football flies overhead. A cooler cracks open with a satisfying hiss. Someone—probably one of the twins—yells, "*Shotgun!*" loud enough to make a few birds take flight.

And me? I'm just standing here, staring like a wide-eyed British idiot, trying to make sense of it all.

"You all right?" Brent's beside me now, nudging my side with a can of root beer. "You've got that look."

"What look?"

"The one that says 'I'm either dangerously fond of you or wondering if your family's going to initiate me with a chili cook-off.'"

I take the can, trying not to laugh. "That obvious?"

"Painfully." He leans in close enough to nudge his shoulder against mine. "Welcome to the Fourth of July."

Apparently, I'm not the only one who got the memo about shorts and bare feet. Every guy here—except for maybe Brent's dad, who's manning the grill like it's a competitive sport—is shirtless or close to it. Tattoos on show. Music loud. People everywhere. It's chaos.

Beautiful, messy, genuine chaos.

"Brent!" a voice hollers from across the garden.

Before I can blink, a blur barrels out of the house and flings itself into Brent's arms.

"Jesus," Brent wheezes, catching the full body of

Cosmo as his youngest brother clings to him like a koala. "Warn a guy, would you?"

"You brought the Brit!" Cosmo exclaims, detaching long enough to peer at me with his too-familiar grin. "Camden *bloody* Crawford in my backyard."

I lift a hand awkwardly. "Hey."

"I still can't believe it," Cosmo mutters, circling me like he's inspecting a new toy. "You. Him. Together. Wild. I'm emotionally unprepared."

Brent's eyes roll skywards. "He's been like this since I told him you'd be joining us."

Cosmo throws a dramatic arm around Brent's shoulders. "You wound me. After everything I did for you two."

"You sent otter memes," Brent deadpans.

"And look where we are now."

Before Brent can retaliate, Tony appears. "You met Calvin yet?" He jerks his head towards the shaded table under a tree, where another twin—Calvin, presumably—is sitting with a guy. "That's Ash. They're disgustingly happy."

"You say that like you're not the one who got all teary having us all together again," Brent mutters.

Tony shrugs. "I get emotional. Fight me."

It goes on like this—greetings, introductions to those I've not already met, jokes flying faster than I can keep up. Brent's sister, Rachel, gives me a warm hug and immediately starts teasing Brent about something he did when he was eighteen involving a piñata and a sprinkler. His mum, Lyn, insists I call her by her first name and offers me a plate before I've even figured out where to sit. His dad, Jo, gives me a nod that somehow says everything and nothing all at once.

By the time I find myself seated under the awning with a plate of ribs, coleslaw, and something suspiciously neon that Brent assures me is "just a patriotic Jell-O salad," I'm sweaty, slightly overwhelmed, and... oddly content.

"Your family's amazing," I tell him as he sits beside me, beer in hand.

"They're loud."

"They're real," I say.

He nudges my foot with his. "You're doing great."

"Is this a test?"

"It's the final exam. If you survive the line dancing later, you get to stay."

I raise a brow. "Line dancing?"

"Oh yeah. One of Rachel's friends teaches it at a community centre. We're all roped in. Even Dad."

This, apparently, is hilarious to everyone but me. And then, just when I'm starting to believe I've passed the vibe check, Brent's mum sits down on his other side.

"Darling," she says, smile wide but eyes sharp. "You look happy."

Brent hums around a sip of his drink. "I am."

"It's good to have you home."

He nods.

"You ever think about staying?" she asks, casual like a bomb dropping in slow motion.

My chest tightens. Brent goes still beside me.

"We miss you," she says softly. "I know England's... whatever it is, but there's always a place here. You know that, right?"

Brent clears his throat, gaze locked on the rim of his can. "I know, Mom."

She pats his leg and gets up just as quickly as she arrived, off to chase one of her nephews—or maybe to stir another tray of something heart-clogging and delicious.

I don't say anything. Not for a long beat.

Brent eventually meets my eye. "That wasn't about you."

"I know," I say.

"But it surprised you."

I hesitate. "Yeah."

"Sorry."

"Don't be."

We sit in silence again, not awkward, just thoughtful.

And then Tony yells something about beer pong and

someone plays the opening notes of "Cotton Eye Joe," and Brent grins, nudging me up out of my seat. "Come on, Captain. Let's see what you're made of."

And despite everything—the jet lag, the humidity, the low hum of nerves in my gut—I follow him. Because in this chaos, in this ridiculous, loud, loving mess of a family... I feel more welcome than I ever have anywhere else, other than back home with my family.

***

WE LOSE BEER PONG. BADLY.

In my defence, I've never played before—and also, Tony is terrifyingly good at it. Like, suspiciously so. Like, were-you-on-a-frat-league-team good. He claims it's all in the wrist, and Brent mutters something about him being "obnoxiously double-jointed," which—frankly—feels like a weird flex to say in front of your boyfriend, but here we are.

"You throw like a dad at an elementary school sports day," Tony announces, pulling a triumphant pose with one foot on a cooler and one hand cradling the winning cup like it's an Oscar.

"I'm sorry," I shoot back. "Do you usually insult strangers at national holidays?"

Brent grins behind the rim of his drink. "He does, actually."

Tony winks. "And if you can't handle that, my brother is way out of your league."

"Oh, I know." I say it without thinking, but the look Brent gives me—soft and surprised, pink rising in his cheeks—makes my chest twist in that now-familiar, ridiculous way.

We drift apart for a bit after that, Brent disappearing with Cosmo and Rachel towards the fire that's being built in the pit in the side yard. I'm nursing a new drink and half a paper plate of someone's famous bacon mac when Calvin drops into the seat next to me.

"Watch out," he warns. "Mom's about to bring out the mini flag cakes. Shaped like stars. Glazed like it's a war crime."

I grin. "Noted."

He nods at Brent across the yard. "He looks happy."

"He is," I say instantly, no hesitation.

Calvin studies me. "You are too."

I shrug. "Trying."

"Man, you look like you're five seconds from folding him into a snuggle burrito."

That startles a laugh out of me. "A what?"

"Don't act like it's not true," he says, jabbing my ribs. "Honestly, we've not seen him like this in ages.

Not since before he moved to England. Don't screw it up."

The warning isn't mean. It's fond. But it still lands with a weight I feel in my chest.

"I won't," I say.

He nods, satisfied, and turns back to wave someone over. A man approaches—Ash, his boyfriend, who presses a hand to Calvin's back as he takes the seat beside him. I get introduced properly this time, and we fall into easy, friendly conversation, mostly about Ash's time in Texas and still failing to wrap his head around the twin chaos.

By the time Brent finds me again, the sun's sinking fast and the sky's bleeding into soft pinks and golds. He looks tired, in that sun-soaked, full-of-food kind of way. His curls are mussed from one of his cousin's kids trying to use him as a jungle gym, and he has a smear of something suspiciously blue near his temple.

I reach up and wipe it away. "Did a cupcake explode?"

"Possibly."

He curls a hand behind my neck and leans in, not for a kiss, just a press of his forehead to mine. It's tender in a way that undoes me a little.

"You okay?" he murmurs.

"Yeah," I say. "Your family's... a lot." And considering just a couple of days ago he met the chaos of my own extended family, he knows I mean it in the best possible way.

He chuckles. "They are."

"But good," I add quickly. "Like, really good."

"You're good too," he says quietly. "You've been great. I know this was last-minute and exhausting."

"It's worth it."

That earns me a kiss, soft and easy, and I soak it up like it'll keep me grounded.

Later, after dusk rolls in and the firepit is blazing, we lie back on a pair of deck loungers, Brent curled against my side. My arm's draped around his shoulders. There's a kid in the distance waving around sparklers, and someone—Cosmo, by the sound of it—is leading an aggressively off-key rendition of "The Star-Spangled Banner."

Brent leans in and says, "You're never gonna survive the fireworks if you think this is chaotic."

I glance down. "Should I be worried?"

He tilts his head. "My dad went to Costco yesterday. There's a crate of explosives in the garage."

"That explains the small cannon I saw Tony wheeling out earlier."

He laughs. It's the best sound.

There's a lull in the noise, and Brent's hand slides beneath my T-shirt, fingers warm on my stomach.

"You're thinking again," he says.

"I'm always thinking."

"You okay?"

I nod. "It's just... surreal, I guess. This is the most welcome I've felt anywhere outside my own family. And even that... doesn't always feel like this." Hell, maybe it's the weather and open skies—so different from Walsall.

Brent doesn't speak. He just rubs slow circles over my skin until my breath evens out.

"You'd tell me," he says eventually, "if it was too much?"

I glance down at him. "Are you joking? I'd burn half the world to stay in this moment a little longer."

He kisses my shoulder, then grins up at me. "That's weirdly romantic and slightly alarming."

"Yeah, well. You inspire that in me."

"You're such a softie."

"Says the man who snuggles like a professional weighted blanket."

"I am the blanket," Brent agrees solemnly.

The fireworks start with a low whistle and a boom so loud it rattles the deck chairs. Everyone screams—some delighted, some startled—and then the sky explodes in a shock of blue and gold.

"Happy Fourth," Brent murmurs, head against my chest.

"Happy Fourth," I say, lips pressed to his hair.

And for once, there's no voice in my head warning me to back off. No shadow of fear about the press, or my teammates, or the weight of what it means to be someone like me in a world that often doesn't let us be soft and seen.

There's just this: Brent, glowing in firelight, smiling against my shoulder, home in the most unexpected way.

And fuck—I think I'm in love with him.

20

Brent

It's surreal—sitting on the back porch of my parents' house, sipping lukewarm coffee while Camden fucking Crawford loads his overnight bag onto the bed of Dad's truck.

I blink at the morning sunlight streaming through the Spanish moss and feel like I've slipped into a fever dream. He's wearing that faded grey tee that clings to his back and does violent things to my sanity, cargo shorts that should look tragic but somehow make his thighs even more sinful, and he's got that laser-sharp focus on his face like packing is a competitive sport.

The man's going to meet his team in Jacksonville, and I'm still trying to wrap my head around the fact that he's been here. With my family. For the Fourth of July. Eating my mom's cobbler and laughing at Tony's terrible

Banana Ball jokes. Letting Rachel teach him how to make devilled eggs while Cal's sat perched on the counter narrating like it was a cooking show.

He fit. Like he belonged here. Like he wasn't a six-foot-something international rugby player with a reputation for breaking defensive lines and jawbones.

And hell, maybe I'm being soft, but watching him these past couple of days—seeing him talk to my mom about his own, leaning into my side during fireworks, ducking his head when my dad called him "son"—it's been... a lot.

In the best fucking way.

I head inside, ducking through the screen door, and nearly run into my mom in the hallway. She's holding a dish towel and looking way too composed for someone who just cleaned up after hosting a holiday for a shit-ton of people and two dogs.

"Morning, sweetheart," she says, then leans in for a kiss on the cheek. "Coffee?"

I lift my mug. "Already caffeinated, thanks."

She doesn't move. "Cam all set?"

"Just about." I scratch the back of my neck, glancing towards the door. "I'll be driving him down to Jacksonville. He's got to meet his team at the hotel."

Mom nods, but I can see it coming—the question. The hesitation. That quiet sort of maternal worry that simmers behind her eyes, like she's trying to measure my happiness with a thermometer she doesn't quite trust.

"Brent," she says gently, "can I talk to you for a moment before you go?"

My stomach drops a little. I nod.

She leads me into the front sitting room—cosy, neutral, the smell of lemon polish lingering in the air. I sit on the edge of the armchair like I'm back in high school waiting for a report card.

Mom perches opposite, wringing the towel. "You know I love that you brought Cam here," she says softly. "We're so happy to meet him. He's... lovely."

I nod. "He is."

"But."

She always had a knack for pivoting with a word like that.

"But," she continues, "seeing you two together—it's wonderful, Brent. It really is. But it also makes me wonder."

"About what?" I ask, even though I already know.

Her gaze holds mine. "Are you ever coming back?"

The question lands like a punch to the ribs. Not because I didn't expect it, but because I don't have a clean answer. Not anymore.

"I don't know," I say honestly. "I used to think I might. But... things feel different now."

"Because of Cam?"

"Partly," I admit. "But it's not just him. It's the studio, the life I've built. The quiet I've found there."

She nods slowly, absorbing that. "You've always needed that. A place that made you feel steady."

I huff out a laugh. "You saying we're chaotic?"

She grins. "Oh, definitely. But you thrive in calm."

I swallow, suddenly aware of how dry my throat is. Mom's looking at me like she's seeing me at five years old again, like she can still peel back every layer of my armour with a single glance. I shift on the seat, my hands half in my pockets, half itching to fidget with something.

"Mom...," I start and then pause, steadying myself. I meet her eyes. "I'm happy. Really happy."

Her expression doesn't change, but something in her softens, just a little.

"I'm not saying I'll never move back," I continue, my voice quieter now. "This house, this family—it's always gonna be a part of me. And yeah, I miss you guys like hell. But right now... Cam's important to me. Really important."

The truth of it settles heavy and warm in my chest as I say it. Like something I've been carrying finally has shape.

I watch her process the words. Her mouth presses into a thin line, not angry, just thoughtful.

"And Exeter..." I glance towards the living room, where I can hear Cam's low voice chatting with one of my brothers. I smile despite the tension in my shoulders. "It feels like home."

Mom doesn't say anything for a moment. She steps forwards, lays her hand gently on my cheek, then sighs, her thumb brushing along my jaw. "I just don't want to lose you to another continent, Brent."

I nod slowly, pressing my hand over hers. "You're not losing me. You're gaining someone who makes me feel more like myself than I ever have."

She blinks quickly, and I pretend not to notice the sudden gloss in her eyes. Then she pulls me into a hug, tight and lingering. I let myself melt into it, feeling twelve years old again—but also more grown-up than I've ever been.

"You always have to follow your heart, Brent. Just promise me—promise us—you won't forget where home started."

"I won't," I whisper.

And then, behind us, there's the unmistakable sound of someone clearing their throat.

My heart stutters as I turn. Cam's standing in the doorway, a duffel bag slung over his shoulder, his eyes a little too unreadable. I have no idea how long he's been there. Long enough, probably.

But that—well, that's a conversation for the drive.

Cam steps fully into the room, saying, "I'm all packed and ready."

I nod and we head to the kitchen so he can say goodbye to the rest of the family. Mom hugs him again, tells him to play smart and stay safe and that she can't wait to see him play. Rachel gives him a thumbs-up, then nudges me with a wink that I pointedly ignore. The twins are already halfway out the door, yelling something about good luck and Banana Ball, and Cosmo's nowhere to be seen—he had to head out early this morning for the summer league he's involved in.

"I'll be back tonight," I tell Mom as Cam and I move towards the door. "But we'll FaceTime before the match on the seventh so you can wish him luck."

She nods and squeezes Cam's arm. "I can't wait for the game, Cam."

Only my parents and Rachel will be at Cam's first game in Jacksonville—Calvin and Tony can't swing it with their game schedule, but they've already promised they'll be there for the final game in Atlanta, when I'll be back in the UK. It's weird, thinking I won't be there to see it live. But I know what this trip has meant, and I'm glad they'll be there to cheer him on.

Cam shoots me a quiet look as we reach the borrowed truck—Dad's, since it's roomier than mine and

Cam can stretch out his long-ass legs. He's not saying much. Neither am I, really.

The drive starts out quiet. The hum of tyres on road is the only sound between us for the first few minutes, but it's not uncomfortable—just... weighted. Like we're both turning over everything that's happened this week, everything we haven't quite said yet.

Cam settles into the passenger seat with a low, gravelly sigh that says more than words could. He doesn't fidget—he never does—but his silence feels heavier than usual. Me? I'm gripping the wheel like the damn thing might escape if I ease up. The air between us feels taut. Like it's waiting for one of us to breathe too deep and set everything off.

I glance over at him as we ease onto I-95. The sunlight cuts across his face in sharp angles, making the faint bruise beneath his eye more pronounced. He's not looking at me, just watching the trees blur by outside the window. There's something almost... guarded about him. Like he's gearing up for a tackle.

"You okay?" I ask, voice soft.

He nods. Just once.

We lapse back into silence. A few miles later, we pass a billboard for boiled peanuts and gator jerky, and normally I'd make a crack. Cam would huff, half amused, half horrified. But right now, I can't summon the nerve.

I think about what Mom said. About permanence. About love and roots and home.

And then I think about Cam. Cam, who is fiercely private. Cam, who plays rugby like it's a war and carries the weight of every single teammate on his back. Cam, who lets me hold him when he thinks no one's watching.

I swallow hard. "Listen," I say finally, just as the truck rumbles past a semi, "about earlier... with my mom."

His head turns slightly. "I heard enough to get the gist."

Of course he did.

I wince. "Didn't mean for you to hear it like that. I was gonna talk to you. I just... I hadn't figured out how to yet."

His brow lifts, gaze pinning me. "Figured out what?"

I breathe in deep, my eyes locked on the road. "That being with you changes things for me. Like... long term."

Silence again. And then, slowly, "Meaning?"

"Meaning I was never really sure if I'd stay in the UK for good. But I could. If you wanted me to."

Cam exhales like I've punched him in the chest. "You'd... do that?"

"If it meant being with you?" I glance at him. "Yeah. I would."

He doesn't answer right away. Instead, he sits there,

turning that over like a stone in his palm. Eventually, he mutters, "That's a lot."

"I know."

"And we've only just started calling each other boyfriends."

"Also true."

"But you'd move countries for me."

"I'd *stay* in a country for you," I clarify gently. "It's not like I hate it there. I've got the shop, I've got friends. I like the pace. But it didn't feel like home until you." He already knows I'm eligible for citizenship next year too.

That gets his attention. He shifts in his seat, finally facing me fully. "You serious?"

"Dead serious." My voice cracks a little, and I smile to soften it. "Though if I'd known you'd tackle the shit out of my heart this fast, I might've bought an emotional helmet."

That earns a low laugh. It's small but real, and the tension in his shoulders bleeds out just a touch.

We're halfway to Jacksonville now, the trees thinning, road signs flicking by like blinks. I risk a glance at him again. "You okay with me being there for the match?"

"More than okay," he says, voice quiet. "I want you there."

"Good." I clear my throat. "Also, for what it's worth, I think our families will get along well."

Cam blinks. "You think? You don't think your mum's going to blame me for stealing you away?"

"She gets very... maternal when she's emotionally overwhelmed. You're a good guy. She can tell."

He huffs out a breath. "Hope she wasn't too disappointed when she realised I'm not dragging you back here permanently."

"She was," I say, only half joking. "But she'll survive."

We fall into a comfortable silence after that. Not quite companionable, not quite settled—but honest. Like something's finally been named between us, even if there's still more road to cover.

And then Cam exhales softly, eyes on the horizon. "I love you, you know."

The truck swerves. Not wildly, but enough to make the tyres groan and the wheel jerk beneath my hands. My heart leaps so fast it slams into my throat.

"What—holy shit." I throw the indicator on and veer towards the shoulder, gravel spitting beneath the tyres as we roll to a stop. Behind us, a car honks loud and long, the shriek of it echoing through the cab.

Cam winces. "Okay, probably should've waited until we weren't on the highway for that, huh?"

I blink at him. My brain's still short-circuiting. "You —fuck, you can't just say that while I'm driving!" I gasp, thumping the gear into Park. "What if I'd crashed? You nearly turned us into a love story and a cautionary tale."

He shrugs, a lopsided smile tugging at his mouth. "Guess I figured it was overdue. Besides, your reactions are never boring."

"Unreal," I mutter, heart hammering like I've just run ten blocks instead of pulled over on the side of a Georgia road. I unclick my seatbelt like a man possessed and launch sideways across the middle console—not gracefully, not smoothly, but with absolutely zero hesitation.

My hands find his jaw, and I kiss him. Hard. Open-mouthed. Desperate.

His beard scrapes my fingers, coarse and warm and familiar as hell. I can feel the faint smile tugging at his lips even as we kiss, like he knows exactly what he's done to me, like he planned this. And God, I don't even care.

The kiss deepens. He groans low in his throat, and I swear I feel the sound vibrate straight through me.

By the time we finally break apart, breathless and flushed, I'm pressed halfway into his seat and gripping the back of his neck like he might disappear if I let go.

"I love you too," I whisper, forehead resting against

his. "You absolute menace. I can't believe you just dropped that on me mid-drive."

His smile softens, and he reaches up to tuck a piece of my hair behind my ear. "You didn't crash."

"You're lucky I didn't explode."

"You're lucky I'm not making a joke about that," he murmurs, lips brushing mine again.

I laugh. Then I kiss him again—slower this time, more sure, like I'm trying to memorise the shape of this new beginning. Because yeah, we've still got a thousand miles to go in so many ways. But this? Us? It's the start of something real. Something that feels terrifying and exhilarating and exactly right.

And okay, yeah—his team's arriving soon, and I should probably let him rest, but all I can think about is how good he looked this morning with my family, how he smiled when I stole his bacon, how he reached for my hand under the table like it was instinct. I just really hope we manage to steal a spare hour or two before duty calls. Because if I don't get to fuck him into the mattress before rugby reclaims him, I might actually combust.

With that in mind, I don't waste time pulling back onto the road to get us to Jacksonville. I drive perhaps a little quicker than I should, but my focus is hard on the road. It has to be. If not, just the thought of being buried deep inside Cam would make me come in my pants.

By the time we reach the hotel, Cam's thigh is bouncing with nervous energy, one hand gripping the handle above the door like it might snap off. He's been mostly quiet since I climbed back into the driver's seat— his "I love you" still echoing somewhere in my chest, louder than any music could compete with.

We pull into the circular drive of the hotel, a classy brick-front place a few blocks from the stadium. He murmurs a distracted "thanks" when I park, but he doesn't move to get out right away. He just sits there, like he's trying to steady himself for what's next.

"You good?" I ask.

He turns to me with a look that makes my blood heat and my heart ache. "Yeah," he says, voice low and a little hoarse. "More than."

We're barely through the lobby when his phone buzzes. He checks it and exhales roughly.

"Coach. They're ten minutes out. Meeting in half an hour." He glances at me with a smirk I feel down to my spine. "So, you know, no pressure."

I don't waste a second. "Check in. Room. Now."

He chuckles, shoulders shaking as he heads to the front desk. I stand there like a man possessed, eyes on him, barely able to keep still. It's not just lust—not this time. It's all the emotion bottled up from the past week: fear, comfort, honesty, exhaustion, and now this—relief. And desire. Always desire.

We take the elevator in silence, but the moment the doors close behind us in his room, I move.

His bag drops to the carpet with a thud. I push him back against the door, the soft click of the lock registering only dimly as I claim his mouth in a kiss that's rougher than I mean it to be.

He moans into it, hands finding my hips, and pulls me in tight. "You gonna do what you said in the truck?"

I grin against his mouth. "Every goddamn word."

I kiss him again, deeper now. His beard scrapes my skin as our mouths slide, tongues tasting, testing, then devouring. The heat between us spikes, thick and urgent. My fingers grip the hem of his shirt, and he lifts his arms to help me peel it off.

"You sure we've got time?" I murmur, even though I'm already walking him backwards towards the bed.

He nods, eyes blazing. "Yeah. I need this."

His honesty slams into me like a freight train.

Cam's never been shy with me, but there's a rawness to this moment. A need to feel grounded. I know what this is. Not just sex. Not just release. It's about connection. About saying *I love you* in a language we both speak fluently.

We fall onto the bed in a tangle of limbs and breath. I

roll over him, kiss my way down his neck, his chest, over every scar and mark I can find. He's solid and strong and so fucking responsive—like every brush of my lips is another thread pulling us tighter.

"Brent," he murmurs, fingers threading into my hair.

"I'm here."

"I want—" He swallows hard, hips rising towards mine. "You. All of you."

My breath catches. "Yeah. Okay. Same."

Clothes disappear. Skin meets skin. There's no time for slow, no room for hesitation—not today. But even in the urgency, there's a softness underneath. My hands are everywhere. So are his. He keeps murmuring my name like it's an anchor. I prep him with care—slow, attentive strokes that have him trembling under my hands. His breath stutters, hips twitching with each glide of my fingers, every quiet word of reassurance I murmur against his neck. His skin is flushed, hot beneath my palms, and when I kiss his nipple before drawing it into my mouth, he lets out a soft, wrecked sound that curls straight down my spine.

When I finally ease into him, it's not just the tight heat that steals the breath from my lungs—it's the way he exhales my name like it's the only thing keeping him tethered. His back arches, legs shifting to pull me deeper, and I still for a second, overwhelmed by the feel of him around me, the moment heavy and raw and entirely ours.

"God," I rasp, forehead pressed to his. "You feel… fuck, you feel incredible."

"So do you," he pants, wrapping his legs around me, urging me deeper.

The rhythm builds—fast and greedy but still laced with something reverent. Every thrust is a vow I don't know how to put into words. Every kiss I press to his shoulder, his neck, the corner of his mouth—it's a promise whispered through touch alone. The heat between us grows fierce, our breaths tangled, our bodies moving in sync like they've always known how to find each other. I don't know how long we stay locked in that rhythm—seconds? lifetimes?—but when he comes, it's with my name broken across his lips. Raw. Shaking. The sound of it unravels me. My spine turns to liquid. My heart feels too big for my chest. And still, I hold on tighter.

I follow a few seconds later, buried deep, vision splintering behind my eyes as everything inside me lets go.

Afterwards, we lie tangled in the mess of sheets and sweat and emotion, Cam's arm draped over my chest, his breath slowing against my shoulder.

"Shit," he mutters after a long pause. "We're gonna need a shower."

"And new sheets," I add, grinning into his hair.

"And maybe an alibi."

I laugh, chest shaking under his weight. "Your coach said in the conference room, not presentable. He should've been more specific."

Cam hums and kisses the side of my neck. "Guess I better get moving."

I nod, but I don't move just yet. Because holding him like this? Feeling his heartbeat slow against mine, his muscles finally relaxing—it's something I'm not ready to let go of.

21

Camden

The locker room smells like liniment, fresh sweat, and nerves.

I'm already half-dressed in my warm-up kit, pacing slow circuits between the benches, pretending I'm calm when my gut's one wrong look from tying itself into a sailor's knot. Most of the lads are in their own pre-match routines—stretching, chatting low, some even joking—but my brain won't switch off.

Because today isn't just a friendly. Today, Brent's family is here.

His parents are *here*.

And I feel like I'm about to be evaluated by the Board of Eternal Boyfriend Viability.

I scrub a hand down my face, exhaling slowly through my nose, and try to focus. Jacksonville's lads are already out on the pitch. We're next. I should be thinking about scrum formations and lineouts. Instead, my brain's shouting, *Don't trip in front of Jo and Lyn*, like that's somehow tactical advice.

I reach for my water bottle, distracted by a ping from my phone on the bench beside it.

> COSMO:
> HOPE YOU WIN TODAY, FUTURE
> BROTHER-IN-LAW 🌝

I blink. "What the fuck—"

Another message flashes up before I can process.

> COSMO:
> TOO SOON? TOO BAD. TOLD THE GROUP
> CHAT.

Well. That explains the other notifications.

A chorus of pings pops up. My phone practically vibrates itself into a coma. I unlock it and see the explosion of chaos in the Love the Game group chat.

> JAY:
> WAIT, WHAT? COSMO. DID I MISS AN
> ANNOUNCEMENT? IS CAMDEN
> CRAWFORD DATING YOUR BROTHER??

> COSMO:
> BITCH, PLEASE. OF COURSE HE IS.
> THEY'RE PERFECT. I KNEW IT.

> JAY:
> WHEN DID THIS HAPPEN?

COSMO:
LET'S JUST SAY I HAVE GREAT INTUITION
AND MATCHMAKING SKILLS THAT RIVAL
OPRAH.

TY:
WAIT. WAIT. YOU KNEW?? HOW?

COSMO:
PSYCHIC GAY ENERGY. ALSO, I MIGHT'VE
INTRODUCED THEM WITHOUT KNOWING
THEY'D ALREADY MET.

JAY:
OKAY, BUT ALSO—CAM, YOU IN
JACKSONVILLE? THERE'S A PANEL NEXT
WEEK. A QUEER ATHLETES TALK, PART
OF THE SPORTS INCLUSION SERIES. IF
YOU'RE STILL AROUND, YOU SHOULD BE
ON IT.

COSMO:
WHAT. WHY DIDN'T YOU ASK ME, JAY?

JAY:
YOU'RE NOT THE INTERNATIONAL RUGBY
HEARTTHROB, COSMO. CHILL.

COSMO:
THAT'S SOME SORT OF DISCRIMINATION.
I'M JUST NOT SURE WHAT.

I snort—actually snort—and sink onto the bench, the weight of nerves briefly replaced by pure hilarity.

"Everything okay?" Rafi asks, nodding at my phone.

I glance up and nod. "Just Cosmo being... Cosmo." He's one of the few people in the group I mention by name—I'm not willing to break anyone's trust.

"You mean Brent's brother? The one from the banana team?"

"Banana Ball," I correct, because apparently I care about the details now. "But no, that's his other brother—actually brothers... the twins. This is the one who plays college hockey."

A small chorus of chuckles rises from the other side of the room. One of the backs calls out, "Tell one of the twins we're still waiting on our signed banana bats."

"Pretty sure that's a euphemism," someone else mutters.

I shake my head and tuck the phone away. *Focus, Crawford.*

But then again, maybe letting myself feel something before a match—nerves and all—isn't such a bad thing. Especially when it's about Brent.

He's up in the stands somewhere. And even though I didn't ask, I know exactly where he'll be sitting—row F, section 208, probably bouncing his leg, trying to act chill for his parents and sister. I can already picture him, one arm slung across the back of the seat, eyes tracking me from the moment I step out onto the field.

And yeah, okay—maybe I like that.

I've been in front of bigger crowds than this. Played on bigger stages. But none of that compares to knowing Brent will be watching.

He saw me go watery-eyed over mashed potatoes a

few nights ago because his mum said she was proud of me for "making her boy so happy."

She meant it. I saw it in her eyes. And it fucking floored me.

"All right, lads," Coach calls, pulling us all into a huddle. "Five minutes."

I zone in, eyes sharp, body twitching to move. There's still time before kick-off, but my brain finally quiets the outside noise—Brent's family, Cosmo's declarations, Jay's surprise panel invite—and drops into focus.

Until I get another ping. Brent this time.

> Brent: FYI, Cosmo asked permission to claim you as family. I said yes. I figured you'd be flattered. Or terrified. Maybe both.

I grin as I type back:

> Me: Terrified. Definitely. Flattered... yeah.

Another ping follows.

> Brent: You've got this, Captain. We're proud of you.

And just like that, the nerves settle into something more solid. I tuck the phone away, stand, and nod towards the tunnel. Just before we leave, my phone buzzes in my boot bag one last time.

> JAY:
> WE'RE FINALIZING THE PANEL FOR
> THURSDAY. YOU IN? WOULD LOVE YOUR
> VOICE ON IT.

I chew the inside of my cheek. It's not the time to decide. But maybe, just maybe, this trip's about more than rugby. Maybe it's about showing up—in more ways than one.

I'll have a think and let him know after the game. I head on out with my team.

Outside, the crowd hums with energy. It's not a packed house, but the vibe is good—lots of families, a decent local turnout, banners for both sides. The sun's high, the heat brutal. The American flag flaps lazily on the sideline.

We jog out to warm-ups, and I glance towards the stands, spotting Brent instantly. Of course I do.

He's standing beside his parents, sunglasses low on his nose, a smirk on his lips. He clocks me and gives a casual little wave. His dad does too. Rachel nudges him, whispering something, and Brent blushes.

I want to die and also kiss him stupid.

Focus, I tell myself again.

But even as we run drills and prep for the match, I

keep checking that row. And every time I do, he's watching. Even when I fumble a catch during warm-up. Even when my water bottle spills down my front. Even when I nearly trip on the sideline marker.

He doesn't laugh. Not really. But I feel the grin from here.

Kick-off approaches. The ref checks in. Line-ups are confirmed.

I adjust my gum shield, nod to the lads, and take my place on the field. Brent's out there watching. It's time to give him something worth seeing.

THE FLORIDA HEAT ISN'T EXACTLY SUBTLE.

By the time the second half kicks off, I'm already half melted inside my boots, and the back of my neck feels like it's baking under the afternoon sun. Still—there's energy in the air. A kind of buzz that's different from a regular league match. It's not do-or-die like the Premiership fixtures back home, but the stakes are still there.

This tour's about outreach. Visibility. Building bridges between the UK rugby scene and the slowly growing sport on American soil. Which means we're not just here to win. We're here to impress.

And impressing is a lot harder to do when your

boyfriend's parents are watching you from the shaded stands and your entire lower back is soaked in sweat.

Brilliant.

The Jacksonville team's solid—rough around the edges, maybe not as tight on formation, but quick and agile. They're hungry in that way teams with something to prove always are. They're giving us a proper game, and I respect the hell out of them for that.

Well—most of them.

There's one player in particular—a back, I think, maybe a centre—who keeps turning his charm up to eleven every time we cross paths. Dark hair, white gumshield, a smile that's probably broken a thousand hearts.

When we shook hands at the pre-match dinner last night, he'd introduced himself as Pen, thrown me a wink, and said something about liking "a man who leads from the front." I thought he was joking.

He's not.

Every time we get into a scrum, or pass within arm's reach, or even lock eyes from across the pitch, he shoots me this grin. Like we're sharing some private joke. Like we've already got history.

It's... disarming.

Not because I'm interested—because I'm very much not—but because it's the kind of attention I'm used to getting from the press or fans. Not from someone in boots and headgear who's meant to be focusing on the bloody game.

At one point, he actually winks at me mid-tackle.

A fucking *wink.*

I blink at him, stunned enough to hesitate half a beat before rejoining the ruck. "Focus," I mutter under my breath, trying to drown out the weird tension building at the base of my skull. I'm a professional. I have a job to do.

Still.

After the next play, I jog over to the wing for a breather and glance at the stands, searching for a distraction—and find it instantly.

Brent.

He's standing, water bottle in hand, sunglasses shoved up in his curls, his shirt sticking to his chest from the heat. He's smiling—properly smiling—and it's aimed at me. It hits like a cold shower and a jolt of caffeine all in one.

I know that smile. It's not about the game. It's for me.

My chest eases, and when the whistle blows for the restart, I'm already rolling my shoulders and settling back into formation, mind cleared, focus sharp.

Screw Pen and his grin. I've already got everything I need.

We pull out a win by five points. It's not a slaughter,

but not nothing either. The final whistle goes, and the whole pitch erupts into applause and claps on the back. The US team's still in high spirits, even after the loss, which only makes me like them more.

As we shake hands again, Pen shoots me one last smile. "If the captaincy doesn't work out," he says, "you've got a backup career in charming the pants off the opposition."

I blink. "You winked at me mid-tackle."

"I was giving you a compliment." He grins.

I laugh, a little incredulous. "That's not how this works."

"Isn't it?" He winks again, then pats me on the shoulder and walks off, still grinning.

I shake my head and jog off the field, muttering, "Bloody Americans."

By the time I reach the tunnel, Brent's waiting—cool bottle of water extended like a gift from the gods, and his All Access pass hanging around his neck. "How do you feel?" he asks as I take a long drink.

"Sweaty. Exhausted." I grin. "Victorious."

He tilts his head. "And marginally flirted with?"

I choke on the water. "You saw that?"

"Cam, the man blew you a kiss during the second half. I was ready to throw a banana at him."

"I didn't notice the kiss."

Brent raises an eyebrow. "Sure."

I narrow my eyes. "Jealous?"

He shrugs, smug. "Nah. I'm the one who gets to help you out of that kit later."

Heat spreads under my skin, and not from the sun. "You're the worst."

"I'm *your* worst."

I shoot him a sidelong glance, warmth blooming behind my ribs. "Yeah. You are."

He walks with me back towards the changing room, fingers brushing mine as we go. "Come on, Captain. Let's get you cleaned up. My parents are already planning dinner. Something about ribs the size of your face."

"And fireworks?"

"Oh, babe." His grin is lethal. "You have no idea."

By the time we're in the locker room, I'm buzzing. Not just from the win—which was tight but satisfying—but from the entire atmosphere. The Jacksonville lads were great sports, and the vibe of the crowd was rowdy in a way that reminded me of home, even if most of them were still figuring out what a scrum was.

But under the adrenaline, there's this dull tug of sadness. I keep thinking about Lachie.

He should be here.

I can almost picture the way he'd be yelling for me across the pitch, calling me out on my positioning or barking reminders from the sideline while stuffing his face with a hot dog. He'd have loved this—mixing with the Americans, cracking jokes about the accents, and calling the Jacksonville captain "mate" until the poor guy started saying it unironically.

I shake off the thought. It's nearly midnight back home, so Lachie's probably fast asleep. Or not. Who knows. I'll shoot him a message later, send over a few pics and let him know how it all went. He'll want the play-by-play whether he admits it or not.

Jay's comment in the group chat lingers too. A panel next week? It sounds like a good opportunity—and I know what it means to show up publicly. Still, I'm cautious. I haven't said yes yet. I'll reach out to my agent later, see what the logistics are. Tomorrow I've got a full day off, and I already plan to spend it with Brent and his family. The day after that, there's training in the morning, but I'm holding the afternoon sacred—for Brent.

Because fuck if I'm not making the most of every minute with him.

As I'm about to put down my phone, I notice a new chat from Jay—not the group chat, but a private message.

JAY:
SO, THIS ISN'T PUBLIC, BUT I'LL BE
THERE NEXT WEEK AS A GUEST.
THOUGHT IT MIGHT BE COOL IF YOU
CAME TO THE PANEL TOO—MY
BOYFRIEND'S ACTUALLY ONE OF THE
SPEAKERS.

My eyes widen. Jay? With a boyfriend? He's barely said a word in the group all year, and definitely never dropped that info.

> ME:
> THAT'S AWESOME. SO, YOU'RE SEEING SOMEONE…
>
> JAY:
> YEAH. FOR A WHILE NOW. NOT PUBLIC, THOUGH. LIKE, I TRUST THE GROUP, BUT HE'S NOT EVEN IN IT. JUST A FEW CLOSE FRIENDS KNOW.
>
> ME:
> TOTALLY GET IT. I WON'T SAY ANYTHING. WHAT'S THE PANEL?
>
> JAY:
> LGBTQ+ VISIBILITY IN MEN'S SPORTS. NEXT THURSDAY. WE'RE DOING IT AT A YOUTH CENTRE NEAR ATLANTA. WASN'T SURE IF YOU WERE STILL IN THE STATES UNTIL COSMO'S BIG FUTURE-BROTHER-IN-LAW ANNOUNCEMENT 😄
>
> ME:
> LOL. YEAH, I'LL BE HERE. HEADING TO TALLAHASSEE NEXT WEEK, BUT NOT UNTIL FRIDAY.
>
> JAY:
> THAT SHOULD WORK OUT. WOULD SERIOUSLY MEAN A LOT IF YOU CAME. YOU AND OTHERS LIKE YOU ARE KINDA THE REASON I STAYED IN SPORTS, YOU KNOW? BACK WHEN YOU CAME OUT— SEEING THAT… IT MATTERED.

I freeze. The words hit hard. I don't even know what to say to that. Warmth floods my chest. It's a strange kind of gratitude, the kind that humbles you.

> ME:
> SHIT, JAY. THAT'S... WOW. THANK YOU.
> I'LL BE THERE. NO WAY I'M MISSING IT.
>
> JAY:
> APPRECIATE YOU, MAN. REALLY. SORRY I
> DON'T TALK MUCH IN THE CHAT—I
> BARELY REMEMBER BEING ADDED. BUT
> WATCHING YOU, WHAT YOU'VE DONE...
> IT'S MEANT MORE THAN I'VE EVER SAID.
> ALSO, I SHOWED MY BOYFRIEND YOUR
> SPEECH FROM LAST YEAR'S EQUALITY
> DINNER. HE CRIED.

I snort softly, shoulders hunching with a weird mix of pride and embarrassment.

> ME:
> GLAD IT HIT HOME. IF I CAN MAKE JUST
> ONE PERSON FEEL LESS ALONE, THAT'S
> THE GOAL, YEAH?
>
> JAY:
> YOU DID. AND YOU STILL ARE.

The screen blurs a bit, and I blink quickly, then type one more message.

> ME:
> THANKS, JAY. TRULY. I'LL SEE YOU
> THERE.

I set the phone down, my chest full and tight in a way that feels... good. Like something is settling into place. Like maybe all this—the pressure, the spotlight, the fear—has been worth it.

And hell, maybe that's why I came out in the first place. For more than myself. For guys like Jay. For the next generation.

I step out of the locker room and find Brent waiting just outside the media area, laughing at something one of the press coordinators says. He spots me instantly, and that grin softens.

This is why I keep going.

This is what I'm playing for.

The media have been ushered back out to the field for the post-match photo ops with the team. It's a PR thing. "Grow the sport, show off the international camaraderie," and all that. Still, I don't mind. Our opponents were solid players and good guys. We'd even all shared a buffet dinner last night at a hotel conference room. It had been loud, chaotic, and surprisingly fun. I'd spent most of it trying to keep up with the jokes and the low-key trash talk.

And yeah... Pen.

Pen is back again. Number 14. American. Fast as hell. And apparently now the king of flirt. He'd been subtle at dinner. A few extra-long glances. A wink when I refilled my drink. A low laugh when I accidentally dropped my fork. But now? Now, it's like he's on a damn mission.

He leans in when we pose for the team photos, his arm brushing mine. "That was a hell of a try, Crawford."

"Thanks," I reply, trying not to look like I've swallowed my tongue.

"You always move like that? Or were you just showing off for me?"

Jesus Christ.

I glance towards the edge of the field where Brent stands, talking to one of the Seagulls staff who tagged along on the trip. He's in sunglasses, his tattooed arms crossed over his chest, posture relaxed, mouth curved into that smug, unreadable half-smile.

Fuck. He's seen this.

Pen follows my gaze and stills. "The fuck?" he mutters. Then, louder, he hollers, "Brent Parks?"

Brent, who clearly didn't catch the first part, lifts his chin, eyes narrowing slightly as he tries to place him. Then his brows shoot up.

"No fucking way. Luke Penby?"

Pen—or apparently Luke—grins wide. "The hell are you doing here, man? The twins here?"

"Nah," Brent says, stepping closer, shaking his head in disbelief. "Cal and Tony have a schedule clash. I can't believe you're here. The twins always said you were a menace. Looks like that hasn't changed."

Pen shrugs one shoulder. "I was thirteen and high on Gatorade most of the time."

Then, like it's nothing, like it's just Tuesday, he smirks and says, "Damn, Brent. You're hot AF now."

And that's about all I need to hear.

I step forwards and wrap an arm around Brent's waist, yanking him flush to my side with a possessiveness I don't bother hiding. "Easy there, mate."

Brent laughs under his breath but leans into me, his body warm against mine. "Cam," he murmurs. "You all right?"

"Nope," I mutter. "You've got ex–boy-band energy staring at you like he wants dessert, and I'm not in the mood to share."

Pen raises both hands, grin widening. "Hey, no judgement. Just didn't realise you were already taken."

"I'm not 'taken,'" I say, before adding, "I'm very much involved. Big difference."

Brent huffs out a laugh. "That's splitting hairs."

"Not when it comes to this," I say quietly, meeting his eyes.

Pen whistles low. "Damn. Okay. Got it."

We finish up the photos—mercifully without more flirt-flashbombs—and head off the pitch. Brent's hand brushes mine once, then finds it completely. Fingers threaded. Just like that, I feel grounded again.

He squeezes. "You okay?"

I nod once. "Yeah." But my heart's still racing.

Not because of Pen. Not because of the game. But because of this. Of him. Of the way one look from Brent calms the rush of everything else. Like a grounding wire straight to my chest.

He's only here a few more days before he heads back to the UK. Back to his studio. His life. And yeah, I'll be training, travelling, doing team press, focused on tour matches... but the thought of not seeing him? Not feeling the weight of his hand in mine, the steadiness of his voice late at night?

It's going to be shit.

Two weeks apart isn't forever. But when you've finally found something—someone—that fits in all the ways you didn't realise you were missing, even a day feels too long. I squeeze his hand tighter and tell myself I've got this.

Because loving someone like him? Yeah. That's worth every mile in between.

22

Brent

Ten days. That's how long it's been since I kissed Camden goodbye at the hotel in Tallahassee and watched him disappear into the lobby to be with his team. Ten days since I drove back to Savannah with my heart all out of rhythm, the phantom heat of his kiss still clinging to my mouth. Ten days of mornings without him and evenings where the quiet of my flat stretches too wide, too hollow.

Which is ridiculous, really. I survived twenty-nine years without Camden Crawford in my life. But now? After weeks of having him in my bed, in my space, wrapped around me like he belonged there? Ten days feels like ten fucking months.

And the bastard's having a good time.

Don't get me wrong—it's well earned. His second

game in the States went brilliantly from everything I've heard. His team won, the crowd was wild, and he even managed to dodge the press shitstorm that had been hounding him before. The photos I've seen—sent by my mom, no less—show him sweaty, smiling, bruised, and surrounded by fans like a goddamn local hero.

Then came the panel.

Apparently, one of the guys in his group chat asked him along for a queer sports panel. Camden joined, got loud about visibility in pro sports, and my inbox exploded. Cosmo has not shut up about it.

"Why didn't I get to be on the panel?" he grumbled the other day. "I have opinions. I've done stuff. Brent, tell your boyfriend he owes me a platform."

"You're still in diapers," I replied. "You've got plenty of time to be loud and famous."

"Ugh. You're just bitter you're missing it all."

Okay, so maybe I was.

Back here in Exeter, life feels like it's trudging forwards. The shop's running fine—Carrie's keeping the admin tight, and I've got a new apprentice coming in next week. Clients are happy. My sketchbook's full.

And yet.

Camden's not here.

He's not hunched on my sofa, watching crap TV and pretending he's not the world's worst liar when I catch him staring. He's not hogging the covers or kicking my calves in his sleep or sneaking kisses behind my ear like he's not six foot two and made of granite.

So yeah. It kind of sucks.

The upside? One more game.

The final friendly is today—in Atlanta. It's not televised, but I've got the stream booted up on my laptop, and my Wi-Fi has never been under more pressure. My folks are there, so are the twins, and Cosmo managed to make it after wrapping up some training stuff early. They all met up with Cam beforehand.

Apparently, Pen was there too.

That particular bit of information had been dropped casually—too casually—by Camden when he called me twenty minutes ago from the locker room.

"You're watching?"

"Obviously."

"I'll give you a sign."

"What kind of sign?"

"A good one. You'll know."

Then, like it was an afterthought: "Oh, and Pen rocked up. Said he was in town and figured he'd stop by to take in the game."

I'd groaned. Loudly.

"He's just watching. Don't worry."

"I'm not worried."

Cam had laughed. "You're so worried."

"I'm not. Just... he's a flirt."

"He's also not the guy I left pressed up against a hotel headboard ten days ago," Cam said. "That was you. You win."

Jesus.

The locker room noise had picked up, muffling whatever smartass thing I might've said next. Cam told me he had to go but promised to text after.

Now, I sit cross-legged on the couch, my coffee cold on the table, and my laptop perched on a stack of coasters as the match timer counts down. And then I see him. Camden runs out with the team, loose and powerful, his kit clinging to sweat-dampened muscles like sin.

He doesn't look for the camera, but as they pan down the line-up, his fingers flash a quick sign—two taps over his heart, then a subtle salute.

Fucking hell. That's for me.

I grin like a total idiot and reach for my mug.

The game kicks off, and it's everything I hoped for. Exeter's playing sharp, aggressive, fast. Camden's dominant in the scrum, a fucking wall of force, and despite the friendly nature of the match, he's not holding back.

My phone buzzes with a message from Cosmo.

Cosmo: Your boyfriend is terrifying. He just flattened a guy like a lawnmower.

Me: I taught him that.

Cosmo: Liar.

Me: Okay, fine. But I'll take credit anyway.

I glance back at the screen, and for a moment, I just breathe. Camden's out there. My boyfriend. My chaotic, sweet, brooding, secretly romantic boyfriend.

Yeah, the last ten days have been lonely. But watching him like this—seeing him shine, doing what he loves—it's worth it.

Still, I can't wait to have him back.

My phone buzzes again with a message from Cosmo a little while later.

Cosmo: Don't freak out, but...

Fucking hell. If a sentence has ever been designed to induce an instant cardiac arrest, it's that.

I click the attachment, and my gut twists.

It's a photo—no, two. Both snapped outside the stadium, obviously pregame one.

A second message comes through. This time, it's a link.

One of them shows Camden in his Exeter travel kit, laughing at something Pen says. Innocent enough—until you notice Pen's arm slung around Cam's shoulders like they're best mates from way back.

The second photo? Pen's hand is on Cam's ass.

My *boyfriend's* ass.

I inhale sharply, pulse rocketing. Not because I think Cam's done anything wrong. I trust him. I do. But it's not just the photos. It's the text beneath them.

"Rugby's most low-key out player seems to be making up for lost time. Is tighthead Camden Crawford sampling the American delights on tour? First spotted with a mystery man before departing the UK, now seen getting friendly with Jacksonville player Luke Penby. The Seagull flies free, it seems."

My mouth goes dry. I barely process the rest—some rehashed bullshit about Cam's coming out years ago, how he's never discussed his dating life, a quote from some old coach about how Cam "leads with discipline."

Fuck that. Fuck them. And fuck whatever bottom-feeding opportunist thinks it's okay to speculate about someone's sex life because they're queer and happen to be in proximity to another man.

I blink at the screen, then drag my hand over my face. Cam's going to be so pissed off. He hates this kind of attention. Loathes the spotlight unless it's about the damn game. Which it never is, not really. Not with queer

athletes. We're either symbols or scandals. Never just...
people.

I check the clock. Halftime.

Please, please, don't let him have seen this.

If he's smart—and he is—he won't check his socials during the break. Still, I can't stop the gnawing frustration curling in my gut. I head for the fridge and grab myself a beer. My crappy coffee is definitely not going to cut it.

I try to focus on the stream, but my chest won't stop tightening. The second half's starting now, and all I can think about is how fast the internet moves. How easily this shit spreads. There are already comments—tweets, quote tweets, tags.

Then another alert.

Different account.

Different headline.

"Meet Camden Crawford's Mystery Man"

This one includes a blurry cropped photo of me and Cam—taken God knows when—walking down the street. It must've been from one of those few days before we left for the States. His hand is low on my back. My face is half shadowed, but someone's put the pieces together, no doubt the asshole who stopped by the studio a few weeks back.

"American. Tattoo artist. Source claims his name is

Brent Parkinson. Could Cam be collecting American conquests?"

I rub my eyes with the heels of my hands. Fucking hell. They've named me—well, kinda.

This is it. I've officially become the thing Cam wanted to avoid: a distraction.

Even if Cam doesn't see it right away, someone on the team will. Or his coach. Or worse, one of the shitty tabloids back here, where they'll clickbait the whole damn narrative.

God, I wish I was there right now. I want to be at the stadium, to see him walk off that field and into my arms so I can say, *"I know this is a mess, but I'm here."*

But instead, I'm halfway across the fucking world, staring at my screen while his life gets picked apart by people who don't know the first thing about him.

Another buzz.

Another headline.

I close the app before I can read it fully. Just seeing the name-drop of the guy who sold his story a few years back is enough to churn my gut.

Instead, I turn back to the match, forcing myself to focus. He's out there playing. Still leading. Still driving his team forwards with every ounce of himself. His form's tight, and he's focused. But something in his shoulders looks tense now. His jaw's locked up.

Has he seen it?

Maybe... maybe I'm spiralling.

I mean, it's a couple of pictures. Gossip sites thrive on drama, yeah, but the attention span of the internet is measured in hours. And honestly, maybe the whole "Cam gets around" headline won't gain as much traction as I think. Most people will forget it by morning. Maybe the media cycle will move on.

Still.

Cam won't.

Even if it's just a whisper, he'll hear it like a scream. He's private, guarded, and careful as hell about his reputation—and this? This isn't just a footnote. It's personal.

I sigh and swipe my palm down my face, pacing my small flat like it'll help. The light from the laptop screen flickers as the commentators talk stats and substitutions, and I can't help but bite my lip hard enough to taste blood.

"Hold it together," I mutter to myself. "He needs you steady. Not losing your shit." But it's easier said than done. Because Cam, he means too fucking much. And the second this game ends, he's going to walk into a media storm. And I won't be there to block the wind.

It's less than forty-five minutes after the game that Cam calls me. I scramble for my phone so fast it nearly launches off the edge of the counter. "Cam?" I answer breathlessly, like I hadn't been pacing the entire sitting room since the final whistle.

He doesn't start with hello, just "Hey. You seen the bullshit?"

I freeze. My spine goes rigid. "Uh. Yeah. Cosmo sent it."

A beat of silence follows, and my stomach twists.

Then Cam huffs out a laugh. "Yeah, well, Pen's got grabby hands and zero brain-to-body filter. He smacked my ass for luck. It wasn't a thing."

"You sure?" My voice is low, wary, careful. Not because I doubt him, but because I've seen how this stuff gets out of control.

He makes a noise halfway between a scoff and a sigh. "My boyfriend"—the word sends a ripple through my chest—"is in England. Not Jacksonville. Not named Pen. And most importantly, my boyfriend's not a clueless flirt who calls his own mum 'bro.' So yeah. I'm sure."

My chest tightens. Not in panic this time—but relief. I pinch the bridge of my nose and let out a breath I didn't realise I'd been holding.

"I don't give a shit about any of it," he says firmly. "The photo. The headline. The innuendo. Your parents were standing ten feet away when it happened. They saw it. They laughed." He pauses, voice softening. "They know I'm not stepping out on you, Brent. And that's all I care about."

My throat thickens. "Yeah," I murmur. "I guess I was just worried. Not about trust. Just... you dealing with it all. Alone."

"I wasn't alone. Not really," he says quietly. "I had your voice in my ear as soon as I read the BS." A pause. Then he says, "And I got you now."

I lean back against the counter, eyes stinging, heart pounding. *Jesus. This man.*

"Listen," he says. "I've got a final media spot in twenty minutes. Just local stuff—wrap-up for the tour. If you're okay with it, I'm going to mention you."

I blink. "Mention me?"

"Yeah. I was going to say something vague about someone waiting back home, but... screw that. If they're going to talk about you, they can at least get your name right."

My stomach swoops. "You sure?"

"I'm sure. You're not a rumour. You're real. And I'm not hiding that."

The air leaves me in a rush. "Camden," I breathe. "You're gonna kill me."

He chuckles, low and warm. "Just trying to keep things interesting."

Silence laps between us for a moment—soft, full, heavy with something tender and whole.

"I love you," I say, because I need to. Because I can.

"I love you too," he replies, quiet and sure. "And I'll call you after."

Then he hangs up, and I stand here alone in my kitchen with the widest grin on my face and the giddy weight of something that feels a hell of a lot like peace pressing deep into my chest.

Let the headlines say what they want. I've got the truth. And the truth is—I'm his.

It's well past my bedtime when my phone vibrates on the nightstand.

> Camden: You should be asleep. But if not… [link]

My breath catches. I sit up straighter in bed, brushing crusted sleep from my eyes as I tap the link. It takes me to a local US sports outlet's page, already updated with the interview he did barely an hour or so ago. My heart skitters.

The video loads with the buzz of background chatter

and stadium noise fading into a calm hush as the interview begins. Cam's seated on a low bench, shoulders broad and relaxed, still in his branded polo shirt. The camera picks up the soft glisten of sweat on his collarbone and the angry bruise under one eye that I instantly want to kiss better.

The interviewer, a neatly dressed local anchor with a crisp Southern lilt, offers a smile as she begins. "Camden Crawford. Tighthead prop for Exeter Seagulls, British international, and—after today—a real crowd pleaser here in the States. How's the tour been treating you?"

Cam tips his head, smile crooked. "It's been brilliant. Different, but brilliant. The fans, the players we've met, the energy—it's been unreal. I think we've all enjoyed shining a little light on the sport over here."

"Three friendlies, three wins, one a close one," the interviewer counts off. "Not bad for an international exhibition series."

Cam chuckles. "We'll take it. More importantly, it's been about building community and interest. Rugby's a sport that thrives on heart, and it's been great sharing that with new faces."

The interviewer leans forwards slightly, interest sharpening. "And speaking of heart... I've got to ask. There's been quite a bit of social buzz the last few days. Rumours of a certain someone? An American someone?"

Cam shifts slightly, the smile on his face morphing—

softer, more real. "Yeah. There is someone. My boyfriend, actually."

My breath catches as I watch.

Cam continues, his voice level. "He's American but lives in England full-time. He flew out with me for a bit of the tour—got to show me what a real Fourth of July looks like."

"You mean fireworks and grilled everything?"

Cam laughs. "Exactly. And family. A lot of loud, welcoming, amazing family."

The interviewer's grin widens. "Is that the first time you've shared that publicly? About having a boyfriend?"

Cam nods once. "Yeah. It is. But... I'm proud of him. Of us. He's been a huge support—quietly, without ever asking for recognition. That's just the kind of man he is."

I swipe a hand across my face, heart doing weird backflips.

"Will we get to know who he is?" the interviewer prods gently.

Cam doesn't falter, but his expression shifts—protective now. "This is the only time I'll be speaking about my personal life publicly. While we're not hiding, Brent Parks and I are also not making a spectacle of our relationship. He's not in the industry. I want the focus to stay on the game, on my team. But he's a big part of my life. And that matters too."

There's a pause. The interviewer nods with quiet respect. "Understood. I have to say, it's refreshing to see an athlete so grounded. What's next for you?"

Cam leans back slightly, confidence tempered by fatigue. "Recovery first. Then back to Exeter. We've got our sights on next season already. A bit of downtime, but not much. Still... I'll be visiting here again, I reckon. Got a few good reasons to."

I let out a shaky breath, eyes stinging a little. Because damn if this man isn't everything.

The interviewer finishes with a handshake. "We'll be watching, Camden. And I'm sure your fans on both sides of the Atlantic will be too."

As the screen fades out, I just sit here, phone limp in my hand, heart too full to move. In three days, Camden will be back.

And I've never wanted anything more than to hold him again and tell him exactly how proud I am.

Fuck, I can't wait.

23

Camden

The bell over the door jingles as I step into Black Salt Ink, the sound oddly comforting despite the nerves buzzing just beneath my skin.

Christy looks up from the front desk, her knowing grin already in place. "You're early," she says, her voice pitched low with amusement. "That alias you gave me was shit, by the way."

I smirk and step fully into the shop, the air thick with antiseptic and the low hum of something warm and familiar. "Figured it wouldn't fool you."

She flicks her gaze towards the back, chin lifting. "He's in his room. Head down. Completely oblivious."

Perfect.

I nod, give her a grateful look, and move past the waiting area, every step somehow quieter than usual—

despite the pounding of my heart. I haven't seen him in nearly two weeks, and somehow, that feels both ridiculous and monumental. The US tour was short by professional standards. But in Brent-time? It's felt like a fucking decade.

I pause at the threshold of his workroom.

The door's open, the late-morning light slanting in through the frosted window and catching in the strands of his messy dark hair. He's seated at his drafting desk, sleeves pushed up, head tilted slightly as he sketches something I can't see. His lip ring catches the light every time he draws it between his teeth, something he does when he's really focused. He's wearing a charcoal T-shirt that clings lovingly to the planes of his back, stretched just enough that I catch the outline of his shoulder blades when he moves.

God, I missed him.

There's a tenderness in the moment, the way his brow is furrowed in concentration, the pencil in his hand moving with quick, practiced ease. It's a side of him I've only recently come to know—the artist at work, utterly absorbed and stunningly unaware of how beautiful he looks when he's thinking.

I lean against the doorframe, letting the seconds stretch.

This—being here, watching him in his element—is

worth every lie I told to get here early. I haven't even told my brother I landed this morning, let alone Brent. But the way my chest swells just standing in this doorway, the way my mouth aches from holding back a grin... it was the right call.

Finally, he senses something. Maybe the shift in light. Or just that inexplicable gut feeling that someone's watching.

He glances up, blinking once, then twice, like he doesn't quite believe what he's seeing.

"Cam?" His voice is soft, rough with surprise.

I shrug one shoulder, unable to keep the grin off my face. "Thought I'd drop in. You know, get some work done. Figured I'd go with a fake name and everything. Keep you on your toes."

Brent's chair scrapes back as he rises, that dazed look on his face melting into something warmer. Something breathtaking. "You absolute bastard," he says—but he's smiling like he might kiss me into next week.

I open my arms just in time to catch him.

He collides into me, arms banding around my back, the scent of ink and soap and Brent flooding my senses. His unshaven face lightly scrapes my jaw as he buries his face against my neck, and I exhale like I've been holding my breath since the plane took off from Atlanta.

"Missed me?" I murmur, voice low, amused.

"Like hell," he says against my throat, his hands splaying across my back, fingers digging in like he's making sure I'm really here. "You're early."

"Couldn't stay away." I run my fingers through the back of his hair, letting them tangle in those dark strands. "Three weeks before training starts. I plan to spend every damn second I can with you."

He pulls back just enough to look at me, eyes roving over my face like he's committing every line to memory. "You should've told me. I would've booked the day off."

"Would've ruined the surprise."

Brent's eyes narrow slightly, like he's pretending to be annoyed, but the curve of his mouth betrays him. "You're lucky you're hot."

I kiss him.

There's no fanfare. No hesitation. Just lips meeting lips with the kind of ache that comes from too much distance and not enough time. His hand slides to the back of my neck, anchoring me to him as he deepens it— tongue sliding along mine, teeth grazing my lower lip just enough to make my knees threaten to give.

"Christ," he breathes when we part. "You taste like airport coffee."

"Still gonna make out with me?"

"Obviously."

We're both grinning now, and something settles in

my chest—heavy in a good way. Like a weight I've been carrying has finally been set down.

Brent pulls me fully into the room, closing the door behind me with a quiet click. "You serious about that tattoo session? Or was this whole thing just an excuse to ambush me?"

"Why not both?" I stretch my arms overhead and drop into the client chair. "But yeah. If you're game. I've got time today."

Brent circles me, slow and considering. "I've got some time in a couple of hours. I've an appointment due."

I shoot him a shit-eating grin. "Make that now since I'm your next booking." I arch my brow, totally pleased with myself.

He snorts out a laugh. "Christy set that up? You're Brian?"

I nod, watching him like I haven't had a proper drink in days. "Maybe. I can be charming when I need to be."

"Ain't that the truth."

"So, this sleeve we've been hashing out...," I begin, letting my voice trail off just enough to watch the way Brent's eyes flick up from my arm to my face. His lips twitch, and that damn lip ring catches the light like it knows it's a weapon.

He leans in slightly, fingers brushing my forearm

with a featherlight touch. "You mean the one that brought you striding into my shop, all growl and business, working out if I was good enough?"

"You being good enough was never an issue," I retort, not even trying to hide my grin.

"Mm-hmm." He tilts his head, sketchbook still in one hand. "You were already plotting how to get in my pants."

"Debatable," I say, though I'm fully grinning now. "But not inaccurate."

Brent sets his sketchbook down and moves between my knees, resting his palms on my thighs. The look he gives me is pure mischief with a dash of fondness that tightens something warm in my chest.

"Then let's make this full circle, Captain," he says. "Shirt off. Let me see what I've got to work with."

The way his voice dips on that last word shouldn't be legal. My breath catches despite myself, and I huff out a laugh as I strip off my tee and toss it onto the nearby chair. I sit up straighter under his gaze, chest bare, muscles already reacting to the attention.

He drops his gaze, sweeping over my right arm—the completed piece he didn't ink—and then to the blank canvas of my left shoulder and bicep. His fingers skim my skin, mapping the areas we've talked about. There's reverence in the way he touches me now, not just as an artist or a lover, but as someone who knows what this means to me.

"I've been thinking about starting up near your collarbone," he murmurs, voice suddenly all focus. "Using that shoulder swell to anchor the first visual weight. Flowing around the deltoid, echoing the structure of the other side without being a copy. Balance without mirroring."

God, he's sexy when he talks shop.

I nod, swallowing. "Sounds good."

"I'm still not completely sure about the final transitions past your elbow, but we'll talk about it, and I'll sketch it out later this week," he says, thumb brushing along the top of my pec absently, like he doesn't even realise he's touching me. "But I've got the outlines ready. If we start today, we can rough in the core flow and get the stencil down."

"You always this smooth when you seduce your clients?" I ask, voice gruffer than I mean it to be.

Brent smirks, stepping back. "Only the ones I'm dating. And love stupidly much."

My chest pulls tight, heat washing through me in a way that's got nothing to do with the temperature of the shop.

"Lucky me," I manage.

"Luck had nothing to do with it," he says, already

turning towards his station. "You barged into my shop with forearms like artillery and the grumpiest goddamn frown I've ever seen. I was doomed from day one."

I laugh and lean back in the chair, watching the way he moves—sure, graceful, the way he always is when he's in his space. It hits me then, not for the first time, how much I missed him over these last couple of weeks. And how fucking glad I am to be here now.

Because this? This feels like home.

Even with the needles, and the ink, and the low buzz of the machine warming up behind me—this is where I want to be.

With him.

And if I have to endure a few hours of pain and his smug teasing to make art that stays with me forever? Hell, sign me up. Especially if I get to feel his hands on me the entire time.

Brent flips the stool around with a practiced flick of his foot and rolls it into position beside the chair. "All right, Captain Crawford. Get comfortable."

I chuckle low in my throat. "You say that like you don't enjoy bossing me around."

His lips twitch as he pulls on his gloves. "Oh, I do. But only because you look like sin when you listen."

I stretch back into the curve of the chair like I own

the damn place. "So what you're saying is I'm your favourite client."

He taps the tray beside him and checks the fresh needle cartridge. "I didn't say that."

I shoot him a look.

He grins as he preps my skin. "But yes. Obviously."

After he's applied the stencil, the machine hums to life, a sharp little buzz that crawls over my skin before he's even touched me. He leans forwards, one gloved hand steadying my arm, the other guiding the machine towards the top of my shoulder.

"You ready?" he asks, all teasing gone from his voice.

I nod, already braced. Then the first sting hits. Hot, precise, a slow burn as the needle drags that fine black line into the muscle of my shoulder. It's pain, but it's also something else. Something grounding. It pins me here, in this chair, in this room—with him.

Brent's breath is steady as he works, his touch confident. His body leans in just enough that I catch the scent of his cologne—something warm and woody and definitely unfair. The sleeves of his T-shirt ride up just a little, exposing strong forearms dusted with ink. I focus on that. On him.

"You know," I murmur after a minute, "this is how all this started."

He huffs out a laugh, eyes not leaving the line he's

pulling. "Me stabbing you? I thought I only did that in my head."

I grin. "Me coming in here to talk tattoos and walking out with a crush I tried to convince myself I didn't have."

He glances up just briefly, that damn lip ring caught between his teeth. "How'd that work out for you?"

"Terribly," I say. "I fell. Hard. Fast. Full tilt."

There's a beat of silence, soft and charged. His gaze flicks up again, warmer this time. "Yeah," he says quietly. "Me too."

The machine buzzes on. He leans closer as he works the curve of the design around my bicep, thumb dragging gently across the skin as he wipes excess ink. I flinch slightly at the contact, but not from pain. From heat.

The whole damn room feels hotter with him this close. My skin's singing—not just from the needle, but from the way his fingers settle on me with something just shy of reverence.

"You're doing good," he murmurs. "Better than most. Some big guys get cocky and end up squirming like toddlers."

"Rugby players don't squirm," I shoot back.

He tilts his head. "You sure about that? 'Cause I've seen you post-match. You whine when you're sore."

"Lie," I mutter, even though he's not wrong.

"You're lucky you're cute."

"I'm lucky?" I say, voice catching as he starts a new stretch of linework just under my arm. "I'm the one getting art and innuendo."

"And a free show," he adds. "You've been staring at my mouth for ten minutes."

"Don't flatter yourself."

He just smirks.

The session flows from there—me drifting in and out of conversation, him focused and maddeningly hot while he works. And somehow, the pain of the tattoo becomes background noise compared to the pulse in my blood every time his fingers brush too close to my ribs.

When he finally lifts the needle, stretches his back, and murmurs, "Break time," I'm both disappointed and relieved.

He leans over me again, a paper towel in one hand, the other braced on the headrest near my temple. "Want water?" he asks softly.

"No. I want you."

He blinks.

"After the session," I amend quickly, voice low.

His grin returns, slow and wicked. "Good. Because I've got plans."

And just like that, I feel the hum of anticipation slide right under my skin—just like his ink.

Brent barely finishes wiping down the ink before I'm already shifting in the chair, wound tighter than a goddamn drum. His voice—normally smooth and low—is in full professional mode as he starts rattling off post-ink care instructions.

"You'll need to wash it gently tonight. No direct sunlight, no—"

"I swear to God," I cut in, sitting up slowly, the muscles across my chest and arm pulling, "if you don't stop talking and kiss me, I'm going to lose my mind."

Brent's mouth quirks. That lip ring catches the light, and I'm done.

"You know," he says, pulling off his gloves, "I usually like to be courted before being jumped."

I roll my eyes and stand, crowding into his space. "You courted me with needles and filthy grins. That's on you."

He snorts a laugh, but it dies the second I press in, our bodies aligning like magnets with unfinished business. One of his hands finds my waist. The other skims low. Too low. And I almost moan.

But the sharp clang of the front doorbell cuts through the haze.

Brent stills, groaning quietly. "Christy's out front."

I pull back a breath, only enough to whisper, "So?"

"So, unless you want an audience...." His voice is gravel now. His restraint is admirable, but unnecessary.

"Wouldn't be the first time I've bitten back a noise," I say. "But you make it bloody difficult."

Brent mutters something under his breath that sounds like "You're going to be the death of me" before grabbing my hand. He drags me through the hallway and out into the reception area like a man on a mission. "I'm done for the day!" he calls.

Christy looks up from the desk, barely hiding her smirk. "Oh? That wouldn't have anything to do with your mystery client turning out to be your boyfriend, would it?"

Brent doesn't stop walking.

"It's a good job I cleared your schedule, hey, boss?" she calls after us, clearly enjoying herself.

He flips her a casual two-finger salute. "Remind me to give you a raise."

I'm still laughing as the door swings shut behind us. The sunlight hits my fresh ink—stinging faintly beneath the wrap—but I barely feel it. All I feel is him.

Brent lives a short walk from the studio, and we take it fast. My legs eat up the distance, driven entirely by need. I've never been this impatient to get someone alone before. And maybe it's not just sex. Maybe it's the closeness. The hunger. The magnetic pull of being apart too long.

The second the door closes behind us, I spin him around, press him against it, and kiss the breath out of both of us.

His hands go to my waist, pulling me in. I shove my fingers into his hair, tasting the salt of his skin, his breath, the low groan in his throat that sets off a chain reaction in mine.

He tastes like home.

"I missed you," I say against his mouth, my voice rough.

"I can tell." He palms my arse. "I could feel you staring at me the whole damn session."

I grin into his mouth. "Not my fault your stupid sexy face makes it hard to focus."

His laugh rumbles through my chest, hot and low. Then, before I can blink, he hitches his arms under my thighs and lifts me.

"Brent!" I bark out, half shocked, half thrilled, arms flailing for a second before I lock them around his shoulders. "Jesus, are you trying to rupture something?"

He grunts under his breath, adjusting his grip, and keeps walking—like I don't weigh nearly two and a half stone more than him.

"You weigh less than the tattoo chair," he says, breath

warm against my ear. "And I move that solo every morning."

"You are so full of shit," I laugh, tightening my grip around his neck as my back hits the hallway wall for a second—his mouth crashing into mine like he's making a point. It's fast, filthy, and God, I want more.

"You think I can't handle you?" he murmurs against my lips.

I snort, breathless. "I think if you throw your back out mid-thrust, it'll kill the vibe."

"Then I'll just get creative," he growls, tightening his grip with a cocky smile and carrying me the rest of the way with purpose. His shoulders strain under my hands, muscles flexing like he's showing off.

Maybe he is.

And maybe I like it.

When he kicks open the bedroom door and half drops me onto the mattress, I bounce once—legs splayed, chest rising—and he's on me before I can so much as blink. Hands everywhere. Mouth dragging a trail down my jaw like I'm his reward for surviving two weeks apart.

"You're a menace," I murmur, fingers sliding under his shirt, feeling the warmth of his skin, the cut of his ribs.

Brent looks at me, eyes dark with something wicked. "You say that like you don't want more."

I grin, tugging him in. "I want everything."

And I mean it.

Brent watches me for a beat, gaze roaming my face like he's memorising the moment. Then his hands lift, fingers ghosting over my hips, slipping under the hem of my T-shirt like he's asking permission with the touch alone.

"You're sure?" he murmurs, voice low and almost reverent. "It's been a long day, and I know your arm's—"

I kiss him before he can finish. Not gentle, not patient—just full-on, mouth to mouth, tongue sweeping his bottom lip until he opens to me. His groan is immediate, muffled but hungry, and suddenly we're moving together again—uncoiling tension that's been wound too tight for two weeks.

"I don't care about my arm," I pant when we break apart. "I just want you."

His pupils blow wide at that, and I swear I can feel the moment he gives in completely. We fumble our way out of shirts, jeans kicked off in haste, our mouths barely leaving each other for more than a breath or two.

When we finally fall back onto the bed—him over me, skin to skin—everything goes soft and sharp at the same time. I run my hands along his back, feeling the curve of his spine and the shiver that races through him when I drag my fingertips lightly up to his nape.

Brent kisses me again, slower this time, almost careful—like we're both trying to savour every second. His hands are everywhere, brushing the curve of my hip, cupping my jaw, sliding across my chest in a way that sends heat spiralling through my gut.

We move together in a rhythm that feels familiar now—like we've been doing this forever. There's no awkwardness. No nerves. Just... us. Tangled up in each other and breathing the same air.

I arch up, his name a whisper against the curve of his ear, and he responds by mouthing down the line of my throat, across my collarbone, and lower—his hands warm and grounding on my sides, steady even as everything inside me turns molten.

When I groan his name, he lifts his head just enough to meet my eyes. There's heat there, yes, but something else too. Something solid, grounded, and real.

"I really missed you," he says simply, voice rough and full of meaning.

I wrap my arms around him, hauling him back down so we're chest to chest, heart to heart. "I missed you too," I murmur, and the words taste like truth on my tongue.

We move slowly after that, letting the weight of our bodies and the intimacy of skin-on-skin speak louder than anything else. There's no need to rush—just the need to feel, to be felt, to lose ourselves in each other after being apart.

Brent's hips press into mine, deliberate, claiming. His mouth finds the side of my throat, warm lips dragging over the edge of my jaw before he bites—not hard, just enough to make me gasp. I slide my hands down his back, feeling the tension in his shoulders, the coiled restraint in the way he holds himself. It makes me ache in the best way.

He lifts his head, eyes burning into mine, and there's something wordless in the look we share. His fingers trail down my chest, teasing with maddening precision, grazing over sensitive skin like he's memorised every spot that makes me squirm. And maybe he has. God, maybe he always has.

When he finally pushes in—slow and sure—I suck in a breath that punches straight through my chest. Not just from the stretch or the burn, but from the overwhelming rightness of it. The press of him inside me, the weight of his body above mine—it's not just sex. It's something deeper. We're not just skin to skin. We're soul to soul. And everything in me opens up to let him in.

Brent leans down, forehead to mine, our noses brushing. We breathe the same air, locked together in a rhythm that's slow, unhurried, yet somehow still urgent with everything we haven't been able to say in the last two weeks.

We move together like a promise—tight, deliberate, relentless. Every thrust rewrites a memory. Every kiss is a vow. His lips find mine again and again, greedy and reverent, and I hold on to him like he's the only thing anchoring me to the moment.

And maybe he is.

It's not long. I wish it were longer. What I really wish is that I weren't this wrecked from travel, my body this keyed up from being away. But my control slips fast and hard, and when I come, it's with a bitten-off curse and my face buried in his shoulder. Brent follows a beat later, hips jerking, fingers bruising my waist as he spills into me with a groan that makes my toes curl.

Afterwards, the silence is thick with the kind of intimacy that can't be faked. He rolls off me carefully, breath still heavy, his arm slung lazily over my stomach as he nuzzles against my neck.

I huff, tugging the edge of the blanket up. "That was... too fast."

He kisses my jaw. "Too good."

I grunt, letting my eyes slip shut. "Don't get cocky."

"Pretty sure I just did."

I groan, swatting him without any real heat, but my lips won't stop twitching.

Brent shifts, his fingers lacing with mine beneath the sheets. "You okay?"

"Exhausted. Sticky. Bruised. Mildly embarrassed by my overzealous dick." I pause. "But yeah. I'm okay."

He kisses my shoulder. "Welcome home, Captain."

I turn my head just enough to press my lips to his hair. "Yeah," I murmur. "Home."

And just like that, I let myself rest. Not because I'm tired—though I am—but because for the first time in a long damn time, I feel safe enough to.

Because Brent is here.

And so am I.

Epilogue
Camden

Five Years Later – Exeter Stadium

THE ROAR OF THE CROWD IS STILL ECHOING IN MY ears as I stand at the centre of the pitch, chest heaving, sweat drying on my skin, and gold confetti clinging to my jersey. The scoreboard behind me glows like a dream: Exeter Seagulls—League Champions. Final whistle. Final game. Final win.

I should be in the locker room by now, half-drunk on champagne and shoulder-deep in teammates' hugs. But I'm not.

Because tonight isn't just about rugby. Tonight's about him.

Brent stands on the sidelines, right where I told him to wait. He's in faded black jeans, his studio hoodie pushed back to reveal that inked throat I love so much. His hair's longer now, curling a little at the ends. There's silver at his temple these days—probably my fault—and he's never looked more annoyingly beautiful.

When our eyes meet, he grins. Slow. Knowing. Proud.

I jog towards him, heart rattling like a drum. And yeah, maybe the grass is damp, and maybe I just played eighty minutes of brutal rugby, but nothing—*nothing*—is stopping me.

Brent raises a brow when I slow to a stop in front of him.

"You planning on lifting another trophy?" he teases.

I smile. "Something like that."

He opens his mouth to speak, but then I'm dropping to one knee, right here on the field, on the soggy pitch beneath a hundred stadium lights. Brent goes utterly still. The noise around us fades to a dull hum—reporters yelling, fans screaming, champagne spraying somewhere behind me—but I barely hear any of it.

I only hear my own voice.

"I knew," I say, "the moment you kissed me in that alley five years ago, that I was never walking away from you."

Brent's lips part. His eyes shine, even in the floodlights.

"You've held me together," I continue, "when everything else was falling apart. You've made my home feel like more than bricks and a bed. You've made me feel like more than muscle and grit. You've loved me—all of me—even when I didn't know how to let you."

I pull the ring box from the pocket of my warm-up jacket and open it. It's simple, a platinum band, and etched on the inside with the word *home*.

"Marry me," I say, voice tight. "Let's make this forever."

Brent doesn't hesitate. Not for a second. He lets out a stunned, choked laugh—and then he's dropping to his knees, crashing into me with the kind of kiss that steals the air from my lungs and floods my chest with fire.

"Yes," he breathes, arms locked around my neck. "Yes, Cam. Of course, yes."

The crowd must've realised what's happening, because the roar kicks up again—louder. Someone throws a flag over us like a cape. Someone else's voice breaks through, shouting, "Get a room!" and I swear it's Cosmo's from the box seats.

But none of it matters. Because I'm kissing my fiancé.

My fiancé.

When I finally pull back to slide the ring onto his finger, Brent's face is flushed, his grin wide, and his voice a little breathless. "Guess I'm finally part of the team now," he says, tilting his head towards the field.

"You've always been the best part of it," I say.

And when we stand—fingers laced, foreheads pressed together, the whole damn stadium watching—I know this moment will live in my bones forever.

We won the league today.

But I already won the only thing that really matters.

Curious about Cosmo and Jay? Check out **The Poster Boy** by **EM Denning** to read Jay's story and **Puck Shots** by **Becca Jackson** for Cosmo's. Plus, you'll meet other members of the **Love the Game** group chat by reading the whole series available on Amazon: https://reader links.com/l/4922388

Love the Game

READ THEM ON AMAZON:

HTTPS://READERLINKS.COM/L/4922388

OFFSIDE PLAY BY BECCA STEELE

BARN BURNER BY JODI OLIVER

THE POSTER BOY BY EM DENNING

FULL TILT BY BECCA SEYMOUR

PUCK SHOTS BY BECCA JACKSON

TOP SHELF BY EM LINDSAY

PLAY WITH ME BY CORA ROSE

NEW RULES BY WILLOW THOMAS

Bonus Scene 1
Camden

The pub isn't anything fancy—just a converted barn on the outskirts of Exeter, string lights twisted along the ceiling beams, a fire crackling in the old hearth, and someone's playlist bouncing between retro pop and indie acoustic.

But it's perfect. Because everyone's here.

Brent's family—jet-lagged and slightly overdressed—have taken over the corner booth near the bar, his mum already two glasses into a celebratory rosé and quizzing my brother about regional accents.

"I just think yours sounds more Shakespeare than Camden's," she says earnestly, leaning in. "Is that a West Midlands thing, or are you secretly in the theatre?"

My brother doesn't quite know where to look.

Meanwhile, Cosmo's flitting from group to group like a social butterfly in leather boots and a super-tight tee. At some point he stuck a glittery "Team Groom" badge on both Brent and me, and we haven't been able to remove them without him popping up like a cursed sprite.

Tony and Calvin are over by the pool table, attempting to teach Rachel how to break like a pro. Judging by the gleam in her eye and the way Calvin's dramatically covering his groin with both hands, it's not going well.

And then there's Lachie, leaning casually against the bar, a pint in one hand and his other arm draped around the shoulders of his partner. They've been joined at the hip all evening, which does something to my chest—seeing Lachie relaxed, happy, safe. It wasn't always guaranteed.

"You planned this, didn't you?" Brent murmurs, slipping up beside me.

I shrug, lips tugging upwards. "Maybe."

Brent sips his drink, then tilts his head. "Even the part where my mom cornered your nan in the loo and now they're planning joint Christmases?"

I chuckle. "Okay, that bit I didn't plan."

"Mm." Brent slides an arm around my waist and presses a kiss behind my ear. "Still. Pretty amazing."

I lean into Brent, not so subtly dipping my head and

inhaling his fresh citrus scent. "Didn't want to celebrate without them. Without you."

He turns to me slightly, hand firm on his hip. "You did all this while playing eighty minutes of rugby and proposing to me in front of a full stadium?"

I smirk, feeling thoroughly damn proud of myself. "Yeah. I multitask when I'm in love."

Brent exhales a laugh that's half sigh, half swoon, then leans in. "So... how long do we have to stay before we can sneak out?"

I arch a brow. "Sneaking out on your own engagement party?"

"I have plans," he murmurs, lips brushing my jaw. "Plans that involve you, no clothes, and at least one celebration blow job."

A cough spills out of me, right into my pint. "Jesus Christ."

"What? I'm romantic."

"You're shameless."

"You love it."

I do. I really, really do.

As the night stretches on—filled with too-loud toasts, impromptu dance-offs, and one suspiciously competitive trivia round hosted by Cosmo—I can't help but grin so hard it aches.

This? This is everything. The team. The win. The man by my side. The family we've built and inherited.

And the rest of our lives starts now.

Bonus Scene 2
Brent

There are exactly four things I'm trying to keep together right now:

1. My suit.
2. My hair.
3. My brother Cosmo's volume.
4. My composure.

I'm only winning on one of those. Maybe two, if you count "slightly tousled" as a hairstyle.

"Are you sweating?" Cosmo hisses, popping up like a caffeinated meerkat from behind a hedgerow. "Brent, this is not the vibe. Grooms don't sweat this much. Not even in gay weddings."

"Did you just say 'gay weddings' like we're hosting a niche TikTok event?"

"Don't change the subject. Where's your handkerchief? Dab. Dab!"

I swat him away as delicately as I can manage while standing under a rose arch in a Devon garden with fifty of our closest friends and family—and one llama.

Okay. The llama was not our idea.

That was Lachie.

Apparently "it's not a wedding without an emotional support animal," and "the farm was already booked for another party, so we got the llama at a discount." I've stopped asking questions at this point in my life.

But even with the weird animal cameos and the complete lack of breeze, I wouldn't change a thing.

Because in about thirty seconds, Camden Crawford —the love of my life, my grumpy, talented, endlessly sexy rugby-playing fiancé—is about to walk down the aisle towards me. And I've never felt more ready for anything.

The string quartet (also Lachie's idea, because he "knew a guy") swells with the opening bars of "Can't Help Falling in Love." There's a ripple of shifting chairs, and then... then I see him.

And everything stops.

Cam is—fuck, he's beautiful. Strong lines softened by the summer light, navy suit tailored to within an inch of its life. No tie, just a few buttons undone at the collar, and that signature scowl-smile hybrid he wears when he's trying not to be emotional.

He fails by the time he's halfway up the aisle. His jaw clenches, and his eyes go all glassy. He doesn't cry, though—he's not a public crier—but he does look at me like I'm the only thing in the world that makes sense.

Cosmo mutters behind me, "You're totally gonna ugly cry."

He's not wrong.

The ceremony's short. Sweet. We wrote our own vows.

Cam clears his throat when it's his turn. "You make me better," he says simply. "Not because you ask me to be, but because you see me—even when I don't. You've never tried to fix me. You just held the space until I wanted to step into it. I love you, and I want to choose you, every damn day."

Someone sniffles. I think it's my mom.

I go next. "I didn't expect you. I definitely didn't plan for you. But you took up space in my heart so fast, I didn't have time to second-guess it. You're fierce and loyal and generous in all the ways that matter. You call me on my shit and then hold me after. I love you. And if I ever forget to say it—just look at my face. It'll be right there."

We exchange rings, ignore Cosmo's stage whisper of "Kiss him like you mean it!" and wrap the whole thing up with the most perfect, grounding kiss we've ever had.

It's home.

It's us.

The reception is low-key chaos, because of course it is.

Rachel's managed to convince Calvin to choreograph a full wedding dance with backup dancers (the twins and all their partners, naturally). My mom gives a beautiful, tearjerking toast. Cam's dad tells an inappropriate story involving Camden's childhood crush on a lifeguard named Carl, which earns him a headshake and a glare that could sink a ship.

Lachie and his partner do a surprise poem toast. Cosmo somehow ends up as the officiant and the DJ. And the llama—now called Dennis—makes a return appearance in the group photos.

Later, under the fairy lights and half-melted candles, Cam pulls me into a slow dance. No cameras. No guests. Just us, swaying like the night can't touch us.

"You good?" I murmur, fingers laced behind his neck.

He nods. "Best day of my life."

"You didn't even threaten anyone today. Proud of you."

Cam huffs out a laugh and presses a kiss to my temple. "You've mellowed me."

"God help us all."

We don't need to say much more than that. The day's been full. The future is waiting.

But this moment? This is ours.

And it's everything.

About the Author

Becca Seymour is a British/Aussie author and the #1 gay romance best seller of the True-Blue series. Known for "steamy and endearing" and "emotionally profound love stories" (InD'tale Magazine) her books have been nominated for multiple RONE Awards.

Becca has a sweet tooth for marshmallow-hearted monsters, swoon-worthy supernatural studs, and everyday guys and basketball players with hearts of gold. If you like your MM romance sweet, spicy, and occasionally action-packed, slip into stalker mode and fall hard for her True-Blue and Minnesota Eagles men—and maybe a shifter or monster two.

To check for updates head to my website:
https://beccaseymour.com
https://landing.mailerlite.com/webforms/landing/r9f0i4
Plus, join my Facebook group:
https://www.facebook.com/groups/rommancewithbeccalouisa/